THE HEART CASTS NO SHADOW

SUSAN HOLT

INLET PUBLISHING

FREE DOWNLOAD

Sign up for Susan's New Releases mailing list and get free short stories. Go here to get started: *www.susanholt.org/free*

ABOUT THE AUTHOR

Susan Holt lives in New Zealand. She believes stories can change the world and is doing her utmost to make this a change for the better.

ISBN: 978-0-473-50139-6

Published by Inlet Publishing New Zealand.

To Mum.
Thank you for my reading addiction.

In memory of Marianna (Mudz) Minhinnick
(1973 – 2019). Your laugh caught at my heart,
lifted it forth, and let it fly. Sleep well, babe!

1

Yern was choking.

On the far side of the room, Rhonwyn craned her neck to stare over the crowd. Yern's lips became an unhealthy shade of blue, his eyes bulged. All the other competitors and their families were transfixed. Something had gone down the wrong way.

Yern's mother, in her best clothes, held his shoulders and shook him. Her pudgy body rattled in unison with his. Foam exploded from his mouth, all over the blue winner's ribbon draped across his chest. And all over his mother. Green foam, Rhonwyn noted. Yern's body spasmed as his eyes rolled back and he collapsed to the floor.

How did choking produce foam?

The witnesses gulped and those closest to the incident edged away and regrouped closer to Rhonwyn.

He was dead. The winner of the competition was dead.

Rhonwyn eyed the food she held in her hand. What had Yern choked on?

The tidy-crew in their black tabards scurried from their positions near the doors. They removed Yern's body, wiped the floor, and led his stunned mother away.

"Well, what do you think of the weather?" said a frozen-faced family member of one of the other competitors. "Wet for this time of year, huh?"

"Yes," began his neighbour, a ruddy man with bulging eyes. "I couldn't get home for flooding two days ago. Ridic—" His breath drew in as he realised his own audacity. His eyes flashed towards the Enforcers ranged around the edge of the chamber. His voice squeaked with the strain of his forced cheer, "Greened up the grass, though. Just lovely. What an amazing competition. So close."

Rhonwyn turned away from the conversation, her heart still drumming from watching Yern die. She imagined her father, Hywel, standing near, his warm brown eyes shining in his weathered face. Her breathing calmed.

"I've never seen anyone choke like that," she muttered to his memory, "What will happen now?" When she'd lost in the final game, Rhonwyn had resigned herself to returning home, her one chance of gaining access to the king gone. She'd been relieved, to be honest, unsure she could do what the Resistance wanted. Far cleverer people had failed before her – and had been executed for their efforts.

The mayor, his face chalk-white, consulted with his assistant and strode over to Rhonwyn.

Her stomach tightened as he stationed himself in front of her, his jaw set. "Well, Rhonwyn. Congratulations." He snatched her hand and pumped it up and down. The mayor's assistant handed him the winner's ribbon – newly stripped from Yern's body. The mayor draped it around Rhonwyn. A rank, acidic smell rose from where the foam had been. The mayor stepped to the side and raised his voice. "Rhonwyn mi Hywel, winner of the Gymbal championship."

Rhonwyn, daughter of Hywel, forced a smile as she looked at the crowd, their over-enthusiastic applause bouncing around the council chamber like panicked birds looking for a way out.

The congratulations began all over again. The handshaking hurt after a while. Her little finger felt particularly sore. She couldn't help but wince when the last few well-wishers stepped forward and proffered their hands.

Once the mayor disbanded the after-party, no one stuck around. They didn't even pretend to linger, and the group of thirty collided with each other in their haste to get out. Trapped by the ribbon around her, Rhonwyn watched them go.

The mayor's assistant had a quick word with her before she left: "You know where to go tomorrow? And the time?" Despite these being framed as questions, the woman didn't wait for an answer. She thrust a small slip of papyrus at Rhonwyn and stalked off towards the offices at the back of the chamber.

Rhonwyn studied the note, crumpled from the speed of its delivery. It read, *"Sunrise. Palace gatehouse."* The date was in the top right corner, the royal seal at the bottom.

So, a whole night to enjoy the last of her freedom. How *kind* of His Majesty. Rhonwyn sneered at the papyrus before brightening. This was also a free pass. She could break a few rules tonight and show this to the Enforcers. They would have to let her go.

That could be fun. She glanced sideways and caught the image she still held of her father. He was with her – he felt real. She could see him as he rubbed his hands together, grinning, just like he used to before one of their adventures. They'd had so many – Papa was always with her.

"Of course." She nodded to the memory in her mind, the figure of her father's shining face. "You may as well come on this one, too." She fixed him with a glare. "But you have to be *quiet*!" She flashed a grin at him.

And so she set off – alone, but not alone – towards the exit. The sole sentry watched her without looking at her. He was waiting for her to leave, so he could lock up. How many times had she passed him after a city event? No one talked to him, but he wasn't exactly a collaborator. This was her last chance to meet him.

On a whim, she stopped at the chamber door and looked him in the eye. He blinked back in surprise.

"Peace to you," she said. "What's your name?"

His eyes slid sideways before he answered. "Peace to you, miss. I am Gerwyn."

She stuck out her sore hand. "Well met, Gerwyn."

After a brief pause, Gerwyn took it and gave her a tiny smile. "Well met, miss." His deep voice crackled; he didn't use it much. He looked solid, but held her so gently. Where did he live? Did he have a wife? Children? Where had his land been? She could ask him. But she mustn't get him in trouble just because she wouldn't have to bear the consequences.

"Be well and happy, Gerwyn." She used the old blessing.

His smile grew. "Be well and happy, miss."

Yes, well. Too late for that.

"Come on, Papa," she muttered, eliciting a startled look from Gerwyn.

She'd forgotten herself. Rhonwyn must remember not to do that once she got to the palace, or there would be trouble. Again.

As she walked down to the narrow road, she tossed the winner's ribbon away. That rare bit of prettiness in their stark world had the stench of death upon it; she didn't want to keep it. Seeing no one nearby, she also warded off the evil spirits, pressing the middle finger of each hand together before her to form the unbreakable circle.

She'd just whipped her hands down to her sides when an omnibus turned into the road and whined its way towards her. The power came from the sun-catcher on the roof, courtesy of His Majesty, King Risick. No one else knew how the magic worked. She clambered aboard and slipped into a space around one of the upright poles. Although five men clung to it already, they wordlessly squeezed her in. The black-smeared workers, now being trucked home, filled the tiny wooden cabin. Eyes to avoid, silence to hold.

She studied the king's-eye on the ceiling instead. In every omnibus, every public building, and on every street, these sickly yellow globes kept track of every citizen's movements, though no one knew how. More magic. Somehow the king knew if you broke the rules, and there was no escaping the consequences.

Rhonwyn rode back to her home district. She hadn't travelled so far away from her precinct for years, though everywhere in the city looked the same. The omnibus whined off into the distance.

A light breeze made the ends of her tabard flap. She adjusted it and pulled her undershirt down over her brown leggings. The sun was setting at the end of the long avenue, its light revealing the unevenness of the pavement. People meandered up and down, the most relaxed they could be in public. They could even converse a little. The families with children had gone home; official bedtime for children was sunset.

Rhonwyn strolled down the path, imagining her father at her side so she would relax. She nodded at some of the familiar faces. None of these neighbours knew yet that she'd won the Gymbal championship; that they would never see her again after today. They would know after Announcements. Then those who knew her might seek her out to say goodbye.

She would survey everything available before she picked where to go. Since she could eat away from the dormitories for once, she could allow the delicious aromas to tempt her as she passed.

The exercise yard was next, where everyone gathered to perform the daily physical workout. Would she have to do exercises in the palace? She'd never been enthusiastic about them. Though, she had to admit, they sometimes made her feel better. The grass in the yard was roped off and unnaturally flat – so no one would get injured. A bright green splash of softness in the grey sea.

Her father would have suggested Rhonwyn come back later, jump over the ropes and walk about barefoot. She tittered, making a passing couple glance at her. Papa had always been up for adventure. Between planting and reaping and all the rest of his chores, he'd often stolen away with Rhonwyn. He'd shown her the joys of the forest around them, picnicking in secluded glades or at the tops of hills, just to look out over the natural beauty. The city didn't have gardens, except for these grass squares. Everything else was paved.

Yes, that's what she would do later: walk on the grass. And the Enforcers wouldn't be able to hold her for it.

It took her some time to pass by the exercise yard, and then the chimes of Announcements interrupted Rhonwyn's circuit. With an Enforcer nearby, she wasted no time finding a screen and waiting for it to start, others assembling around her while the chimes continued to ring out. When the last cadence sounded, Rhonwyn laughed at herself. She could have ignored it. She had her excuse folded in her pocket. Too late now.

Everything stopped during Announcements. A crowd of murmuring people assembled around the panels.

King Risick's emblem appeared on them: the silhouette of a face with yellow eyes and a snake emerging from his mouth, though the king had a tongue like everyone else's.

All noise died away when the face of the presenter materialised. Not for the first time, Rhonwyn wondered how they got his face on the panel and whether it hurt him. There were the usual things: what weather they expected, changes in routine, more rules to obey. Distracted, Rhonwyn nearly missed the announcement about herself.

"Today's winner of the Gymbal tournament, Rhonwyn mi Hywel, will be honoured with a place in His Majesty's court.

She will have the privilege of playing King Risick himself and become the Royal Gymbal Opponent now that Walethyn ma Talog has stepped down. We congratulate her on her achievement."

And that was it.

What had happened to Walethyn ma Talog? And would it happen to her, in her turn? The surge of fear made her want to lean into her father's chest again, but she could only imagine him standing next to her – and make sure she didn't lean.

Today was the day for King Risick's weekly message. Rhonwyn swallowed hard.

His trumpet fanfare blared out. At the sound, Rhonwyn automatically drew one foot back and went down on one knee, as did everyone else in the city. Only the Enforcers could just bend at the waist and then, straightening, look for anybody who wasn't paying attention. Every head tilted back, every eye was on the screen.

When Risick appeared, he was looking down. So when his brown eyelids opened on his sulphur-yellow irises, Rhonwyn felt her stomach shrink. She had never got used to it.

"Citizens of Merynbyl," he began. The double-toned sound of his voice made the hairs on the back of Rhonwyn's neck stand up. Not only were there two distinct notes in his voice, they were pitched so that lower notes sounded at the same time. The buzz of them was hard to listen to through the panels. What would it be like in person?

"Boros production is down again this month," he stated.

She drew in a deep breath. Who would pay for that? It happened a couple of times a year and, every time, the king demanded someone pay the ultimate price for the lack. Why boros production was so important, Rhonwyn had never discovered; it just was. It didn't seem to produce anything anyone needed.

So they were to watch another execution. Rhonwyn braced herself. She should be used to them by now.

"I have determined where the fault lies and after this I expect production next month to make up for the deficit," he said.

King Risick backed out of the frame as it widened to reveal the bare, grey room he stood in.

A man knelt on the floor. A flicker of movement at the edge of the picture indicated the guards holding him had moved away as Risick turned to face him.

Sweat glistened off the thickset man's pale skin. They'd sewn his lips together; dried blood from the stitches crusted his chin. The orange panel on the front of his tabard indicated he was a mining manager.

First the man tried to escape, pushing himself off the floor and scrambling towards the door.

Risick extended a lazy hand, pinched his fingers and thumb together around the air. He flicked them back as though he was a Wise One throwing herbs over his shoulder in a ritual. The man, with nothing touching him, flew backwards and slid headfirst towards the king's feet.

Where had His Majesty's magic come from? No one else could do such things. Not even the Wise Ones, who'd known all the spirit stories, healing herbs, and genealogies.

The man's eyes bulged in fear, looking up at Risick's disdainful face. Flipping over, he changed his tactics, bursting up with his hands outstretched and grabbing the king by the throat.

Though he was the first in a long while to lay a hand on His Majesty, he made no impression. Risick just sneered as the poor man struggled to throttle the royal throat.

Rhonwyn heard a soft, "Very good!" before the king swung his right arm around in a circle, coming down hard on the man's forearms.

They snapped. For a moment, Rhonwyn saw jagged bone sticking out of the man's flesh. There were low gasps from people around her and Rhonwyn winced. If only she could reach out and hold her father's hand.

As the man crumpled to the ground, staring at his useless arms, Risick gripped the man's neck and squeezed. His immense strength easily crushed the man's throat. In fact, he squeezed all the way through the flesh. The man's face distorted as the king's hands separated his head from his body. His spinal cord held on, however, and the head flopped back between his shoulder blades as Risick let go and stepped back, smiling. The body thudded onto the blood-spattered floor.

The king turned back to his watching audience and approached until his face filled the screen. Flecks of blood dripped off his nose.

"Don't let me down, will you?" he said, his gaze holding until Rhonwyn shivered and had to look away. When she looked back, the screen was empty.

The crowd around her rose at different times. It took a while before quiet conversation began again, people moving back into the groups they'd been in and wandering off.

Rhonwyn wasn't so hungry anymore. Perhaps some exercise would help. She would walk around the block.

A small smile warmed her face when she discovered the memory of her father shuffling his feet, tugging on his hat, and otherwise being his usual comforting self nearby.

The next building she passed was the uniform stockist. She looked through the window at the racks of tabards. Light green for builders, teal – like hers – for manual labourers, yellow for administration, and on through the colours, up to red for the Enforcers. Then there were black, white, and various shades of brown, each a coloured piece of fabric attached to the top front of their grey tabards. Because of her current designation as a seamstress, she knew where every stitch went.

What colour was she going to wear in the palace? How did His Majesty's Gymbal Opponent dress? She had no idea. The palace was a mystery. Not one of the Resistance infiltrators had lasted there longer than two days.

Rhonwyn changed her focus and studied her reflection in

the window. Blue was good for her: it made her freckles fade a little under her hazel eyes, and somehow her shoulder-length mouse-brown hair didn't look so scruffy.

Tall, she looked clumsy and ill-proportioned. She hoped her new colour wouldn't make her look too ugly.

"You're beautiful," she imagined her father murmuring into her ear.

A smile growing on her face, Rhonwyn turned away and spied a man in the shadows between the uniform stockist and the next building. He was looking at her.

Her stomach clenched as her smile wilted.

3

Kephlen turned and walked out of sight down the alley between the buildings. Rhonwyn was meant to follow him. She must be discreet.

She'd known he would contact her before she entered the palace. Why did seeing him make her so nervous?

Trying to keep her breathing even, she strolled closer to the uniform stockist's window and pretended to examine the other uniforms. Anyone who was about to change their job would do that, wouldn't they?

She walked to the end and performed a slow turn to check where the nearest Enforcer was. At least she could spot them easily in their bright red clothes. The closest was a long way away and occupied in questioning a pale man with an ochre tabard.

Rhonwyn slipped into the alley and hurried towards the back of the building. There must be a blind-spot – where the king's-eyes couldn't see them. It got darker the further she went; Kephlen had snuffed some of the lamps.

She heard a hiss just behind her, "Rhonwyn!"

She whirled around and found Kephlen standing in a recess between a drainpipe and a rear exit. Rhonwyn stepped into the cramped space with him.

"Well done," said Kephlen. He meant for winning the tournament. He was beaming, his dark green eyes sparkling in the dim light, his white hair luminous.

"We were lucky," she whispered. "Yern won the actual competition."

Kephlen's smile disappeared. "Someone else won? I thought—"

"Yern's dead. He choked on something. It was awful." Rhonwyn squirmed at the memory. "If he hadn't died, I wouldn't be getting in."

Kephlen's head retracted in surprise before he blinked it away. "Are you ready? This is the last time I'll see you for a while."

"Yes. I'm ready."

"Rhonwyn," he said, his voice wavering. "You will have to conceal your ..." He held his breath before releasing it all at once. "... your conversations with your father. You understand that, don't you?"

Rhonwyn's eyes lowered and she attempted a laugh, her face warming. "Yes. I'll try."

Kephlen gazed at her, frowning, before he pulled her into a rough embrace. "You'll be fine," he whispered. His voice sounded choked.

Rhonwyn hugged him back. Kephlen had worked with her father in the city. In the six years since she'd been declared barren, her already small group of friends had dwindled to nothing; married off into other sections. When the king had executed her father, she'd been allotted a tiny room in the singles' apartments.

She'd discovered living alone wasn't truly living. That was why she'd joined the Resistance – something had to change.

But once she was in the palace, she wouldn't see one face she could trust. Isolated, she would have to decide how to do her spying with no advice from anyone. She would only have her wits, and a Resistance contact who visited the palace. She didn't even know who that contact was.

Kephlen drew back and cupped his hands around her head, the heels of his thumbs against her jaw. "Your father would be proud of you, Rhonny. Remember that." He kissed her on the forehead. His chin was bristly, just like Papa's had been in the evening.

Rhonwyn swallowed hard. "Thank you."

He stepped back and released her, his gaze steady. "You're a clever woman. Just collect as much information as you can – whatever might be useful for getting rid of Risick. And never write anything down."

She snorted. "You know I'm not good at my letters."

"Yes, well." Kephlen flashed a lopsided grin, but it was short-lived. He leaned towards her. "If they catch you, it'll be years before we get someone inside again, if ever." He looked around. "Don't go back the way you came."

A lump swelled in Rhonwyn's throat. "Farewell Kephlen. Be well and happy."

His jaw clenched, he nodded as he stepped back into the shadows. He would wait until she was gone before he left another way.

After one last look at Kephlen, Rhonwyn turned and walked down the alley, her heart thundering.

To see him again, she had to find information to depose the king. If she lived, perhaps she could have friends again. Until then, she was alone.

After leaving Kephlen, Rhonwyn made her way around the district, checking her options as she went. Horseshoe throwing and table games – Gymbal included. She would play that for the rest of her life; she could give it a miss tonight.

Food first. Pangs of hunger, activated by the delicious aromas drifting out of the eating establishments, finally overtook the butterflies she'd felt.

"Let's try *Glyn's*, shall we, Papa?" she said, and bit her lip.

The host's eyebrows shot up when she showed him her palace note, and he took her straight upstairs to a table with a view over the city. She was surprised to see trees surrounding a lake behind the buildings across the street – she hadn't known there was any green besides the exercise yards. The sun, still illuminating the sky, had set in front of her. Huge pink and orange-edged clouds hung far above. The local apartments stood over to her left.

Rhonwyn could see half the other districts. Every one the same shape, they were set out on the plain in a grid. One exercise yard, two tall concrete apartment buildings, a central section where the regular services were, and the support services quarter. All square, grey and functional. The omnibuses wound from the edges, through the districts, to the boros mine entrance, right in the centre of the city.

It was extraordinary what Risick had accomplished in his

twelve years in power. Rhonwyn, however, was now convinced that kind of speed was far from beneficial for her people. He must go and she was going to help.

Over to her right the palace precinct sat upon its hill. Taller than everything else in the area, it loomed over them, dominating the landscape. Rings of security walls at its base meant no one knew anything about it. That was why the Resistance were sending her in. Towers and multi-storeyed buildings huddled together inside. The royal enclave was its own little town, and no one knew which building was the actual palace. They made deliveries at one gate where the supplies disappeared. They were consumed by the unknown number of people who lived there – King Risick, his cronies, and all those assigned to cater for their needs. All the best supplies.

The best supplies in *Glyn's* seemed to make their way to Rhonwyn's table that evening. The staff behaved as if this was her last meal. Friendly and attentive, her server gave her everything she requested and more, suggesting wine that complemented the main course, and recommending one particular dessert. He barely even blinked when she asked for an extra – half-filled – wine goblet for the other side of the table.

"Here's to you, Papa." She raised her goblet in a toast to his image, seeing his crinkled smile in her mind's eye. At least he'd taken his hat off at the table.

This would be the last time she could do this.

The cook even emerged from the kitchen briefly. She assured him she would recommend his skills to the palace. It seemed the kind thing to say.

As she wandered home afterwards, she remembered her mother's words to her when Rhonwyn was seven summers of age: "Be kind whenever you can. Especially to your Papa." Hours later, her mother had been dead, the child she'd been struggling to deliver following soon after.

Tears pricked Rhonwyn's eyes and the void in her heart twisted. She looked around.

She must keep herself composed on the street.

After watching her father being killed during the Announcements, her soul had run away and hidden, leaving her body empty and unaware of anything but the sudden reality of this loss. A friend had found her and led her home – she barely remembered how they'd got there.

She'd been lucky. If anyone else had discovered her, babbling incoherently out on the street after curfew, Rhonwyn would have been turned in, deemed unproductive, and terminated.

Since then, she'd found she needed to pretend her father was still here – imagine him standing nearby, or speaking gently to her – to stop herself losing her mind again. Manchyl, the god of chaos with his chittering demons, was always ready to take her soul.

She stopped at the exercise area. After looking around, she took off her sandals and stepped over the low rope. The grass was soft and thick. She walked a few paces, enjoying the sensation.

"Excuse me, miss."

The stern eyes of an Enforcer were looking her up and down.

"You know you're not supposed to do that." The woman's square face was grim. "I will have to—"

Rhonwyn held up her hand. "I know. Don't bother." It felt amazing to say that, despite the automatic rush of fear she'd felt at the sight of the red tabard. She withdrew the palace note from her pocket and held it out, trying to suppress a grin.

The Enforcer's brows descended as she peered at the piece of papyrus. When she straightened, she was still frowning at Rhonwyn.

"Going to be trouble tonight, are you?" Her eyes were a challenge and one fist now sat on her hip.

Rhonwyn took a slow breath and let it out in a rush. "No, probably not. I really can't be bothered. I'll go home soon. I've got an early morning."

So much for a wild night out. Well, she needed to be alert for her entry into the unknown world behind the forbidding walls. Letting down her guard would be too risky. Besides, she had no one to celebrate with. Except her father's memory.

The Enforcer looked at her askance before chuckling. She hadn't expected such speedy acquiescence.

"I'm glad to hear it." With a nod, she returned Rhonwyn's note and left her to it.

Rhonwyn didn't spend much longer on the field; the moment had soured. Would there be grass in the palace? She doubted it. After putting her sandals back on, she walked to the singles' apartments, lit one of the lamps standing inside the door, and trudged up the concrete stairs to her room.

Big enough for a bed, a chair and a table, it was in the middle of the building, so there was no window, thank the heavens. It hadn't just been her who'd taken a while to get used to the near-invisible glass; more than one of her neighbours had put their head through their window, forgetting it was there. And it meant she didn't have to remember to light the lamp outside.

The requisite alarm and viewing panel were on the wall, next to the alcove where she kept her clothes. A message shone on the panel stating the alarm would go off to wake her in time for her morning appointment. The all-knowing state had intervened again. She pressed the button to make the glowing note disappear, before using the washroom she shared with three others at her end of the hallway.

In a daze, Rhonwyn got two cups of peppermint tea from the kitchen and settled down in the chair to think.

She frowned when she finally spotted the extra cup.

"Oh, Papa," she murmured. "I really have to stop this."

5

In the pre-dawn light, she dressed and packed her few belongings into the bag she found outside her door – state-provided. She didn't have much. She'd left a picture of her father with Kephlen for safekeeping, assuming nothing would be private in the palace. All she would have were her memories and a woven blanket her mother had made. In one of its corners she had sewn the elaborate button Rhonwyn had pulled off her father's shirt when she was a toddler, back before Risick had appeared and everything had become plain and all the same.

At the palace gate, she presented her note to the guard, who squinted at the thing, his tongue jammed between his teeth, before he rummaged through her bag.

Satisfied, he motioned her through. Rhonwyn stood watching the world she knew disappear as he slid the gate shut. That could be her last view of freedom.

It was hardly freedom, though, in the true sense of the word, and the loneliness had become unbearable. She squared her shoulders and set off up the short path to the inner gate where she presented her papyrus invitation once more. They summoned a guide who led her onward and upward through the labyrinth that was the palace precinct.

After the second corner, the guide – a girl with a pale, round face and straight black hair pulled into a ponytail – turned to her. Her brown eyes glinted in a smile.

"I'm Kymra, one of the housekeeper's assistants," she said. "I'll be taking care of you. My parents work in the stables. I've been working for Mistress Berwyn since I was fourteen summers." She took a deep breath and paused before talking again, more slowly. "Well met, Rhonwyn." She rolled her eyes. "I talk too much." Kymra giggled as she blushed and they moved off again.

Rhonwyn smiled, surprised to find someone so open. "Peace to you, Kymra. It's a pleasure to meet you. How long have you been the housekeeper's assistant?"

"Nearly a year. How old are you?"

Rhonwyn chuckled at the girl's bald question.

"Twenty summers."

There were a few moments silence as they continued.

"So, where are we going now?" she asked the girl, who was biting her own lip.

"I'll take you to your quarters and get you settled in," blurted Kymra. "Then we'll visit Mistress Berwyn." She beamed. Kymra seemed full of energy and suppressed excitement. Rhonwyn could tell she was burning to divulge everything that popped into her mind.

Smiling, she let the girl loose: "What else? How do things work in here?"

As they continued up the hill, Kymra told her how the housekeeper had selected her from the palace families as her assistant, and how glad she was to be out of the stables.

Rhonwyn took careful note, as she would with every conversation now. She must gather as much information as possible and Kymra seemed like a good source, though Rhonwyn wasn't sure the girl would know anything significant.

That had been one of her father's games – observation. "Notice everything," he'd said. "There are clues everywhere."

But that had been for finding mushrooms in the forest.

The sun had risen, yet the two women were still in shadow. The tall buildings shut out most of the dawn. Rhonwyn could see the glint of it hitting the top storeys and moving down their lengths. Most of them were sandstone that became a lovely shade of orange in the warm morning light.

Rhonwyn stumbled and had to concentrate on where her feet were going. It was the moisture in the air that drew her attention again to her surroundings. As Kymra prattled on, Rhonwyn looked around in astonishment at the forest that had appeared on each side of the broad, winding road they followed.

Kymra noticed her surprise and tittered. "Beautiful, isn't it? It's the first part of the palace grounds." Further on, she nodded towards a path on the left. "There are paths all through it. They're lovely to walk along when you get time off. You can even do it in the middle of the night; they have torches on them." Halfway through the forest she pointed over to the right. "Go a little way down there and you'll come to the snake house, with the pit out the back."

Rhonwyn wasn't sure she'd heard right. "A snake pit?"

"Yes. His Majesty loves snakes," said Kymra, "and they are amazing when you see them in the snake house – behind the glass." She wriggled in discomfort. "But they're scary when they get put in the snake pit."

Kymra shivered and became quiet for the first time. It didn't take long for her to perk up, though, as they left the forest for the cultivated garden.

And what a garden it was. The ground was completely flat. Within large expanses of trimmed grass were neat hedges surrounding beds of bright flowers and succulents. The riotous colours were warm in the dawn light, some blooms still opening after their night's sleep.

"I thought there were only buildings up here," said Rhonwyn. "It's extraordinary." She couldn't believe her eyes. She'd expected everything to be dull and lifeless under the close control of the king.

Kymra grinned and then indicated with a flourish what lay ahead. "And then there's the palace itself. Also extraordinary, I think you'll agree."

In the distance, at the end of the now straight road, was the most alien and elegant building Rhonwyn had ever seen. She slowed as she took it in.

The front of the palace spanned the width of the gardens. It seemed to consist entirely of arches. The arch at the end of the road – its entrance – rose two-thirds of the way up the majestic edifice flanked by three similar arches on each side. Each wing ended with a pair of towers. A row of partly-filled-in small arches – sleepy eyes – joined one set of towers to the other above the main arches and added the uppermost storey.

A large red hemisphere sat atop every tower, each with a spike protruding from its top. Rhonwyn had never seen anything like it.

Behind the entrance arch was the tallest tower. Made of gold, it glowed in the morning light. Its colour differed from the front section of the palace. Was it a separate building altogether?

"Amazing, isn't it?" Kymra said.

Kymra pointed out features as they passed them. "The menagerie is over that way. There's the fountain over there. Its outlet runs around the side and off the back."

The water sprang straight up from the ground and pattered into the round pool at its foot. Rhonwyn had never seen water make those kinds of shapes. How did it do it? Was this more magic by King Risick? Was he the god of water?

The two women finally arrived at the entrance arch. Its door opened into a hallway. Kymra turned left. On both sides of the corridor hung picture after picture, and at the end was an enormous portrait of King Risick. He stood erect, his unnatural eyes staring out, his languid hand resting on the head of a huge striped cat.

Turning right, they came to a vestibule with an ornate staircase leading to the upper floors. At the bottom another large feline – this one sand-coloured – sat motionless in a glass case.

"His Majesty killed that with his own hands and had it preserved," offered Kymra.

Rhonwyn could believe it. But there weren't big cats like that in Merynbyl, were there? Where had he found the creature?

They ascended the stairs, turned left, and reached the end of another corridor before Kymra opened a door and ushered Rhonwyn into her new quarters.

Just inside the door was an interior wall that created a short corridor and provided privacy even when the door was open. The bed sat on the other side of this wall. Hers was a corner room with windows on two sides, both with heavy curtains. On the left was another door. Kymra opened it.

"Here's your washroom."

"I've got my own washroom?"

Kymra nodded. "Yes. His Majesty wants you rested and ready for your Gymbal matches with him."

Rhonwyn felt a flutter of anxiety which Kymra seemed to sense.

"You'll get used to him," she said. "Everyone's nervous when they first meet the king face-to-face. In fact bowing to him can be a relief." The side of her mouth rose. "A moment for you to collect yourself." Her expression became serious as she instructed Rhonwyn. "I should have told you this at the beginning. Lucky we didn't see him – you never know when you will." She began what was obviously a well-practised speech. "When you bow, you need to get on both knees and fold yourself right down. Like this."

She demonstrated the correct pose on the floor in front of Rhonwyn, her forehead nearly touching the ground, her arms tucked in at her sides. She'd had a lot of practice.

When Kymra sat up, Rhonwyn thanked her. Kymra stayed where she was, however, looking up at her.

"I need to make sure you do it right – it's part of my job. Would you please join me on the floor here, Rhonwyn?" she asked.

"Of course," replied Rhonwyn and knelt across from Kymra to

get her lesson.

Once this task was complete, they rose for the rest of the tour of Rhonwyn's room, which had far more storage than she needed, having so few possessions. The bed was luxurious and wide.

"And then there's the view," said Kymra and led her over to the double doors made of windows and opening onto a small balcony. Rhonwyn could see the Meryna hills in the distance, their contours standing out in the morning light. When they reached the railing, Rhonwyn gasped and staggered back, her stomach lurching.

Kymra giggled at her. "It's a surprise, isn't it? You'll get used to it." She held Rhonwyn's shoulder to reassure her.

Rhonwyn, taking a deep breath, shuffled forwards again, clung to the rail, and peered over the edge, her pulse pounding in her ears.

Her gaze fell down and down until, hundreds of feet below, she scanned the rumpled floor of the valley, still in darkness. The light of the sun wouldn't reach there for hours.

Kymra, her eyes sparkling, went on talking. "His Majesty wanted a cliff here, so he somehow made half the hill collapse. Apparently it was amazing to watch." She pointed to Rhonwyn's left. "See? That's the stream going off the edge."

Rhonwyn looked as instructed and saw water plummeting off the precipice. It separated as it fell, becoming a mist. A slight breeze bent it to the side.

A small building stood off in the same direction. It sat, impossibly, on a column of rock that jutted up, far out in the valley – a finger that grew up from its floor. A thin tether led out to it from the corner of the palace. No, that wasn't a tether, it had windows – it was a corridor. What supported it?

"What's that?" she asked Kymra, nodding at the building. She wasn't ready to let go of the rail yet.

"That's His Majesty's private chamber. No one goes in there except him. I've never seen him go there, though. I wonder if he ever uses it. He's always awake. And busy."

The ultimate in privacy. If the king held a secret to his downfall, it would be there. Rhonwyn must find a way in. Could she overcome her fear of falling enough to traverse the thin line that hung over the endless nothing?

Kymra remembered something else. "You have new clothes. I'll show you. You must clean up and change into them."

In the wardrobe were several sets of strange-looking garments – of all different colours.

Rhonwyn looked at them, mystified. "Which ones do I wear? What colour?"

"They're all yours," said Kymra. "You can wear whatever colour you like. And you can ask me for another set anytime. I'll get them made and delivered to you in a couple of days."

Rhonwyn couldn't believe her ears.

Kymra turned to the door. "I have to go now. I'll be back in half an hour, just after seven. Then I'll introduce you to Mistress Berwyn and give you more of a tour." She waved and left, closing the door behind her.

Rhonwyn stared at the door and shook her head. She hadn't understood all Kymra had said. What, for instance, was a clock? Or an hour? And ... after seven *'whats'?* She wandered to the balcony and gazed out on the stunning view – from a safe distance. The line of sunlight was inching closer along the valley floor. The squashed half of a hill sat a mile away. The surreal imprint of a giant hand was visible in its grassed-over pile of debris. That hillock must be what had sat outside the window originally.

Magic, definitely.

She returned to the wardrobe and stood, unsure which colour to pick. In the end, she chose a deep green with an exotic pattern around the edges.

She was accustomed to leggings, undershirt, and tabard. These long pants were a loose fit under a comfortable short-sleeved top – closed at the sides. She completed the outfit with a pair of simple sandals. Everything was perfectly tailored to her. How had they known her size?

As she waited – fighting the impulse to picture her father pacing back and forth – Rhonwyn stored her things away and spread her blanket over the end of the bed.

She heard the airy pealing of a bell ring out seven times – all in a row. What did that mean?

Someone knocked on her door. Rhonwyn ran to it.

Kymra stood there, a startled look on her face. "You know, if you don't want to answer the door, you can just say, 'Come in' and I'll let myself in."

Rhonwyn's eyebrows rose.

Kymra looked at what Rhonwyn was wearing and nodded. "You look good. Nice colour."

Rhonwyn smiled as Kymra stepped back into the hall. As they walked, Rhonwyn kept looking down. She'd been wearing the blue for so long, the new colour kept drawing her attention from the edge of her vision.

They made their way back down to the ground floor and towards the rear of the building. More people were around now.

Rhonwyn continued to stare at the magnificent interior. She couldn't help but stop when they encountered the door to an enormous room, filled with birds. Surrounding the area just past the entrance was a cage in which people could stand to watch the hundreds of feathered creatures all around them. Even the roof was a closely woven mesh of wire. With all the colours, calls and movement, Kymra had to drag her away.

Directly under Rhonwyn's room was Mistress Berwyn's office. Rhonwyn and Kymra waited outside and watched as person after person came and went after receiving instructions.

Eventually, an authoritative voice called out.

"Kymra!"

Kymra and Rhonwyn walked into a large, busy room. On every flat surface lay pieces of papyrus – some collected and bound with string. Assorted bolts of fabric were piled on a table in the far corner and three staff members worked at side benches.

Mistress Berwyn herself was an older woman with short, dark hair beginning to grey at the temples, and light blue eyes in her elfin face. She pursed her lips in thought as she regarded a single square of papyrus. A young woman – around Kymra's age – waited next to her, her hands clasped before her apron.

These hands were paler than the rest of her skin. They must be covered in flour.

The two younger girls exchanged a look.

"Alright, Vylen," said Mistress Berwyn. "This looks acceptable. Point out to Cook that His Majesty does not like this vegetable. He must exchange it for another." She held up what was apparently a menu and jabbed her finger at the offending line. "He should know by now what His Majesty likes and dislikes."

Vylen muttered, "Yes Mistress," and winked at Kymra as she scuttled from the room.

Mistress Berwyn frowned, peered at the list in front of her, and then up at Kymra and Rhonwyn. Her face cleared, and she smiled. This softened her features. She stood and skirted the table.

"Rhonwyn mi Hywel, the new Gymbal Opponent," she said. "Well met." She held out her hand and shook Rhonwyn's, which caused Rhonwyn to wince. She'd forgotten about yesterday's hand-wringing; it now seemed a lifetime ago.

"Peace to you, Mistress Berwyn," replied Rhonwyn.

The woman was business like. "My job is to run the king's household. I know everything that goes on here and make sure His Majesty is comfortable and has all he needs. I also take care of his retinue." She nodded at Rhonwyn, her eyes widening briefly. "If you need anything, first go to Kymra. If she's not able to help, come straight to me. Kymra is very capable, so I don't expect to see you often." Her expression was wry. Rhonwyn could sense Kymra beaming.

Mistress Berwyn went on, "If His Majesty needs your services, he will summon you. I recommend you attend him immediately; His Majesty must not be kept waiting." She paused for emphasis. "I also advise you to come to his audience at three o'clock today."

Rhonwyn frowned.

"It will help you become accustomed to court life and get used to His Majesty's proximity. It overawes most people. The

King finds it tiresome if the fuss goes on for too long."

Rhonwyn jumped in. "Wonderful. I will do that. But please explain: what is 'three o'clock'?"

At this, however, Mistress Berwyn glanced at Kymra. "Teach Rhonwyn how to use the clocks." To Rhonwyn she said. "Forgive me. I'm a busy woman, as you can see, and just wanted to meet you. I need to know all the members of the household by sight. I'll leave you in Kymra's hands. A good morn to you."

At this, she returned to her seat, checked her list, and called out for the next person. A burly man with thick, black hair and matching eyebrows bustled in and took a position, arms folded, next to Mistress Berwyn. They conferred in murmurs.

Kymra took Rhonwyn out the door and along the next corridor.

"I'll show you the throne room," said Kymra.

They hadn't gone far when a wondrous door caught Rhonwyn's eye. Inlaid with tiny white designs and figures, the dark wooden door was delicate and exquisite. Again, the artistry in the palace amazed her.

"Actually, this is where we're going," said Kymra. Beyond was a room lit by sunshine – through the roof far above.

Rhonwyn stalled on the threshold, mesmerised by the multicoloured glass roof. It looked like it was made of fish scales, some blue with green flowers embedded within, others opaque white with marigolds. The warm morning sun streamed in, enhancing every colour. Other panels contained unfamiliar birds with large, fanned tails, some blue, others entirely white. What were they?

Intricate designs covered the walls, gold on a deep red or turquoise background.

Kymra finally got Rhonwyn further into the room so she could close the door. Gold and turquoise striped columns made two parallel rows through the oblong room. At the top of each column were two gold ducks facing outwards. Between the ducks, human-looking figures with wings all knelt facing in one direction – towards the throne. Each figure had two faces – one on the front of its head, the other on the back. The images made her shiver.

Steps led up one side of the throne to a platform with cushions and a padded, ornate back for the king to lean against. An umbrella stood suspended over it.

As Rhonwyn stood gazing at all the opulence, there came a dry voice from behind her.

"Like it, do you?"

The sound of it sent darts of fear down Rhonwyn's back. Only one voice sounded like that, its multiple tones far too familiar. She whipped around and stared.

King Risick stood before her, an arrogant tilt to his head, his sulphur eyes staring directly at her face.

They narrowed as she looked back – frozen.

He wasn't as tall as she'd thought – the height her father had been. He wore clothes of the same, strange design as hers, but more elaborate. The swathes of cloth accentuated his slim build before tapering down to his near-naked feet. He looked alien somehow.

Rhonwyn suddenly spied Kymra in the corner of her eye, already kneeling and bowed over on the floor next to her.

She gasped and dropped to the floor, trying to remember where to place all her limbs.

"That's better," said the king. She heard him step closer to her. "Who are you?"

Was she supposed to talk to him from this position? Would he be able to hear her?

She spoke as loudly as she could. "My name is Rhonwyn mi Hywel, Your Majesty. I'm your new Gymbal opponent." Her voice quivered.

"Gymbal opponent?" He huffed. "I didn't realise you were a woman. I can't tell with these ridiculous names."

Was she meant to answer that? Probably not. Rhonwyn stayed silent.

"Alright, get up." He sounded irritated.

Both women stood to face him. Rhonwyn's heart was racing in her chest.

King Risick inspected Rhonwyn. "Well, I hope you have some skill. These buffoons bore me to death and I need some distraction." He thumbed behind him and Rhonwyn realised there were five other people standing there, watching.

He sniffed. "Well, I'm too busy for a game now. I'll call you soon. Be ready."

He sauntered past her. One of the people with him raced ahead and opened the door that Rhonwyn and Kymra had just entered.

The king was gone. Rhonwyn let out a breath she hadn't realised she was holding. Her father's memory had emerged with her fear and, in her mind, he was sneering at where they'd last seen the man, his fists on his hips.

"Just you wait, boy," he muttered.

Kymra seemed to sense how rattled Rhonwyn was and took her straight back to her room. She then stayed to teach her how clocks worked. Rhonwyn suspected Kymra hoped to distract her with what appeared to be a complicated subject.

"If it goes through the numbers twice, why are there only twelve hours on it? Why not all the hours of the day at once?"

This stumped Kymra. "I don't know. I never thought about it."

"And why twelve? Why not ten? Who decided how long an hour was?"

Kymra shrugged. "The king?"

Kymra had grown up with clocks and hadn't questioned how they worked, or why. Rhonwyn should do the same.

"I suppose that's how it is. Sorry. Carry on," she said.

Kymra was holding a small clock in her hand as she explained. She'd taken it from a shelf in Rhonwyn's room. It seemed the things were everywhere. In fact, Rhonwyn was told, they ran the entire kingdom. The bells that told everyone to start and end work and to have breaks, happened according to the clocks.

They had all been set to the same time.

Once Rhonwyn got the basics of it, she realised how useful it could be – everyone working within the same framework.

Learning about measuring time did distract her from the nervousness left over from meeting King Risick. She hadn't made a good first impression. If he didn't like her, she was sure he would get rid of her in a heartbeat.

Kymra outlined the general timetable of the palace, including mealtimes. Certain days of the week featured particular activities. Everything was centred around keeping the king happy.

There were time periods when His Majesty was more likely to call upon his Gymbal opponent, and Rhonwyn had to stay near her room. At other times, though, she could do whatever she liked and, if he needed her, someone would come to fetch her. Kymra asked Rhonwyn to tell her what she was planning to do during those times, so finding her wouldn't take long.

How would Rhonwyn know what to plan? Would that allow her time to find out the information she needed to get rid of Risick?

There were plenty of things to do, Kymra reassured her. All the resources of the palace were at her disposal.

Rhonwyn had always had her days filled for her – with chores on the farm, or her seamstress duties. The bell rang, you did the next thing. It was strange having so little of her day organised.

"I can really go anywhere I like?"

Kymra's smile faded only fractionally. "Everywhere within the palace walls, yes. There will be signs telling you where you can't go. There aren't that many. I suggest you take a big walk around the palace grounds today – get to know what's where. And remember, you can ask me for suggestions."

When Kymra finally left, Rhonwyn fidgeted for long moments. Lost without her guide, and with her belly writhing at the thought of coming across the king again, she fell to walking in circles in her room before stopping herself.

"Come on, Rhonny. You can't stay in here all day."

Her jaw fixed, Rhonwyn stepped out the door and retraced the halls back to the entrance. Spying some stairs near the exit, on a whim she climbed them.

They took her to the space above the entrance. The tiered areas and seats reminded Rhonwyn of the auditorium of the common hall – made for villagers to stand or sit in.

The ceiling above divided into nine arched areas and contained beautifully painted designs. Some sections resembled the sky with billowing clouds. Others had swirling designs in fawn and light green like the maps Rhonwyn remembered from the Wise One's workroom wall, where she'd been taught her letters.

The opening to the lower floor was surrounded by a fence made of wrought iron beaten into stalk and leaf designs. Woven within these was the figure of an eagle with two heads.

Which folklore character did that figure represent? Bwelys was the goddess of the air and birds, but looked like a normal woman. Fylus was the dark-skinned god of the earth. All the gods looked like people.

Domysh the faerie was a trickster. But a creature with the wrong number of limbs wouldn't fool anyone.

Perhaps it was the demons. They could look like animals. Normal animals, though, not anything with four arms or two heads. Rhonwyn had wondered if King Risick was a demon, but he was a man, not an animal. Even if he behaved like a demon.

Rhonwyn gasped, startled by the scuff of feet nearby, and sprinted back down the stairs and out the entrance without looking behind her.

The sun was well up now and she wandered the formal gardens, which were even more splendid and varied in the full light of day. Rhonwyn felt almost happy looking at them.

More than once, she had to dispel the image of her father walking alongside her. He would have enjoyed this place, but this was something she must do on her own.

Nervous of missing the set events, Rhonwyn made sure she was back in her room well before lunchtime. She circled the room again and again.

The sound of feet outside her door had her hurrying to open it. But Kymra wasn't there. Instead, Rhonwyn came face-to-face with two narrow-eyed men, one brown, the other pale. They had been passing and their heads turned as the door opened.

Rhonwyn gasped, withdrew and slammed the door shut. She heard the men chuckling as they carried on down the corridor. She stayed where she was, listening as more people passed by.

When the door rattled with a sudden knock, she leaped back in fright.

Rhonwyn eased the door ajar, peered through it, and could breathe again.

"Time for lunch," said Kymra, beaming.

The roar of many voices greeted them in the dining hall, as people jostled in all directions. King Risick sat alone at one end of the room, already consumed with wolfing down food from the dishes covering every inch of his table. It looked on the verge of collapsing under their weight. Unlike everyone else on Merynbyl, he didn't eat with his hands, but used metal utensils. Rhonwyn found it hard not to stare. She'd never seen anyone eat so fast. The other diners gave him a wide berth. There were fifty other diners in the room plus the servers running to and fro.

"You should only need one plate," said Kymra, eyeing the two that Rhonwyn had automatically picked up.

"Oh, silly me." The heat of a blush rushed up Rhonwyn's neck.

"Well, I must go. Enjoy your meal." Kymra's departure left Rhonwyn watching what others did and then searching for an unoccupied seat.

The king expected the palace occupants to use utensils at their tables as well. It took her a while to figure out how to hold the things, slyly spying on her table companions.

The food was spicier than Rhonwyn was accustomed to. She asked one server to bring water to ease the heat. Apparently, though, water wouldn't help. He kindly brought her a cup of something that would, which was the most delicious drink she'd ever had. It had a tang, but was sweet with a delicate fragrance, and took the burn away immediately.

She glanced again at Risick. He was still eating at an alarming rate. How could anyone who ate so much be so slim? She pulled her gaze away.

The woman next to her leaned over. "Don't worry, dear. Stare all you like. He doesn't notice anything when he's eating." The woman's eyes were bright and friendly and she gave Rhonwyn a huge smile. Her clothes were resplendent in bold and varied colours.

"Peace to you," said Rhonwyn.

"Well met. I'm Felenya. I sing for His Majesty. You're new, aren't you? What are you here for?" Felenya enunciated every word and was easy to hear through the babble in the background.

"I'm Rhonwyn. I arrived today. I'm His Majesty's new Gymbal Opponent."

"Aah!" The sound was long and broad. Felenya smiled again, a little cheekily this time. "Do you play other games? I've never been very good at Gymbal, but I do love a good game."

"Oh, absolutely, yes. I would be happy to play something with you. Is there somewhere particular to play games?"

Felenya laughed, the hoots echoing around the eating chamber. Some glanced in her direction. "You don't know where the games room is? Well, well, you are new." She continued chuckling, though Rhonwyn didn't feel laughed at.

She'd not expected to discover so many friendly people in the palace.

"How long have you been here?" she asked her table-mate.

"His Majesty has put up with me for ten years now. He loves music." Felenya's eyes widened at Rhonwyn and she leaned in again, her voice dropping only marginally. "He loves lots of things: dancing, singing, wrestling, art, colour. All sorts of activities." Her eyes slid away at that point and Rhonwyn took that to mean that not all the things His Majesty loved were fit to be mentioned.

Felenya introduced Rhonwyn to the people either side of them. Felenya seemed to know everyone. She had such a big personality; it would be hard *not* to know her.

Rhonwyn tried another dish and coughed and spluttered again before grabbing the soothing drink the server had brought her.

"You'll get used to the food," Felenya reassured her, "His Majesty always has it spicy. In fact, his is much spicier than ours. I don't know how he eats it. Everything he does, he seems to go to extremes. It's all or nothing with him."

It surprised Rhonwyn that Felenya felt free to express what almost sounded like a criticism of the king, with no fear of censure. She didn't even look around. Perhaps the palace inhabitants weren't watched as closely. She could only hope. But if that was so, why had the previous Resistance members who'd managed to get in been found out so quickly?

When the meal was over, Kymra met Rhonwyn at the door to continue her tour of the palace. Taking her again through the front entrance, she showed her the tiered area Rhonwyn had come across in the morning. She told Rhonwyn it was for public audiences. Further in, an extraordinary hall of columns – four rows of them – spanned the full width of the building. The columns were peppermint green and two different pinks in stripes, with gold filigree at the top. Large mirrors placed at both ends of each row gave the illusion of the rows continuing forever in both directions.

The beauty of the palace complex again amazed Rhonwyn.

"Kymra, where did the design for all these things come from? The king?" she guessed.

Kymra nodded. "He drew and described it all to those who built it and insisted that they do it exactly as he'd ordered. I believe he once said he designed it so he could feel truly at home." She frowned. "That's a funny thing to say, isn't it? Of course he's at home."

Yes, it was a strange thing to say, but Kymra had obviously never thought along these lines before. Rhonwyn must be careful; perhaps she was asking too many questions. That kind of thinking might get Kymra in trouble.

8

At three o'clock – Rhonwyn counted the three chimes from the clock in the hallway – she managed to find the throne room again. This time, it overflowed with people. Some watched, others queued for the attention of the king.

Rhonwyn slipped in and found an out-of-the-way place from which to observe. The number of people crammed in created a sharp, sweaty odour.

The king sat on his throne, ankles crossed, bare feet drawn up underneath his thighs, and leaned against the cushions behind him, his eyes narrowed.

As time passed, and the seemingly endless line of people approached one by one, the king leaned further and further forward and fidgeted, his movements jerky.

Mistress Berwyn was nearby, pushing forward the next supplicant and ejecting those who'd had their turn. The king showed little patience with anyone who hesitated or provided too much detail. He interrupted, badgering them to get straight to the point. This made them more flustered – and he more annoyed. Those used to the process spent as short a time as possible presenting their reports. Others were more timid.

At one point – when the king seemed particularly agitated by a man gibbering about horse prices – Mistress Berwyn nodded to Kymra. She came forward and placed a glass globe full of what looked like smoke on one end of the throne's platform.

The king snatched the end of its long, decorated tube and sucked on it, breathing deeply. When he breathed out, smoke snaked from between his lips and from his nose. Soon his eyes glazed over and he appeared calm; he fell back into his cushions and gazed off into the distance as though in a dream world.

Rhonwyn had seen people smoke many years ago – the activity was prohibited now – but it had never looked like this. Men had puffed from a pipe in the evening after coming in from the fields, or at community meetings. Nor had Rhonwyn seen it affect someone so drastically.

Finally, after the clock chimed five times, the line of people petered out. Audience time was over. The smoke in the glass globe was diminishing, too. Perhaps Mistress Berwyn timed when she gave it to the King, so it wouldn't run out too early.

Rhonwyn was making her way towards the door when Kymra intercepted her.

"The king requests your services," the girl murmured.

Rhonwyn's heart squeezed. She must play well so she could stay long enough to gather information and not give herself away as a spy. She took a deep breath as she followed Kymra. She'd seen how irritated the king became when faced with timidity and was determined to do better this time.

The games room was round, with a high glass roof, like the throne room's. Two comfortable chairs faced one another in its central area with a Gymbal board and its playing pieces on a table between them. A mezzanine jutted out halfway up the walls, under which other games tables were arranged, where groups of people played various games, their voices occasionally ringing into the space.

Rhonwyn had to concentrate on Gymbal. She knew she must impress His Majesty, or her term as Royal Gymbal Opponent would be short. She must do her best for the sake of the people of Merynbyl.

Assuming the more opulent seat was for King Risick, she took the other chair and set the board up for play. She paused at the sight of the playing pieces. They were the most beautiful figurines she'd ever seen, much of their decoration similar to the patterns on the king's clothing – and hers. The board was wider and the levels more elaborate than Rhonwyn was used to. She felt her gaze intensify.

"Everything does the same thing, Rhonny."

She started. In her anxious state, her father's voice was almost audible to her – and harder to ignore.

The greatest challenge was the mind game. She needed to relax and not be so nervous. She assumed he preferred to be challenged – even beaten – by his opponent.

Was that right? Would he get angry if she won? No one had said. Well, she would find out, wouldn't she? She would simply do her best and hope.

Rhonwyn's pulse throbbed in her ears as she sat waiting, sitting on her hands so she wouldn't fidget. Looking up, she began studying the chandelier above her. Three enormous rings were chained to one another with at least twenty lamps dangling off them, all at varying heights.

"Well?" came a voice.

Rhonwyn slipped to her knees, barely glancing at His Majesty, and curled into a bow. Did the king always enter rooms so quietly?

"Enough," he said after a moment.

She straightened and resumed her seat as the king settled in across from her. Servers brought snacks to him. Rhonwyn hoped he wouldn't cover the pieces with bits of food and then saw the image of her father laughing at her. The king could do anything he liked.

Stop, stop, stop. That would get her in trouble.

They sat for a moment, Risick looking her up and down, before he leaned forward and moved his first piece – not the regular opening move. He was trying to throw her. Rhonwyn swallowed her smile and made her own move.

The king huffed a laugh, his mouth wrinkling into a wry

smile as they continued. She'd passed that test, it seemed.

As usual, the two players spent the beginning of the game setting up the terrain while at the same time arranging pieces to outmanoeuvre the other player. Risick played at top speed. Rhonwyn kept her head and slipped her pieces into attack positions whilst using other moves to draw attention away from her tactics. After his first smile, Risick kept his face impassive, giving nothing away. Only when he paused ever so slightly after having committed a piece could Rhonwyn see he might have some doubt.

Risick was a good player. Rhonwyn found herself absorbed in the game and noticed his entire attention was taken with it too. He might be enjoying himself. She certainly hoped so.

At one point she leaned back to discover they had an audience. A man with a large beard and dark eyes and his clean-shaven companion were leaning against the mezzanine's rail, watching.

The play was elaborate and took several different turns before the clock chimed seven times, startling the king mid-manoeuvre. They'd been playing silently for two hours. Her opponent was taking more time now, reassessing the situation before making each move. He leaned back, seized a handful of snacks and threw them into his mouth as he glared at Rhonwyn.

She was about to trap him. Did he realise? Or was this another tactic to put her off? With her heart tripping as it was, it might very well work. Was she meant to meet his gaze? And did she really have him where she thought she did? Self-doubt made her tense. She was hungry too. Hunger helped with concentration, though. Rhonwyn breathed deeply and unclenched her muscles one by one.

"Good girl," she heard her father murmur. In her mind, his weathered face was tilted over the board. He even wore his black peaked cap. His presence calmed her further. She eased forward and made her play as Risick continued to stare at her.

When he took in what she'd done, he leapt forward and

reached for a piece before freezing and drawing back again. His eyes flicked from place to place on the board, assessing one move after another as his brows descended.

He had no way forward. Any move he made would mean the loss of the battle. Rhonwyn held her breath as he searched for a a path out of his predicament. Would he find one? Or would she win … and make him angry? She should have asked whether she was supposed to let him win. Her heart was trying to find a way up her throat.

He looked up at her, sulphur eyes burning, face rock-hard then transforming as he smiled and laughed.

"Very good."

This chilled Rhonwyn to the bone. They were the same words he'd said to the man he'd executed the night before. She forced herself to smile back.

Risick leaned back in his chair. "Excellent." He stretched like a cat, got up and left, leaving Rhonwyn staring after him, eyebrow raised.

He hadn't made the final move: capitulation, where the key piece was handed over to the victor. This left Rhonwyn bereft of the winner's satisfaction. Had he done that deliberately? If he won, would he expect her to capitulate?

Kymra leaned into her field of vision, startling her. "Well done! I'll take you to the dining room."

Rhonwyn blinked. "I'll put the game away," she replied. The set had to be ready for the next game; Rhonwyn had a particular way she stored it so it would be easier to set out.

Rhonwyn realised just how tired she was as she trudged towards the dining area, Kymra chattering beside her. The long period of concentration had taken its toll. It usually did, just more so this time. And it'd been a long day.

Rhonwyn sighed and shook her head. Yes, she was hungry; however, the sensation warred with her exhaustion.

"Are there any dishes that aren't so spicy?" she asked Kymra. "I'm not sure I'll sleep so well with my stomach full of spice."

Kymra smiled and nodded. "I'll make a request with the cook."

"Thank you," replied Rhonwyn.

"I have no idea how that game works." Kymra's innocent smile beamed forth as they passed through the dining room doors. "I didn't know what was going on. And then you won, just like that."

Just like that?

9

Rhonwyn didn't sleep well and woke while it was still dark. Tangled in her bedclothes, she struggled to escape and panicked when she couldn't find the edge of the bed.

Of course. The thing was bigger than she was used to.

That's right, she was in the palace. Rhonwyn lay in the darkness for some time before hearing the faint chime of the clock out in the hallway. Four chimes. Her mind began to turn over.

What time did the sun rise? Didn't the day get longer and shorter when the seasons changed? Did that affect the clocks and how they worked? Were the hours longer, or shorter? Was sunrise at the same time every day?

These questions whirred around in her head until she sat up and threw them off, along with her covers. She was well awake now and felt like getting up.

Was she allowed to walk around the palace at this time of day? Would she be told to go back to her room? Were there guards? She didn't remember seeing a single Enforcer since she'd arrived. Nor had there been the usual list of rules posted anywhere. What were the rules?

And there'd been no Announcements. The usual time for Announcements had passed while she and the king had been playing Gymbal. There were no panels - not that she'd seen, anyway. Things were very different here.

Rhonwyn felt the heavy silence. She was used to hearing people nearby, snoring or moving about. The large rooms must be what made it so quiet. She'd never slept in such a large room, even on her father's farm. She felt even more isolated than usual.

The night was warm enough to go exploring. She would venture out and see what happened. If anyone was up, she would talk to them. That might help.

She thought she'd left some fire sticks next to the lamp, but she drew them along the scraper several times before realising they'd already been used up. The magic that made them spark to life could only be used once. She briefly wondered why that was.

Giving up on lamp light, Rhonwyn rose, dressed, and cracked open her door. The stars, shining through glass skylights, provided sufficient light to wander around without tripping.

Pulling a wrap over her shoulders against the chill, she walked along the corridor and took the stairs down to the ground floor. She got all the way to the palace entrance without seeing a soul. A feeling of freedom gripped her as she wound through the many garden beds, going nowhere in particular. She removed her sandals to walk barefoot on the grass. No one was around to tell her off. No one.

When she finally thought to look up, she gasped. The deep darkness of the sky – with no moon – accentuated the swathe of stars. Rooted to the spot, Rhonwyn stared at the heavenly bodies until her neck became stiff. She lay down on the damp grass then and gazed up into what seemed like eternity.

"Remember we used to do this?"

Back before Risick had come, her father had often taken her out at night. They'd lain down on the top of Byron's Tor, just a short walk away from the farmhouse. He'd wrapped one arm around her to keep her warm and used the other to point upwards.

"There's the Tymbral constellation," he'd said, "See the circles, one inside another? The Archer – he's over there. There's his arrow. And there's the Deer of the Lord, forever escaping the wounds of the hunter."

She remembered her little voice, saying, "Papa, where are the teeth of Gobmyl?" Her father had told her the story only a few days before as he'd been milking one of their cows, the steam rising off his wooden bucket, his head resting against the cow's side. Rhonwyn had loved the story and had already asked him to tell it again.

He'd pointed closer to the horizon. "Down there. When his teeth rise no more, summer is with us in full. See the 'W'?"

"Wa!" she'd cried. He'd been reminding her of the letters from her lessons and she'd exalted in her new knowledge; that was how 'W' sounded.

He'd laughed. "Yes! Do you see it?"

She'd peered into the sky and had seen the down-up-down-up of the letter she'd only been shown the week before. She'd pointed and giggled. "Gobmyl's gnashers, old world smashers!"

Her father had chuckled again and bent to kiss her forehead. "Good girl," he'd said.

No 'W' in the sky tonight. Rhonwyn found tears running into her ears and the stars became indistinct. "Papa?" she whispered. "I'm scared, but I'm being brave, just like you said to. Watch over me. Help me find what I need for the Resistance and not get caught."

She sat up, wiped her eyes, and looked around. What could she see? No one was around. Was that a clue? Could she indeed move freely at night, with no one the wiser? Did they have king's-eyes here? She hadn't seen any. She must pay more attention during the day.

Rhonwyn stood and walked towards the fountain, its water dancing for her alone. The magic worked all the time? Even when the king was asleep? What did that tell her?

She followed the outlet from the fountain's pool to the wall that prevented people walking off the precipice. It was too high for her to see over. The top of the aperture over the stream rose only a hand's breadth above its surface. She knelt down and, leaning over the smoothly running water, peered through the hole.

Light shone through the gap.

The only thing out there was the king's chamber. How could he be awake at this hour? Did he *ever* sleep?

She knew she could see his chamber from her balcony, so Rhonwyn made her way back to her room and ventured out the double doors.

The night hid the vast drop beneath her, so she had less trouble standing at the rail. Yes, light beamed from the king's chamber – an island in the dark. In fact she could only detect the light as it reflected off the decorations hanging from the eaves; none of the windows actually faced the palace.

No one could look in on His Majesty at night. Neither could he look towards them.

What did that tell her? How could she get in there? Where was the entrance? She would have to find a way; she was sure it was important to get in. If she could find out Risick's secrets, perhaps she could discover a way to overpower him and his magic.

Holding tightly to the rail, she leaned over it to see if she could determine where the entrance to the king's chamber was, but the darkness hid it from sight. She would have to wait for daylight.

She returned to her bed and lay on it, fully dressed, waiting for the sun to rise. Would there be any reaction to her nighttime activities? She hadn't done anything wrong, that she was aware of, so hopefully she had no reason to fear.

She woke with a start at a knock on the door. Her heart raced.

She sat up. "Hello?"

"A good morn to you, Rhonwyn," a voice called. "It's nearly time for breakfast."

Kymra was really taking care of her.

"I'll be right with you," Rhonwyn called back.

Checking her hair and clothing, she splashed her face quickly and went out into the hall where Kymra was waiting for her.

"Is it bad to be late for breakfast?" she asked as they headed for the dining hall.

"Not really," said Kymra. "I'm just supposed to take care of you for the first three meals, to make sure you remember when they are. Why is there grass on your sandals?"

Rhonwyn stopped to brush it off and laughed self-consciously – she must be more careful. "I was awake during the night and went for a little walk in the garden. Am I allowed to do that?"

Kymra nodded. "Yes, of course. That sounds nice." She didn't seem concerned at all. Once again, Rhonwyn was amazed at how free the occupants of the palace seemed.

"It was. The stars were amazing," said Rhonwyn. "Is there a list of rules that I should know?"

"Rules?" said Kymra, frowning.

"Yes, there's usually a set of rules to keep up to date with, so we know what we're not allowed to do."

Kymra tittered and looked down. "No, we don't have that here. The only rule is to keep the king happy, really." They turned the last corner before the dining room door. "Are there really lists of rules outside?"

The roar of conversation grew louder as Kymra opened the door for Rhonwyn.

"Yes," she replied and tilted her head at the girl. "Haven't you been outside the palace grounds?"

"No," said Kymra with a wry grin, a tint of red colouring her face. "I'll have to find out what it's like from you sometime. I need to go now. Will you be alright?"

"Yes, I'll be fine. Thank you, Kymra."

So they had freedom, but only within the bounds of the

palace walls. As long as the selected few did what kept the king happy – the task they were there for – they had the run of the place.

No wonder there was so much chatter and laughter. They didn't seem to care what was happening outside.

Rhonwyn's jaw clenched as she watched the girl retreating for a moment before she searched for a vacant seat.

"Yoo hoo!" sang a booming voice over to the right. Felenya was standing at her chair and waving for Rhonwyn to join her. She'd attracted a lot of attention but the king continued eating, his head down.

Bemused, Rhonwyn walked over and joined her.

Felenya chuckled as she resumed her chair, her eyes sparkling. "Yes, everyone sits in the same place every meal."

Rhonwyn's brows rose.

"I tried to sit somewhere different once and got the bum's rush from one irate man." Felenya's version of a whisper was amusing. "Have some of this." She pushed over a bowl full of scrambled eggs.

"Thanks." Rhonwyn grinned. "And thank you for letting me join you here."

This made Felenya hoot with laughter, though Rhonwyn wasn't sure why.

"I heard you beat His Majesty last night. Well done," she added, waving her fork at Rhonwyn. "He likes a challenge. If you can keep him distracted with a clever play, he'll be less ..." She paused and leaned back before she went on. "... more relaxed, believe it or not. I'm singing tonight. Will you come and listen? It's in the throne room – it has the best acoustics."

"Of course I will. I would be delighted. What are acoustics?" She slipped in the question before Felenya changed topics again. The woman slid around subjects like a duck on a frozen pond.

Felenya swallowed and patted Rhonwyn's hand as she thought, and her eyes brightened even more. "That's what a room and its surfaces do to sound. You'll have heard it yourself.

In some rooms, sound falls to the ground and it's difficult to hear and, in others, the sound bounces around gleefully, popping into your ears in a jiffy – sometimes more than once."

Rhonwyn smiled at her description.

"The king himself explained that to me," said Felenya. "Not in those exact words. He's a very clever man – he knows so much. He had me sing in nearly every room in the palace to find out which one worked best for me."

"How often do you sing?"

"Once or twice a week. Sometimes three or four, if His Majesty or one of his visitors wishes. I need to take care of my voice, though, so I make sure it's not more than that. I'm always working on new pieces to sing. We keep the court composers very busy. He has four."

"Court composers?"

"Yes, they invent the music I sing."

"I thought you made it up."

"Oh goodness, no," said Felenya, "I'm not nearly clever enough for that."

"Nonsense, woman," said a passing man, his head bald, his nose knobbly and enormous. He leaned over Felenya. "You just need to practise."

Felenya giggled and flapped her hand. "You're too kind, Urven. Too kind."

She turned to Rhonwyn. "This is Urven – one of the court composers I was telling you about. I'll be singing one of his pieces tonight."

Rhonwyn smiled. "Well met, Urven. I'll look forward to it. I've never really gone to a … a singing thing," she ended lamely.

"A concert, dear," said Felenya.

"Well, you're in for a treat," said Urven. "Felenya's singing is truly of the gods." He straightened and, with a brief wave, returned to his seat just two tables away.

Felenya insisted she and Rhonwyn meet for a game of Twyrn straight after breakfast.

)))●(((

Their hour in the games room was animated and raucous – a complete contrast to Rhonwyn's game with the king. The two older men playing at the next table left after one particularly loud burst of laughter from Rhonwyn and Felenya. They directed frowns at the pair, making Felenya clap her hand over her mouth until the men were gone, and then guffaw even more. Though it was a simple game and required mostly luck, Rhonwyn had a marvellous time. She'd truly not expected to make friends here in the palace, and now she'd met two.

Guilt surged up in her heart. She should be working, not having fun.

Would it be acceptable for her to ask Felenya about the king? Surely that wouldn't be suspicious. She'd only arrived yesterday and new people always asked questions.

"It's so different here," she began, as Felenya shuffled the cards for another game. "I didn't expect it to be like this."

"What were you expecting?"

"I was expecting it to be dreary and ... more restrictive, I suppose, being closer to the king." She studied Felenya's reaction, which was underwhelming.

"Ah, yes, I remember that," she said. "How many restrictions there were outside and how dull it was. And my surprise at how colourful and intriguing everything was in here." Felenya leaned forward. "The king loves colour and flavour, art, and music. His world is full of wonder and creativity. So, the closer you get to him, the lovelier things become."

Rhonwyn stared. It sounded so unbelievable. She nearly asked her new friend to explain why the king, therefore, restricted everyone else's wonder and beauty.

She sensed her father shaking his head. No, that would not be wise.

Felenya answered the question anyway. "He told me he has

to have lots of rules outside because people don't know how to rule themselves. That's what he's for, he says: to teach them how to be productive and to rule themselves. He often gets frustrated with the silly things that people do." She dealt the cards out.

It didn't seem to bother Felenya that the king's frustration resulted in public executions.

Rhonwyn tilted her head. There was actually only one reason she knew the king killed people.

"Do you have Announcements here?"

"Announcements?" asked Felenya. She was still sorting the cards she'd dealt to herself.

"The daily Announcements, with new rules and weather and ..." Rhonwyn gasped at the memory of the last execution she'd witnessed. "... messages from the king. Everyone has to watch them."

"Really? I didn't know he did that. When does he do that?" Felenya flipped over the top card of the deck and looked at Rhonwyn, ready to play.

"He does a message once a week." Rhonwyn placed her first card.

Perhaps Felenya didn't know. Especially since she'd been here for so long. Most of the king's reign in fact. A lot of things had changed in that time.

"You must pay attention, Rhonwyn," said Felenya. She giggled. She'd played a card, picked up another, and snatched up her own and Rhonwyn's card straight away as Rhonwyn had sat watching.

"Oh, dear. Sorry!" Rhonwyn laughed.

Did anyone in the palace know what the king did to the people outside?

10

Rhonwyn spent the rest of the morning exploring more of the grounds. As she entered the stable courtyard, a group of mounted men rattled in. They looked official.

Rhonwyn stayed out of their path at the edge and watched as the riders dismounted and gave their horses to the grooms. All but one wore a sword and a uniform. Rhonwyn had only seen these uniforms in her capacity as seamstress. They were for the bodyguards of the president.

The important-looking one must be the president himself. He had an enormous moustache, a round belly, and legs that looked like they would snap if someone kicked him in the shins. His men had to help him down from his horse, bringing a platform he could slide onto. He vacillated on the last of its steps, attempting to avoid a pile of manure. Rhonwyn struggled not to laugh.

All at once a man loomed over her, his top lip bare, his expression severe. "Who are you? What are you doing here?" One of the uniformed officers, the man had his hand on his sword.

She blinked twice. "I'm R-Rhonwyn. I'm just looking around," she replied, her heart hammering all of a sudden.

"What is your position in the king's household?" he demanded.

This was more like an interrogation. The image of her father had materialised and was glaring at him, arms folded.

"I'm the Royal Gymbal Opponent." She had no way of proving this, however. Perhaps she would be asked to leave.

The man stilled and stared at her from under his bushy greying eyebrows. He inspected her closely.

He eventually spoke again, his voice less pointed. "Well, be sure to stay out of the way, miss." He sniffed and, with one last, narrow glance at her, returned to his fellows. Rhonwyn watched him until he followed the president into the palace. His cohorts were deferring to him, so perhaps he was their captain. He marched them away after the president.

She hurried to the dining room and found what was now her regular seat next to Felenya. She'd lost track of time and wondered how she would ever figure out when the meals were. There were no bells rung to let them know, as there had been outside, in the city. Rhonwyn hadn't realised how dependent she was on them.

The president and his retinue were seated at a table to the side of the king. They made an enormous amount of noise as they enjoyed the food and drink.

The king didn't require a game that afternoon – apparently he was too busy. Kymra came to bring Rhonwyn the news and then decided she would join her for the afternoon; she had a half-day off. She suggested they visit the menagerie.

As much as she enjoyed Kymra's company, Rhonwyn was disappointed. She'd been planning on exploring further to find the door to the king's chamber. She soon forgot her frustration, however, when she saw the extraordinary animals on display.

In one of the larger enclosures were a group of long-haired creatures, black with white chests, their ears protruding from their round heads. Nearly the entire group screamed at each other as they swung with their long arms from tree limb to tree limb, chasing each other. But they seemed to be having a great time. Rhonwyn was mesmerised.

When she and Kymra finally tore themselves away, they found a small glass cube sitting in the sun. Rhonwyn had trouble even seeing what was meant to be on show. She couldn't believe her eyes when she spotted the tiny blue and yellow frogs, smaller than her thumbnail.

"I've never seen animals like these. Where did they come from?" she asked.

"If you look at the little sign here, it shows you what continent they came from as well as what they are." Kymra was pointing at a board hanging just above and to the right of the cube.

"Continent?" Rhonwyn wasn't familiar with the word.

Kymra explained. "It's the piece of land on a certain part of the planet. See here?" She pointed at the sign again, next to the box of writing.

All Rhonwyn could see were a series of blobs of different shapes in a rectangle. She felt her neck heating.

"I'm sorry, I don't understand. What is that?"

Kymra's forehead wrinkled. "It's a map. Haven't you seen a map before?"

Rhonwyn looked again, irritated by her own denseness. "Yes, I've seen the map before, but it doesn't look like this. The Dryze River is up here and the sea is on the left." She used her finger to draw an invisible map on a blank section of the sign.

"Ah! You're talking about the map of *this* area." Kymra pointed again at the blobs in the rectangle. "This is a map of the whole planet."

Rhonwyn took a breath and winced. "Alright, I'm going to have to admit something else: I don't know what a planet is." Kymra had mentioned the word twice now.

Kymra's mouth tensed up, and she cleared her throat.

"It's the big ball of land and water that we live on. This ..." she pointed again to the rectangle with its blobs. "... is the pattern of the land on our planet. See here ..." she used her fingernail to indicate a tiny area on the far right of the rectangle, "... you'll see the shape of land that you're used to seeing in maps."

Rhonwyn peered at the image, crammed into the corner, and felt her jaw growing slack. "There's that much land out there on … our planet?"

"And it's all empty." Kymra's voice rose in pitch. "The king said he couldn't believe how much space we had. Room for lots more people."

Rhonwyn frowned. "Why did he move us all into the city, then?" They'd had so much room on their farms and then, when King Risick had seized power, they'd had to live in tiny boxes close to all the other families, which had caused so much tension.

"The king says it's because it's more efficient," said Kymra, smiling.

Rhonwyn nodded. Of course, Kymra was too young to remember the time before King Risick had taken over and the freedoms they'd had, so she didn't have anything to compare it with. Kymra seemed to think very highly of the king. Rhonwyn must make sure she didn't criticise him to the girl as she was likely to get upset.

Kymra's previous words popped back into Rhonwyn's head. "A *ball* of land and water? Land is flat. And the water would fall off if it was on something round. And how does a rectangle fit on a ball?"

Kymra was speechless for a moment, then shrugged and admitted, "It's just what I've been told – we live on a ball. I don't know how it works."

The questions that had been bubbling up in Rhonwyn's mind sank again. It sounded like Kymra didn't know the answers to them. Who would? She nearly shooed the vision of her father away, stopping herself just in time. He'd passed his curiosity on to her.

Rhonwyn was here for something else, though. She *must* concentrate on what was important: getting Risick off the throne.

Every time they stopped at an animal enclosure, Rhonwyn took the opportunity to study the map again. A red dot marked where the animal inside had come from. Some were from the other side of the rectangle. How had they got here?

Rhonwyn and Kymra's legs finally tired, and they collapsed on the seat opposite the loud swinging creatures called monkeys, and sat giggling at them.

The atmosphere in the throne room was entirely different from yesterday afternoon's. Again, people were everywhere, seated on chairs or cushions. But this time they were relaxed, and the room was full of the warm buzz of conversation.

A small, empty platform stood where the throne had been and the throne itself was over to one side and pivoted so it faced the platform.

Rhonwyn searched for somewhere to sit. Up against a column near the back, three empty seats stood in a row. She perched on one of them and waited, watching the crowd in the atmospheric lighting, provided by lamps positioned around the room.

The audience was resplendent in an array of colours. Those on cushions lay or sat cross-legged, much like the king yesterday on his throne. The president and his entourage sat in the middle of the room, the president in the centre.

Rhonwyn looked up as a smattering of applause erupted from those on her right along with calls of admiration. Some people even stood.

Felenya was entering the room. She looked stunning, her dress shimmering as she ascended the steps. More cheers rose as she took her place on the platform.

The crowd settled, and a beaming Felenya spoke. Her voice was easily heard. Perhaps this was because of the acoustics she'd spoken of. But then, Rhonwyn knew how loud Felenya was normally.

"Ladies and gentlemen, thank you for your generous welcome. It is delightful to see you all." She spotted Rhonwyn, her bright eyes widened in greeting and she nodded with an impish grin. Felenya's face was painted with subtle rosy shades that accentuated her cheekbones and drew all attention to her eyes.

She went on, "And now, may I present to you our esteemed ruler and glorious patron of the arts: His Majesty, King Risick of Merynbyl." She turned towards the throne and folded in the middle, bowing to Risick who'd appeared and stood surveying his subjects.

Everyone in the room rustled to their knees and bowed their heads. Silence reigned as they waited for the word of the king.

"You may rise."

When Rhonwyn raised her head, the king had settled against his cushions, his attention fixed upon the stage. As she looked away, her eye caught another's, looking directly at her. The captain of the president's guard nodded at her.

Nonplussed by his attention, Rhonwyn didn't make any response before the man looked away again. He was standing at the far edge of the president's mob of soldiers, leaning against a column.

Felenya spoke again. "Your Majesty, Mister President, and friends, Urven ma Iwan wrote this first song just last week." She grinned cheekily at the king. "It's my new favourite."

The king flashed a crooked smile at her and a wave of gentle laughter rose and fell.

The audience quieted and Felenya clasped her hands as the sound of a stringed instrument floated forward from behind the platform. Several musicians sat there, including a man who strummed a guitar. One chord rang through the room ... two ... three ... and Felenya opened her mouth and sang.

Rhonwyn had never heard anything like it. The notes soared and floated through the air, trilled and twisted from side to side before falling and rising again. The closest thing in Rhonwyn's experience was the call of a bird echoing in the forest – an old memory.

Felenya sang a phrase and then sang it again, so softly. Her control was extraordinary. Though the song had no words, Felenya relished each note. At its climax, she hit and held a delicate, high tone, trilled upon it, circled amongst the notes surrounding it before returning finally, and letting it dissolve into the air.

Only when there was complete silence did the audience began to cheer and clap. Rhonwyn sat, stunned by the beauty of it and touched to the core.

Felenya gaze sought her out, one eyebrow raised in query. Rhonwyn beamed back, pressed both hands to her heart, and closed her eyes in bliss. When she opened them again, Felenya was taking another bow.

The next song was equally stunning. Felenya truly had a voice from the gods. A variety of instruments accompanied the next few songs. A petite, brown woman played a pipe – Rhonwyn loved its bending, willowy sound. Another played a flute, and still another a set of drums. One stick-thin man stood behind a frame upon which he struck pieces of wood suspended over pipes – a round, full sound. She must ask Felenya about that.

The king was entranced. He lay back, his lids closed as he listened, a dreamy smile on his face. Without those unsettling eyes, he could almost have been handsome.

Rhonwyn's gaze fell again on the president's party. The captain was no longer there. That was a relief.

During the next song, she had her own eyes shut as she listened to Felenya weave her voice with the flute and pipe – up and down, in and out. Rhonwyn smiled in delight.

Someone sat on the chair next to her. Before she could open her eyes, a low voice spoke near her ear – a man's voice. Not her father's.

"Don't open your eyes and don't react."

She'd already jumped, but regained her composure.

"I am your contact to the Resistance. We must not be seen together. During concerts is best. At the back, where we are now.

Don't write notes; they may be dropped and found by others."

The song came to a close and Rhonwyn opened her eyes as the applause began. Both her and her neighbour joined in.

She dared not turn her head towards him, but his uniform was plain to see out of the corner of her eye: the captain of the president's guard. She'd thought she'd recognised the voice – hard and distant. Not one that inspired immediate trust.

"Excuse me. I don't know what you're talking about," said Rhonwyn, her voice as low as his and as casual as she could manage, though her heart thundered. "I know nothing about the Resistance and I wouldn't have anything to do with them if I did. They're trouble."

The next song had begun and Felenya's audience was once again held rapt by her perfect tone. Damn the man! Why did he have to come along during this? She could barely think.

The man grunted. "Of course not. Very good." She felt him move his arm. "Look at your knee now."

Rhonwyn felt a feather-touch and looked down to find a picture of her father standing with her eight-year-old self. Both pairs of eyes were wide and puzzled – neither had understood what the officials meant by 'taking a photo of you' on their first day in the building site of the city. She stared at the lean, tanned face of her father as her chest squeezed.

The man flipped it over and she found Kephlen's lettering on the back: "Trust this man. He is with us." This was the image she'd left in his care.

"Do you have anything for me?" the man went on, tucking the picture away in his jacket.

"No," Rhonwyn replied. Could she ask for the photo? No. Her mind flitted from thought to thought, examining, discarding. The danger she was in heightened every sense.

He then left such a long silence between them that Rhonwyn became lost in the music once more. He startled her when he spoke again.

"I'm not sure when I will return. Be ready to report at

any time."

This didn't seem to require a response, so Rhonwyn gave none. When she opened her eyes the next time, the man was gone.

He hadn't even told her his name.

11

Despite what seemed like great self-confidence on Felenya's part, she was inordinately concerned with Rhonwyn's opinion of her performance.

"So, you really enjoyed it?" she asked – again. They were eating breakfast.

"I've never heard anything like it. It was extraordinary. Thank you so much for the invitation. Am I allowed to come to other ones?"

"Oh, yes. Most concerts are for everyone in the palace grounds. People seem to enjoy coming along, for some reason." Felenya slid a look at Rhonwyn. Was this another appeal to compliment her performance?

"Of course they do. Your voice is divine. They would be mad not to." Would that be enough?

Felenya's enormous grin and giggle said 'yes'.

Many fellow-diners interrupted their conversation that morning to congratulate Felenya on her singing. She enjoyed every minute and knew each person's name.

Just as they finished eating, a tall, bright-eyed woman came up and grasped the singer's shoulder.

"What a lovely performance last night, Felenya. Thank you," she said.

Felenya's rich voice replied, "You're very welcome, Jovla. Are you coming by this morning?"

The other woman looked eager. "Yes, please. The usual time?"

"That's right. I'll see you then."

As the woman walked away, Felenya leaned towards Rhonwyn and said, "She's a wonderful singer. She takes lessons from me. I'm asking her to sing in one of my concerts soon. I hope she won't be too nervous to do it."

"You teach singing?"

"Yes." Felenya tapped Rhonwyn's forearm. "There might be some who ask you for Gymbal lessons, you know."

The thought horrified Rhonwyn. "Do I have to teach them?"

Felenya's face opened out in a smile. "Only if you want to."

After breakfast, Felenya hurried away and Rhonwyn set about searching for the entrance to the king's chamber. First she ventured onto the balcony outside her room to lean over the rail – her knuckles white as she held on for dear life. Strangely, the suspended corridor seemed to stretch out from somewhere even lower than the ground floor. How was that possible?

Once she'd counted the number of windows down and over, she left her room and headed off in the opposite direction to the king's chamber; she still couldn't be sure she wasn't being watched.

Walking along the next corridor, she heard a woman singing, though the sound was faint. It sounded like exercises, the same pattern of notes repeated on changing pitches. That must be where Felenya taught.

Rhonwyn completed an entire circuit of the first floor, making sure no one was following her. She took the stairs down to the ground floor and into new territory. A side corridor led to a courtyard in the centre of the building. Two men wrestled beneath an open sky, others surrounding them, cheering them on. The wrestlers pushed and strained against one another, their feet sliding in the fine dust. Rhonwyn was shocked to discover the king himself standing in a corner, watching, urging, his expression eager. She hurried away, unseen.

Beyond, in the corner of the building right above the cliff

face, another set of stairs led downwards. This was most likely where the entrance to the king's chamber was and, if someone saw her in the area, it might seem suspicious. With no one in sight, she took the plunge and slipped down the stairs to the lower level.

Paintings lined the left side of the corridor she found there. There were doors only on the right side and, as she ventured further, one opened and a tall muscled man strode towards her.

Though Rhonwyn's heart was in her mouth, she took a steadying breath and spoke to him.

"I beg your indulgence," she began.

"Peace to you," he replied, pausing as he reached her.

"And to you. I'm new to the palace and I'm exploring. Are all the rooms down here people's quarters? Are there any common rooms on this level?"

The man swivelled and pointed along the corridor. "Most of them are people's quarters. Do you see the names on the walls next to the doors? That's how you can tell whose quarters they are."

Rhonwyn now spotted these tiny signs. Their writing was in a decorative cursive that matched the pattern on the wall which was why she hadn't detected them before. She wished she'd worked harder on her lessons with the Wise One.

The man smiled. "It took me a while to figure that out myself," he said. "I'm not very good with my letters, so I don't notice things like that. There are two rooms you can visit at the end of the corridor. One's called a library, and the other is a sitting room with an incredible view into the valley."

"Thank you so much," she said. "I'm Rhonwyn, the Royal Gymbal Opponent. Well met." She held out her hand.

"Welcome, Rhonwyn. I'm Brynn, the wrestling champion," he said as he shook her hand. Why was it the strongest people were often the gentlest?

"I was just watching some wrestlers in a courtyard," remarked Rhonwyn.

He nodded. "That's where I'm heading now, to wrestle with the king."

This piqued Rhonwyn's curiosity. "Do you ever beat him? I thought he would be unbeatable."

"Yes I do. Often," said Brynn, looking pleased with himself. "He doesn't use his magical powers when he's wrestling. He says he wants the physical challenge."

Now that was interesting. Could the Resistance use that against him?

"Well, thank you, Brynn." She smiled. "Be well and happy."

Brynn nodded and strode away, disappearing up the stairs.

Another nice person. So many welcoming people here. Except for that captain of the president's guard. He hadn't been friendly at all.

Rhonwyn carried on along the corridor, happier now she knew she had a valid reason to be there. She would find out what a library was.

A double door with glass in it stood on the left. A table sat just inside the door with a lamp, its glow illuminating a cluttered surface, with pens, papyrus, and several rectangular objects that Rhonwyn couldn't identify. In the middle of the room, two other tables faced each other. Both bore lamps and had chairs behind them. On the right were five ceiling-high shelves in a row. She could see no windows in the room at all.

She pushed the door open.

The room seemed empty before Rhonwyn heard a scraping sound from behind one of the shelves. A woman stepped out. Older than Rhonwyn, she was simply dressed, with an odd contraption on her face. A wire frame held two round pieces of glass in front of her eyes and also reached back behind her ears. Her eyes looked smaller through the glass. Why would someone want to make their eyes smaller?

"Peace to you," said the woman. "I thought I heard the door."

"Peace to you. I'm Rhonwyn mi Hywel, the new Gymbal Opponent. I'm exploring and someone told me this was a library."

The woman's face lit up. "I hoped you would find me early on, Rhonwyn. I'm Matuthalyn – you can call me Matu. I'm the librarian which means I take care of the library." It sounded like she had to explain this often. "Do you know what a library is?"

"No," Rhonwyn admitted.

Matuthalyn had a rectangular object in her hand, similar to the ones on the table near the door. She held it up.

"This is a book." She took hold of its edge and pulled it apart. It hinged open and within were black lines on white. She handed it to Rhonwyn and the black lines resolved into writing that was so straight and regular, Rhonwyn wondered who had penned it. She'd never seen handwriting like it.

As Rhonwyn took the book, she discovered the white was wafer-thin papyrus and within the book there were dozens of pieces of papyrus all stuck together at one edge.

Matu pointed at various parts of the book.

"This is a page." She fingered a single piece of papyrus. "There are numbers at the bottom; those are the page numbers." She carried on explaining different parts of the book: the contents, the index.

Rhonwyn interrupted, "The papyrus is so thin."

This got Matu buzzing. "Yes, which is marvellous, as it means you can fit hundreds of pages into one book. Each book generally deals with one subject, like history, or technology, or a story. This one is about stars. You can read them and learn all sorts of things." Her tiny eyes studied Rhonwyn. "We have some books about Gymbal."

Rhonwyn's eyes widened. "You mean, I could learn Gymbal tactics from them?"

Matu grinned. "I'll show you where we keep them."

As they headed towards the shelves, Rhonwyn suddenly realised that on them were hundreds of books, all stacked on their ends. Matu showed her where she kept the four Gymbal books, carried them to one of the tables, and pulled a chair out.

"You can sit here to read them." She took back the book Rhonwyn had been holding. "This ..." she patted the table. "... is called a desk. That's my desk over there." She pointed at the table next to the door. "It's where you'll find me most of the time."

That explained why she was so pale.

"Why are there no windows in this room?"

"Light destroys books."

Spotting Rhonwyn's alarm, Matuthalyn corrected herself. "Well, not immediately, so you can go and read in the sitting room opposite, if you want. It's just that books last longer if you keep them out of the sun. And if you use a desk, you can take notes."

Rhonwyn was now eager to read the books, but she had to ask ...

"What is this, on your face?" She pointed at the contraption that covered Matu's eyes.

Matu laughed. "Oh yes. These are my spectacles." She took hold of the wires leading back to her ears and pulled the spectacles off her face. "They help me see properly."

Her eyes now looked bigger, though she was squinting.

"May I try?" asked Rhonwyn.

Matu hesitated. "Yes. But please be careful with them."

Rhonwyn took them and slid the wires over her ears. The room became blurry and distorted. Her eyes were inside out. She pulled her head back and blinked repeatedly.

"They don't work for me." She took them off as quickly as she could.

"No, they were made especially for me," said Matu as she put them back on. She seemed relieved.

"Are they magic?"

Matu frowned. "I'm not sure. The king had them made for me, so yes, they could be."

Rhonwyn had a sudden thought. "Are there books on magic?"

"No." Matu looked down. "I imagine that's because it's a

dangerous subject. We keep the dangerous books over there, under lock and key." She pointed at the back wall of the library, covered wall-to-wall with cupboards.

"There are books in there as well?" asked Rhonwyn. "Books on magic?"

Matu nodded. "They're restricted. Only the king and Mistress Berwyn have the key to those." She gestured to the books on the desk. "Enjoy your books. I'll leave you to it."

Rhonwyn stood staring at the restricted section for a full minute. Yes, of course they were restricted. The king wouldn't want people learning magic, or they would learn to fight him.

She was trembling as she sat. Those books might be exactly what she was looking for if they wanted to overpower the king. She would have to get the key. How? Certainly not from him. Perhaps Mistress Berwyn.

So many new experiences. She'd only been here two days. She shook her head, opened the first Gymbal book and leafed through it. It seemed only to list the basics of Gymbal, so she put it aside and looked towards the door.

She could take the next book to the sitting room and find out whether the entrance to the king's chamber was in there. That *was* what she'd been looking for.

Rhonwyn returned the other books to the shelf.

The librarian was peering intently at a book and scribbling on a separate piece of papyrus. Was she copying it out? By the looks of her handwriting, it wasn't her who'd written the books.

Rhonwyn crossed the corridor and pushed open the door, blinking in the bright light. The windows in there filled the entire outer walls.

At a safe distance from the windows were several comfortable-looking armchairs. The room seemed empty, so Rhonwyn wandered to the far end to look for the entrance.

No door. Frustrated, Rhonwyn fought down her fear and edged up to the windows to see if she could spy a clue on where the chamber might be. The suspended corridor did indeed end just below where she was. But she couldn't see any further without shoving her head through a window.

The windows were divided in two, with a metal sill at waist-height and latches attached to the upper sections. One was open already, right at the corner of the room.

Taking a deep breath, she gripped the edge of the frame and leaned out into the opening. It had better be strong enough to hold her.

Wrong window. A huge, yawning space opened to the valley floor. The drop made Rhonwyn's stomach flop over itself and her grip on the windowsill tightened.

"If you're going to jump, use another window. That's mine."

Rhonwyn started and swung around to find a woman sitting in one of the armchairs. The back and sides of it were so high, no one could see her unless they were directly in front of her. And she had her legs folded up underneath her. Rhonwyn felt heat rush to her face and her mind raced in circles, trying to think of an explanation for her actions.

"I ... I was just ... exploring and—"

The woman interrupted, "Oh, you've come over from the library. You'd better not throw that book out there, that lady would have a fit." She slurred her words.

Relieved the woman wasn't interested in what she'd been doing, Rhonwyn took a closer look at her. Painfully thin, she had dark circles around her eyes. Her clothes were similar to Rhonwyn's but were a plainer colour and badly rumpled. It looked as though she'd been sitting there for a while. She'd turned the chair away from the door and it was the last one, so was unlikely to be found. Perhaps she was hiding.

"Peace to you, I'm Rhonwyn," she said as she casually closed the window.

"Rhymla," said the woman. Rhymla's head sagged and her body crumpled in on itself. Now that the excitement of Rhonwyn's appearance had worn off, she seemed abruptly disinterested.

"I'm the Royal Gymbal Opponent. What do you do?"

This reanimated Rhymla more than Rhonwyn expected. Her head snapped up. "Oh, *are* you?" she said, one eyebrow rising. "How *interesting*. Well, aren't you lucky?" Rhymla's voice got louder and louder, and her sharp tone became more pronounced. "Well lah-dee-dah for you." She flung her legs out, stood, and began gesticulating, a bottle at her feet tipping over, empty and forgotten. "Oh, that's so *exciting*. And you came to visit me at my window, did you? Aren't you wonderful?"

Rhonwyn was speechless. She'd never seen a drunk woman before. Only her father's friends at the end of market day after they'd been trying out the southern wines, their wives looking on with disapproval.

"Well, it's all yours now. Enjoy." At this, Rhymla tried to stalk away, but stumbled over the bottle. She recovered, kicked it aside and continued unsteadily as the bottle bounced off the wall and rolled behind the chair. She slammed the door as she left.

Rhonwyn was sure there'd been tears on Rhymla's face. So not everyone was happy and well in the palace.

Concerned the bottle would become a hazard, Rhonwyn reached behind the armchair only to find two more similar bottles.

How long had Rhymla been there?

12

The king called for Rhonwyn just after lunch. Kymra came to inform her and accompanied her to the games room to serve the players as needed. Would Rhonwyn ever not be scared to death of meeting the king face-to-face? She had to force herself not to run down the corridor for fear of being late.

As they walked along the final hall leading to the games room, a figure darted to a door ahead and slipped inside. Rhymla. Had she sobered up yet? What had been troubling her?

"Who was that?" she asked Kymra, who frowned.

"I don't know, sorry."

Kymra's excited chattering actually calmed Rhonwyn. The friendship was a boon, even though Rhonwyn was unlikely to take Kymra into her confidence.

As they waited for the king to arrive, the girl prattled on about something clever the king had said.

"He said everything's made up of these tiny things we can't see, called adams. Each adam has a fixed centre and other things whirling around them. He said, 'Even sitting still, we're moving.'" She cackled at this, though the sound seemed forced. Perhaps Kymra didn't really understand the joke.

Well, neither did Rhonwyn. She had to change the subject.

"You look lovely, Kymra. That's such a pretty top."

Kymra responded with a smile and a blush. The top was low cut and exposed the smooth skin of her throat. A pretty pendant hung from her neck, its single stone sparkling in the sunlight. Rhonwyn noticed then that Kymra had painted her face as well.

"Thank you," Kymra replied, "It's nice to look like a woman sometimes." Her dry tone left Rhonwyn puzzled.

The king arrived, adjusting his clothing, and the two women bowed low.

As Risick sat down, he looked at Rhonwyn through narrowed eyes. "Do you think you can beat me again, Rhonwyn?"

He'd remembered her name.

"I can only try, Your Majesty." She'd better not be too cocky.

This made him snigger as he reached forward to make the first move.

The game today was shorter as the king made an error early on, though he didn't seem to realise it at the time. Rhonwyn looked up in surprise after he'd moved the piece, only to see him sliding his gaze towards Kymra, making the girl smile and blush.

Once again, the king didn't make the customary losing gesture before leaving the room. Rhonwyn would have to get used to that. Did he require her to make the gesture if she lost? She was bound to, eventually.

As Rhonwyn put the Gymbal set away, she heard a short exchange near the doorway.

A shocked voice: "Kymra! What *are* you doing?"

Rhonwyn looked over. Mistress Berwyn had just wrenched the door open and was glaring at Kymra.

"I don't know what you mean, Mistress." The back of Kymra's neck was a deep red.

"And your face," Mistress Berwyn exclaimed sharply. "I told you *never* to wear clothing like that, didn't I?"

"I don't see why. The king seemed to like it," replied Kymra, folding her arms as she stared at the floor.

At this, Mistress Berwyn took a sharp intake of breath. "You silly, *silly* girl!" She withdrew, slamming the door so hard Rhonwyn was surprised the glass in it didn't break.

Kymra's jaw was set as Rhonwyn came up to her. "I don't understand what *her* problem is. Just because she's ugly doesn't mean everyone else has to look plain. Horrible cow."

Rhonwyn raised her eyebrows. "I thought working for her was something you wanted."

"Well ..." Kymra paused and looked sidelong at Rhonwyn. "There's nothing wrong with being ambitious." She smiled with a hint of a flush in her cheeks.

"You like the king?"

Kymra drew her head back. "Who wouldn't? He's so clever. He's fascinating!" Kymra pushed the door open. "And attractive," she murmured.

Rhonwyn blinked. "You don't mind the yellow eyes?"

Kymra wriggled with delight. "They're exotic."

Her excitement made Rhonwyn ill. Kymra's reaction to the king was in stark contrast to her own.

Kymra looked up and down the corridor and then leaned into Rhonwyn as they walked along. "You know, Mistress Berwyn actually has a lover." She rolled her eyes. "What does he see in her?"

Rhonwyn eyebrows rose at this morsel of salacious news. "Really?"

"She thinks I haven't noticed. They meet all the time at night. That's the only time she knows the king won't call for her. I overheard them talking once."

"Do you know who it is?" asked Rhonwyn. She felt a twinge of guilt for using Kymra like this.

"One of the music composers," said the girl.

"Not Urven?" Rhonwyn grimaced, thinking of his bulbous nose.

"No. The one that plays the guitar for Felenya. I don't remember his name."

"What does he looks like?" she asked.

"Oh, he's old," said Kymra, as if being old was unattractive in itself. "But really, who would want *her?*" She shivered and made a face.

"Where do they meet?" Rhonwyn had begun to whisper.

"In his room, I think." Kymra's expression was coy. "She leaves her keys with me when she visits him."

By this time, the pair was approaching Mistress Berwyn's room with its usual bustle of activity. Members of staff walked in and out constantly.

"Why have you brought me here?" asked Rhonwyn.

Kymra stopped, then doubled over in giggles. She eventually recovered enough to say, "I didn't bring you here. I suppose you just came along because we were talking."

Rhonwyn snorted. She'd got so used to Kymra taking her everywhere.

"Well, I've got to get to work," said Kymra. "Are you going to help me?"

Rhonwyn laughed. "No. I think I'll go back to the library. See you later."

She spent some time inspecting other books in the library before pulling out the one on Gymbal she'd started that morning.

"There are so many interesting topics in the books in here," she commented to Matuthalyn at the door on her way out. "Lots of them I don't recognise at all."

Matu perked up and nodded. "Yes, I know the feeling. I'm actually reading through them all. Well ... trying to, anyway. I started at the first shelf and I'm halfway down the back of it. It will take a long time. It's fascinating, so fascinating!"

She sounded like Kymra.

"That's very ambitious," said Rhonwyn.

Matu chuckled. "Yes, it is. I don't know if I can do it. I'm going to try, though. Doing that much has already taken me over three years." Her face sobered. "I've learnt all sorts of things."

Rhonwyn drew in a breath. "Goodness! The whole lot will take ages." She pointed to the large pile of papyrus on one side of Matu's desk, every inch covered with handwriting. "Do you write it all down?"

"Only since I found out that taking notes helps me to remember it better." She held up a handful of the papyrus. "They're only key thoughts, though – not the whole thing."

Rhonwyn's brow furrowed. "Perhaps I should do that." Though the thought made her nervous – she hadn't practised writing since she'd become a seamstress.

"Well, if you decide to, here's where I keep the papyrus, and the pens and ink, too." Matu indicated a shelf just behind her.

Rhonwyn tried a few chairs in the sitting room and finally settled on the one Rhymla had been in; the most comfortable one. Rhonwyn imitated her by drawing her legs up into the seat, leaving her sandals on the floor.

It took a while for her to get used to reading again. She encountered a word she was unfamiliar with and went back to Matu to see if she knew it.

"Here's the best thing in the world for that." Matu handed over another book she kept on the shelf behind her. "Search for it in here; they're all in alphabetical order."

Rhonwyn did as Matu said and discovered the meaning was written next to each word. The book seemed to have every word that ever existed in it.

"I used it all the time when I started reading the books," said Matu. "It really helped." Matu pushed her spectacles back up the bridge of her nose with her index finger. "Why don't you take it with you?"

As the afternoon wore on, the sun shone further and further into the sitting room and made it hot and stuffy. Rhonwyn opened several windows to let in some air. As she did, she made herself more familiar with the position of the corridor that led out to the king's chamber.

Eventually she was forced to retreat to the library; the sitting room was simply too hot. She sat at a desk and used the papyrus and a pen to note down some more interesting stratagems outlined in the book, so she could combine them with her other moves. She even scratched out diagrams to take back to her room to memorise.

By the time she had to go to the evening meal, she was halfway through the book, her piece of papyrus marking where she was up to. Her intention was to go straight back to it afterwards, but she was waylaid by Felenya, who insisted they play Twyrn again.

"And what have you been up to?" asked Felenya.

"I found the library yesterday and I've been reading a book on Gymbal. Very useful," Rhonwyn said.

"A library? A book? What are they?"

Rhonwyn explained. Felenya didn't get as excited as Rhonwyn had. She couldn't see what use it would be to her. Singing was 'doing' and you couldn't write that down.

Nevertheless, Felenya asked to see the library once they'd finished their game. A visit from the renowned palace singer quite flabbergasted Matu. It rendered her speechless for a full minute. Felenya was gracious, though she didn't stay long. She was impressed, however, by the view from the sitting room.

She took an enormous breath and held her arms out wide. "Somewhere you can truly breathe." She stood before one of the open windows as the sun's light reddened, then disappeared.

The room was still warm though, and the pair dragged two of the nearest chairs close to the windows and sat, chatting about the family they'd left behind. Down the other end, near the door, four men murmured amongst themselves as they drank together.

"You have no one?" Felenya asked. "I'm sorry to hear that. I missed my parents for an age when I was brought here."

"Are they still alive?"

Felenya lowered her head and said, "I don't know." The topic seemed to make her sad. Soon after, she excused herself.

Although the men were still there, they made little noise so Rhonwyn retrieved her book and settled into the comfortable chair, turning it to face away from the door. She'd brought a lamp from the library.

She was jolted awake hours later by a bone-juddering

scraping sound. Her heart pounding, she peered through the gaps in the side of the chair. Her lamp must have gone out.

Lit by another lamp sitting on the floor next to him, the king muttered abuse and shoved aside the two chairs Rhonwyn and Felenya had moved towards the windows. He was scowling.

Why was he moving furniture at this time of night?

He stalked towards Rhonwyn, who held her breath and froze. Surely he hadn't heard her? But he passed just behind her chair and approached the wall.

Rhonwyn swivelled.

He slid aside a small section of the wall to reveal a compartment. Within was a grid of numbers, lit from behind. 8 – 4 – 2 – 6, he pressed with his long, brown fingers, a tiny squeak sounding with each push.

Rhonwyn jumped as a metallic grinding began. A long rectangle of floor tilted up into the empty space. A trapdoor. The chairs he'd moved had been on top of it. Beneath was a set of stairs, leading down.

The king strode over, grabbed his lamp and disappeared down the steps. Soon after, the trapdoor lurched closed again.

After a moment's pause, Rhonwyn leapt up. She'd found the door. She could barely breathe for excitement.

She ran to the window. Eventually a light appeared at the far end of the corridor. It moved to the chamber itself, lighting the ornaments hanging from its eaves.

Should she try to follow him? He was already at the other end. He wouldn't be able to see her approaching. She had to give it a go.

Rhonwyn found the wall panel and fumbled to move it aside. She pressed the numbers: 8 – 4 – 2 – 6 and then winced at the rumbling that the trapdoor made. Would anyone hear it?

She dashed down the stairs. As she stood staring along the corridor, the trapdoor began to close behind her. She raced up to stop it, but was too late. The rectangular section clomped down into place.

Her mouth dry, she scrabbled around the walls in the dark before breathing a sigh of relief when she found the same grid of numbers on the wall. She almost pushed the numbers again straight away to get out, but constantly opening and closing the noisy door might attract unwanted attention.

She did her best not to think about the chasm beneath her as she crept along. She imagined she could feel the corridor swaying, but she wasn't sure if it actually moved at all. She finally reached the other end where she encountered a door with no handle. Another grid of numbers was set in the wall.

8 – 4 – 2 – 6 she pressed.

Nothing.

Rhonwyn pushed against the door with all her might. Still nothing.

She peered out the windows on each side to see what was at this end, but there were only bare rock walls on each side of the corridor. And the windows didn't open, anyway.

She threw up her hands. She felt so close ... to *something*. She didn't even know what.

13

Rhonwyn slept in and missed breakfast. She wandered around the empty dining hall and then headed for Mistress Berwyn's room. Her stomach was growling.

She spotted Kymra striding down the hall away from her.

"Kymra!" Rhonwyn called, and the girl stopped. "I missed breakfast this morning. Is there somewhere—?"

Kymra erupted into giggling, making Rhonwyn blink. "Are you sleeping in already? People usually only do that after a month or so, not the first week." She gestured for Rhonwyn to accompany her.

She was still grinning. In fact, she was twitching with excitement and constantly checking over her shoulder as they walked. They rounded the corner of the hall – and were out of view of Mistress Berwyn's room – when she grabbed Rhonwyn's hands and began bouncing up and down around her and giggling. The hallway was empty of people.

"What?" asked Rhonwyn, laughing. Kymra's excitement was comical to behold.

"Oh, I'm so happy!" sang Kymra.

"Why? What happened?"

Kymra took a deep breath and settled herself down and then surprised Rhonwyn by saying, "No, I'll wait. Let's get your breakfast and watch those funny creatures." She then spun around and marched off towards the kitchens. Rhonwyn trailed behind.

The palace cooks were most generous. They wrapped a piece of thin bread around scrambled eggs and ham. Kymra grabbed the roll before Rhonwyn could and sped on ahead to the animal enclosures.

Rhonwyn was mad with hunger and curiosity by the time they reached the bench opposite the monkeys. Kymra allowed her to eat some of her roll before she spoke, even though Rhonwyn could tell she was bursting with words.

When Rhonwyn got halfway through the roll, she shook her head at Kymra, swallowing. "For goodness sake, tell me."

Kymra tittered. "Alright." She took a deep breath and swivelled to face Rhonwyn, clasping her hands in her lap. "The king's chosen me especially to be his consort." She barely took a breath as she went on, "He told Mistress Berwyn to have my things transferred to the consort's quarters – so much bigger than my current room. He told her to tell me he thought I was beautiful, intelligent, and witty, and that he really enjoyed talking to me." Her face was pink. "What? Are you alright?"

Rhonwyn had nearly choked on her mouthful and she could feel the blood leaving her face. She attempted to control herself.

"Consort? What—"

Kymra grabbed Rhonwyn's forearm and whispered, "He wants me to be his wife. That's what a consort is." She clasped her hands in front of her heart and leaned back, closing her eyes. "He's chosen me, of all people." She paused for a moment as a memory seemed to hit her and her expression soured. "Of course, jealous old Berwyn was catty about it. She's so angry. Silly cow! Now she'll have to do what *I* say." She assumed a regal posture, her head held high, then ruined the effect by bursting into childish giggles and looking at Rhonwyn with wide eyes. "I can ask you to teach me Gymbal."

Rhonwyn laughed. "I would love that. You've been so kind to me."

Her friend would disappear so soon? Rhonwyn wanted to

keep the contact – was desperate to. She'd adored the last few days. Despite their age difference, her friendship with Kymra had been a balm to Rhonwyn's soul after being alone for so long.

"Huh!" exclaimed Kymra, her eyes focussed on the middle distance. "Berwyn's face ..." She wasn't even using her superior's title anymore. "It was so pinched, it looked like she was sucking on a lemon. If she's not careful, I'll tell the king about her lover. She's meeting him tonight." And now Kymra spread her hands before Rhonwyn's shocked face. "She's given me so many things to do today. Horrible woman. She's got me until tomorrow morning."

Rhonwyn's stomach hollowed out at a sudden idea: She could use this to get into the housekeeper's office and look for the key to those locked library cabinets. But she resisted the idea. That would be too mean, surely.

But, if that's what it took ...

Rhonwyn assumed the role of conspirator. "Why don't you repay her by doing something to her room while you've got her keys?" Rhonwyn leaned forward and whispered, "While she's with that man overnight you could do anything. I'll help, if you like," she added. This point was crucial. She couldn't meet Kymra's gaze. The playful, furry creatures screamed in the background, ignored for the moment.

The girl's eyes widened. "Oooo! Yes, I could do that. She tells me she's visiting family." Kymra scoffed.

Her young friend sat for a while, her head tilted, as Rhonwyn forced down the rest of her breakfast, though her appetite had evaporated.

Kymra finally spoke. "Yes. That's what I'll do. And yes, I would love your help. You could keep a look out." A smirk twisted her face as she stared at her knees. "I think I know exactly what we'll do."

Kymra came to Rhonwyn's room just after midnight. They crept down to Mistress Berwyn's room and let themselves in. Kymra always behaved as if no one watched and Rhonwyn still hadn't seen anything that looked like a king's-eye in the palace.

Rhonwyn was doing her best not to look too eager to search Berwyn's room. She'd been pacing in her own room, regretting her suggestion to Kymra all day. If the Resistance took Risick off his throne, what would happen to Kymra? Would she get hurt?

Rhonwyn whispered to Kymra, "What shall we do?"

The lamp she held gave the girl's grin an evil cast. "Well, we've only got six hours until I become His Majesty's consort." She blushed at this. "I will find something embarrassing of hers and put it out for all to see."

Rhonwyn bowed her head and sniggered; her young friend's revenge was so petty. Rhonwyn liked that about Kymra, though – her innocence. She frowned. Her innocence. Did Kymra know what becoming a consort was all about?

She took Kymra by the arm before she turned away.

Rhonwyn spoke quickly, her face warming. "Do you know about the wedding night and ... all that?"

Kymra snorted and flicked her hand. "I was brought up around animals, Rhonwyn. I know what it's all about." Her face became a deeper shade of red. "Thanks for asking, though. That's so sweet." She smiled. "I haven't even told my parents. I'll give them the wedding invitation myself. They'll be so thrilled." She shook herself. "I'd better get going; I want to get *some* sleep tonight." She looked at Rhonwyn and sang the next few words. "I won't be sleeping much tomorrow night." Rhonwyn sniggered.

Why would the king want a wife? He seemed to hate people unless they could do something for him. What could Kymra do for him? Rhonwyn's belly churned. There was something terribly wrong here.

"So, what are we looking for?" she asked.

"Something embarrassing," said Kymra. She pointed to the corner of the room. "She sleeps in there. I'll start there and you wait here. If anyone comes in, just tell them – loudly – that you're waiting for me." Kymra searched for something as Rhonwyn peered into the corner. She hadn't seen the door back there. "Let's light this lamp for you." Kymra lit a taper from her lamp and used it to light another she'd found under the desk.

Rhonwyn knew she wouldn't have much time to find the key to the library cabinets, so the instant Kymra slipped through to the next room she darted behind the desk and pulled open one of the cupboards there. The shelves inside that section were crammed full of linen. She shut the cabinet doors and opened the next set. Each set of cabinets had a key in its door, though some were locked and others were not. Even more linen lay in the second cabinet. With the constant turnover of linen, any key hidden there would get swept onto the floor. The rest of the cabinets also held pile after pile of linen. She had to try somewhere else.

Rhonwyn examined the shelves on the side walls. She could hear Kymra rummaging in the next room, so was unafraid of being discovered yet. The well organised storage held no keys. After searching one side, Rhonwyn crossed the room and checked there. Nothing.

Next was the board on the wall next to the entrance. There were timetables and job lists galore. One thing caught her attention – Mistress Berwyn's timetable. Every single minute of the day was taken up with activity. However, the time between midnight and six o'clock in the morning was always clear.

Perhaps that was when the king was in his chamber. The regularity of it was consistent. And now Rhonwyn remembered she'd watched the king enter his chamber last night at almost precisely midnight, which agreed with that theory.

That might be very helpful indeed. The one time of day she could know exactly where the king was.

Rhonwyn stalked around the desk in the centre of the room, searching for somewhere else Mistress Berwyn might keep the key. She hoped the woman didn't keep it on her person all the time.

Perhaps if she sat where Mistress Berwyn usually did, it might present her with an idea. Rhonwyn eased the chair out from under the desk and sat down.

She blinked. She'd never been in such a chair. She was astonished to find its seat spun under her, so she could twist her knees to face in any direction. The movement made no noise at all.

Rhonwyn smiled. It felt so strange and yet it evoked a childlike feeling of mischief within her. Her hands clutched each side of the seat as she pushed sideways with her foot and spun all the way around.

As she came full circle, she straightened her legs, and her knee struck something attached to the underside of the desktop.

She let out a yelp.

The rummaging stopped in the next room and Kymra appeared in the corner. "Are you alright?"

Rhonwyn rubbed her knee and rocked against the pain throbbing through her leg. "Oh, yes, I suppose," she said through gritted teeth. The pain radiated through her lower leg before easing off. She let out the breath she'd been holding. "I hit my knee on something under the table."

Kymra's eyes narrowed. "You were spinning on her chair, weren't you?" She guffawed. "I've done that myself. That drawer really packs a punch when you don't know it's there."

Rhonwyn let out a laugh. "It sure does."

Kymra disappeared and the sound of her searching started again.

A drawer? Rhonwyn leaned over to inspect it. Set back from the edge of the desk, it looked as if it was attached there so it wouldn't be seen.

Rhonwyn pulled it open. A jumble of objects lay inside: a pair of scissors, more papyrus sheets, a ball of string, and a screwed-up piece of papyrus shoved into the back right corner.

Rhonwyn picked up the crumpled papyrus. Something

inside made it heavier than she expected. Her breathing became shallow as she unwrapped it.

Within was a lone key. She dropped the papyrus onto the table top.

This could be the key she was looking for.

It could also be the key to anywhere else in the palace. Rhonwyn held it up to her face and drew the lamp closer to see if any words were carved into the thick, black metal. Its surface was smooth.

If she stole this key and it wasn't the library cabinet key when would she ever get the chance to search in here again?

Rhonwyn looked at the papyrus the key had been wrapped in. She noticed an ink mark on it and flattened it out. On it was one word: Library.

Her body zinging, Rhonwyn was just about to screw the papyrus back up and replace it in the drawer when she stopped. If she could replace the key with another, its theft might go unnoticed for longer.

She slipped the library key into her pants pocket, turned and was just about to take a key from the cabinet door behind her when Kymra spoke from the next room.

"This is perfect. We'll use these."

Kymra was about to return.

Rhonwyn snatched a cabinet key, scrunched it into the papyrus and threw it into the back of the drawer before snapping that shut. Spinning on the chair again, she hoped it would look as if she was still playing on it.

"Look," said Kymra as she walked in. "And I know exactly where we can put them." She didn't seem at all suspicious. She was holding a wad of fabric, which she stretched out to reveal a piece of frayed intimate apparel.

Rhonwyn stood, feeling the key heavy in her pocket. "What are we going to do with those?"

Kymra's grin was wide. "Just you wait and see!"

Kymra came to Rhonwyn's room early the next morning and woke her up. She took her to a spot where they could both watch her revenge. Kymra could barely contain her excitement; Rhonwyn could barely stay awake.

At sunrise each morning, the king's pennant was run up a tall flagpole at the front of the building. It flew over the palace entrance the entire day until sunset.

Somehow Kymra had arranged for Mistress Berwyn to be there just beforehand. In the dawning light, the woman walked out of the front of the palace, looking around. The men who raised the flag were the only other figures in the area.

Kymra's arrangement with the men had them run the pennant up the flagpole and scamper out of sight.

Seeing them disappear so quickly drew Mistress Berwyn's attention and she stared after them and then up at the flag. The girls could see the shock on her face as she peered at what had been added underneath the pennant itself.

Kymra crowed and ran to confront her victim as Mistress Berwyn's hand flew to cover her mouth. Rhonwyn drew closer to hear the exchange, though she made sure to stay well out of sight. She couldn't hear Kymra's words, but her friend's posture conveyed her attitude and Rhonwyn could see the reaction.

At first Mistress Berwyn frowned and sucked in a breath to rebuke the rebellious girl standing before her. Rhonwyn watched as the older woman paused, her face sagging, her eyes welling up. Mistress Berwyn took Kymra by the arm and pulled her into a rough embrace.

Her voice was strained as she spoke over Kymra's shoulder. "Goodbye, dear."

Releasing the startled girl, she kept her head averted as she stalked away to find the men who had strung her unmentionables up the flagpole for the world to see.

Once she was gone, Rhonwyn came out of hiding and approached Kymra as she stood staring after the housekeeper, her brows wrinkled, her mouth pursed.

"That was unexpected," said Rhonwyn.

Kymra nodded and shrugged. "Not as fun as I'd hoped." Her face cleared. "Oh well." Her eyes widened and a smile grew on her face; the girl recovered quickly. "I'd better go and get ready."

She started towards the entrance, turned back, and gave Rhonwyn a quick hug. "I'll see you soon. Thanks!"

"Blessings upon you. See you soon." Rhonwyn smiled as she watched Kymra walk away. She hoped she would be invited to the wedding.

How fast would her promoted friend be replaced and who would the new person be? She could only hope they were as friendly as Kymra.

Since Matuthalyn would be in the library most of the day, Rhonwyn knew she couldn't use the key during that time. She would have to wait until tonight.

Instead of going back to the library after breakfast, to finish reading the book, she went for another walk. She needed the fresh air anyway. The garden was still cool, the sunlight drawing long shadows on the grass. The star shape of a large flower lay before her on the path, the shadow distinct against the white pebbles.

Her father had taught her to determine what time of day it was by the position of the sun. She would try to use that to make it back for lunch on time. She smiled at the memory of the rod her father had placed upright in their garden, and the rocks set in a pattern around it, to measure the passing of time. Rhonwyn remembered her excited search for pretty rocks to fill in the gaps between time's marks, and beautify it as only a little girl could. Her father had been so proud of her efforts.

She'd better stop thinking like this or someone would see her tears.

Rhonwyn returned to the dining room only a few minutes after lunch began and regarded that as success. She and Felenya giggled and chattered loudly over their meal.

Felenya disappeared from the table early; she had a rehearsal that afternoon.

Rhonwyn went straight down to the library, but stopped outside. The sitting room door had a small board hanging from it: *Unavailable for use.*

Her eyebrows raised, she entered the library. Matuthalyn wasn't at her desk, so Rhonwyn went to the shelf, pulled out her current book, and sat at a desk. She stole a look at the cabinets. Did she have time to look now, while Matu wasn't there?

Just as she rose, Matu returned. Rhonwyn took a breath to greet her, but was stopped by the expression on Matu's face – pale and taut.

"What's wrong?"

Matu jumped – she hadn't seen Rhonwyn. She pressed her hand to her heart and came over. She leaned against the edge of the desk, her face downcast.

"Something awful's happened," she began, then paused, and gasped. "I can't tell you any more. I was told to keep it to myself. I shouldn't have said anything." She blinked rapidly, and wandered back to her desk.

What was so terrible it would warrant that kind of secrecy?

Rhonwyn returned to her book, then stopped with a gasp.

"Sorry," she said to a startled Matu, her mind flip-flopping. "I just remembered something." She put her head back down, hoping Matu wouldn't press her about it.

Could she use that sign on the sitting room door to make sure no one was in there when she ventured into the king's chamber? Where did they keep it? Would that raise too much suspicion?

Rhonwyn found it difficult to concentrate that afternoon, and her head and eyes drooped often. Ridiculous. If she wanted to visit the library tonight, she would have to catch up on sleep. She shook her head and stood up, causing the chair to scrape across the floor.

Matuthalyn gasped and started, eyes wide. What was going on with her?

"Sorry. I'm just too tired. I keep dropping off," Rhonwyn explained, smiling sheepishly. "I'd better go and have a rest."

Matu's shoulders relaxed and she uttered a fake laugh. "Sounds like a good idea. I often get dozy in the afternoon. I've been known to fall asleep here at my desk."

"Matu? What does the sign on the sitting room door mean? How often does that happen?"

The librarian's face paled.

"I can't ... oh!" Matu's face relaxed. "Of course ... no."

Matu took a deep breath and began again, her voice shaky. "Yes, the sign does go up there occasionally. It's generally because the room is being cleaned."

"Ah, that makes sense," said Rhonwyn, "I was disappointed when I couldn't go in there this afternoon. So they use it for cleaning, do they?"

Matu became flustered once more. "Well, it's not always for cleaning. They keep the sign behind the door so it can be used for ... any kind of ... event." Her face was becoming more tense by the minute, her jaw working.

It felt like Matu was trying to skirt around something significant. Did it have anything to do with how upset she'd been before?

Rhonwyn woke thrashing and sweating. The sun was streaming into her room and the warmth was being captured and trapped. She should have left the windows open.

She staggered up and closed the drapes. It did nothing to alleviate the heat. She parted the curtains again and opened the doors to the balcony and the windows. A cool breeze drifted through. She stood in it.

How was Kymra's day going? Why hadn't the king's wedding been a big event in the palace? The king himself had been at lunch as usual but Rhonwyn hadn't seen her friend there. In fact, nothing at all had changed.

A knock rattled her door. Rhonwyn ran to open it.

A young woman stood there, Mistress Berwyn beside her. The girl's eyebrow arched as she saw Rhonwyn, who reached up and found her hair was tangled and sticking up. She tried to smooth it down.

Mistress Berwyn spoke first. "Good afternoon, Rhonwyn." Her face was expressionless. "This is Jarysha. She will be your point of contact from now on."

Rhonwyn smiled. "Peace to you, Jarysha."

Jarysha nodded in return. "Well met. The king requires your services, ma'am." Straight to business.

Rhonwyn's heart rate increased. "Er … is it alright if I tidy up a little, first? I was just having a nap."

"Of course," said Mistress Berwyn. "I'll leave you in Jarysha's capable hands." She walked away.

"I'll be right with you." Rhonwyn closed the door on the dour-faced Jarysha and sped around the room, fixing her appearance. Jarysha then walked her to the games room.

The girl – who seemed older than Kymra – did not have any trouble keeping her tongue in check. In fact, she said nothing at all the entire way down. The silence made Rhonwyn more nervous and her chest squeezed when they discovered the king had arrived before them. Had her getting ready made him wait?

Fortunately, he was quite calm – sleepy even. Rhonwyn sat down, once all the bowing was out of the way, and the king made the first move.

It took too long for Rhonwyn's head to get in the game. She regretted not anticipating this possibility and making sure she was awake during the hours the king was likely to call on her. He bested her strategically early on and left her struggling to catch up. The king pushed his advantage to the hilt.

 Despite Rhonwyn doing everything she could to counter his tactics, which made the game long, the king's initial set up was overwhelming and she eventually lost.

Once the last play was made, the king looked at her askance and held out his hand, expectant. Her throat constricted, Rhonwyn picked up her general and gave it to him. It felt more humiliating than usual.

He fixed her with his gaze. "Your efforts were too little, too late. Do better next time."

His lips set in a straight line, he placed her general on the table, rose and left the room, his entourage close behind him.

Jarysha left too, without a word. It didn't look as though she would end up being Rhonwyn's confidante.

Well, at least the king hadn't immediately ordered her execution. She frowned. What exactly had happened to the previous Gymbal Opponent?

Rhonwyn took her time tidying up the pieces from the board.

At the same time, she ran through in her mind the moves the king had made and what she could have done to counter them. If she'd been concentrating, she could have pushed back more effectively, or prevented him gaining the advantage in the first place. She'd not had all her faculties working. That must never happen again.

Rhonwyn meandered towards the dining room. The evening meal was imminent and she looked forward to chatting with Felenya. Indeed, her friend soon had her giggling and shaking her head at her outrageous statements. Felenya described one of the composers that she didn't get on with so well: "He had his mouth on backwards and his overwrought eyebrows were dancing to a different beat entirely."

The sitting room was available for use again afterwards. The same gentlemen were drinking in the same set of chairs as the other night. Perhaps they sat there every night.

Rhonwyn opened the window that Rhymla had called 'hers', noticing the pane of glass had been cleaned, and the putty around it was a lighter colour and soft to the touch.

When she visited the library to look for another book to read, Matu was in her usual place. Did she ever go anywhere else?

"Don't you feel the need for sunshine sometimes?" Rhonwyn asked, then kicked herself – Matu might think she was being insulting.

"Oh, yes, I keep intending to go for a walk and then forgetting to," she replied. "I'll go back to my room soon and take something to read in bed."

"You can do that? Take a book to your room?"

Matu grinned. "If I take a story book, it helps me get to sleep."

She drew Rhonwyn's attention to the shelf connected to the one behind her, farther on from her desk.

"Here. They remind me of the travelling Wise Ones who toured the common halls. They knew all the old stories. Do you remember?"

"Oh, yes."

Rhonwyn's father had regularly taken her along to village events. It had been in the evening, at the end of the harvest or on an annual festival day. Once, there'd been two storytellers, a man and a woman, who'd taken turns telling stories, standing on a wagon above the local families collected in the Wise One's field around a dancing fire. Under a starry sky, each story had transported young Rhonwyn to exotic, mythical places, taken her on adventures with the gods, or made her laugh at the antics of the ridiculous Domysh. One story had scared her into her father's arms – up above the grasping tentacles of the underworld that grew out of the centre of every field. He'd wrapped his arms around her until she'd felt completely safe.

"These are quite different," said Matu, "I've never heard any of them before." She beamed at Rhonwyn. "That's half the fun of it – you don't know what's going to happen." She took a dark blue book from the shelf and handed it to Rhonwyn. "Here's my favourite. Tell me what you think when you've finished it." She yawned. "Well, I'm heading off to bed. Would you put the lamps out when you leave?"

"Of course," said Rhonwyn. She hadn't expected Matu to be going to bed so soon.

"It's been a bit of a harrowing day." Matu's eyes went out of focus and she dipped her head before she turned to the door. "Good night." She absently picked up a book from her desk and left.

"Good night," Rhonwyn called after her.

When Matu's footsteps could no longer be heard, Rhonwyn checked down the corridor and in the sitting room. Empty.

She stood just inside the library door, unsure which task should come first, and listening to her heart beating as her insides tensed. She finally shook herself and started for the back of the library, picking up Matu's lamp as she passed her desk.

She would start on the left and work towards the other end. She must keep an eye out, though. If only Kymra could have been her lookout.

What had happened to Kymra? She hadn't heard anything.

Rhonwyn opened the first cupboard. It was full of books. She flipped one out and opened it, only to find all the words were wrong. The letters all looked familiar, but the words made no sense at all, even when she sounded them out loud.

The next book was the same, and the next. What was the point of these, if no one could read them?

Were they magic books? Perhaps only someone who knew magic could read them, or would know the spell that put the letters in the right places.

A larger, more ornate book stood in the centre. She hauled it out. The cover had a picture on it. A dark figure stared out at her – with sulphur yellow eyes. The king. No other features were distinguishable apart from the eyes, but he was the only one with those.

The figure held a large sabre diagonally across his chest. The hilt was highly embellished and the curved blade looked like it was glowing, an intense blue surrounded it. Could this book be all about the king? Perhaps it could tell the Resistance how to overthrow him.

But when she opened it, the writing was the same as in all the previous books – in magic script.

Rhonwyn slammed the heavy tome shut.

In the next cupboard, a thin rectangular device lay on the shelf. Larger than a book, it looked like a picture frame with no picture. A small square was in one corner. When she fingered it, it wriggled ever so slightly. She pushed harder and started violently when the device made a *bong* and vibrated in her hands. She only just managed to keep hold of it.

Where she might have expected a picture, a large word appeared. Again, it was unrecognisable – a magic word. It disappeared, only to be replaced with a picture of squiggly blue and green shapes. Then a red dot appeared in the centre of the picture and began to throb.

What an odd picture. Why would he want a picture like that?

She shrugged and pushed the corner square again. The picture went black.

How did it do that?

She moved quickly through the rest of the cupboards – endless magic books. Why did the king bother to lock these away when he was the only one who could read them?

What a waste of time.

This propelled Rhonwyn into an almost reckless haste. She strode back to the library door, taking Matu's lamp with her, and slipped into the sitting room. She hung the *Unavailable for use* sign on the door and put one of the chairs up against it – just in case.

The trapdoor opened for the same set of numbers. However, she found no more at the other end than she had previously. She kicked the wall and stalked back along the corridor and out, the trapdoor droning back into place.

What was she going to do? She'd found nothing.

Back in her room, she went out onto the balcony and stood staring at the king's chamber, trying to sort her thoughts out. She would have to keep trying to figure out how to get in. It was the only place she'd seen so far that seemed like it might have what the Resistance needed.

She stared at the isolated building, perched on its finger of rock. The moonlight made the suspended corridor look like a river, or a pathway.

A pathway? Could she walk along the roof?

16

Rhonwyn choked down her breakfast the next day before excusing herself to Felenya. From there she walked straight to the empty sitting room.

Could she reach the top of the corridor from the windows?

Yes, it was possible, though the precipice on each side made her stomach clench. And she would have to get back up again.

Rhonwyn opened the window directly above the corridor and carefully leaned out to inspect the wall beneath. It had enough hand- and footholds for her to climb back up without assistance. The wide window above the door at the other end sat level with the top of the corridor, so she wouldn't have to climb up to it. Hopefully she could get it open.

She leaned back into the sitting room, stretching her back. So, when should she do this? What needed to happen before then?

She would be out in the open as she walked across, and therefore anyone looking out a window would be able to see her. So she had to do it in the dark. In dark clothes. Now she was thankful for being supplied so many different-coloured garments.

Tonight, then. If the weather was good.

Rhonwyn spent the day going from one activity to another, never lingering on one for very long. She couldn't concentrate enough to read. The king didn't summon her to play Gymbal. And Felenya was rehearsing for another concert tomorrow night.

Rhonwyn didn't eat much that evening; her stomach was queasy, though the food was no different. She excused herself early and went back to her room to put on the darkest clothing she had.

Waiting for the sun to go down was the worst part. Though Rhonwyn paced back and forth on her balcony for what seemed like hours, the enormous orange sun didn't seem to move far at all.

She went inside and spied the story book Matu had given her. Soon she was engrossed in it: meeting strange characters doing unexpected things. A small animal talking and hanging bedding out? Rhonwyn shook her head.

She was getting better at reading. She hadn't realised that would happen.

Finally the clock outside her room chimed nine times. All the light of the sun was gone and the moon had yet to rise.

The drinking men weren't in the sitting room, thanks the heavens, so she put the sign on the door and borrowed Matu's lamp again – unlit – and took some fire sticks with her.

She made for the far side of the sitting room, opened the window and leaned out. The night air was completely still.

She briefly visited Rhymla's window. The putty was still sticky, so she used her fingernail to scrape some of it out from the frame and then smoothed the remaining putty down again. She pressed it to the lower, outside corner of her window, stood on the footstool she'd placed under it, and then lifted her leg over the windowsill, to stand on the lower sill, trying not to think about the empty air below her.

When she'd pulled her other leg through, she lowered her feet down to the next footholds and then the next.

Breathe.

Once both hands were clear of the window frame, she reached up and pressed the window shut. The lower corner stuck to the putty. That should keep it shut while she was gone.

Once she had her feet on the roof of the corridor, she looked up to find the window didn't seem far away at all. Her descent had felt like it took forever.

The roof wasn't entirely flat and its surface was slightly slippery. The starlight picked out the lighter colour of the rooftop that led off into the night. To each side was a dark abyss that she knew went down a long way. She must not slip.

Her heart thundered in her chest as she clenched and unclenched her fists. She had to do this; Merynbyl couldn't live under this awful magician anymore. She had to find a way to stop him.

Her arms held out to each side for balance, she shuffled forwards. She stayed to the centre, her feet on either side of the ridge, both at an angle.

What had Kephlen said? *Your father would be proud of you, Rhonny. Remember that.*

Yes, he would.

When she was out over the void, a sudden gust of wind came out of nowhere and Rhonwyn fell to her knees in fright. The breeze died down quickly, though, and Rhonwyn picked herself up, chastising herself for cowardice.

All she had to do was get information to help the Resistance. She didn't have to face King Risick himself. Once she'd done her job, she could keep her head down, play Gymbal the best she could, and wait for the Resistance to make its move.

She pushed herself onto her feet again and looked back. The bright lights shining from the palace windows blinded her and she had to stand with her eyes closed to regain her night vision.

She was only halfway across. It felt like she'd been shuffling forwards forever. Would she have time to do anything once she got to the king's chamber?

If she could get in.

Finally the chamber loomed ahead and Rhonwyn was surprised at how easily she gained access. The window at the end of the corridor, right above the door she'd not been able to open, was broad, and the catch on the other side was rusted. The top of the window hadn't been properly sealed, and rain had dripped down the inside and soaked the metal. She could barely see through the glass.

After she'd grabbed the window edge with her fingertips, wrested it left and right, up and down, back and forth, the catch disintegrated and she was in. She'd finally got past the door.

She pulled up the window – the unused hinges giving a loud creak – and ducked under it, resting it on her back, her hands on the wide inner sill.

Below her, in a small antechamber, a set of three steps led up to yet another door.

Another door? Dismayed, but determined to try every avenue, she made her way along a thin ledge in the side wall and jumped down to the wide top step.

Rhonwyn tried the door. It didn't open. She groaned and leaned her forehead against it.

Why would the king have two locked doors in a row? She searched the antechamber carefully.

Another grid of numbers was set into the wall next to the door. Holding her breath, Rhonwyn punched in the only number she'd seen the king use and was shocked to find it worked. The door buzzed and swung inwards.

She sprang through the door and looked for a clock. She needed to know how much time she had. She finally found one above the door she'd just passed through. It was just before ten o'clock. Two hours to go. It had taken her an hour to come from her room. She'd better leave a good amount of time to get back before midnight – before the king came.

She stared around the room she found herself in. It was dim, but she could see well enough so didn't need to risk lighting the lamp after all.

A bed stood against the wall on the left, a horse-length inside the door. Just a small pad on a shelf, with a blanket and pillow.

This one room took up almost the entire building. As she'd seen from her balcony, all the windows faced away from the palace. Only one door stood on the right. She checked this. It was a washroom.

A large table stood in the centre of the main room, covered in games. The kind of games that one person could play alone. Did the man never sleep? No wonder he was so moody.

Making her way towards the back of the room, Rhonwyn saw movement in the corner of her eye, and whirled around, her heart rearing out of her chest. A moment later she was shaking her head. A mirror off to the side, next to the washroom door, was reflecting her own face. She breathed a sigh.

Against the far wall was a set of cabinets. She tried to pull them open but found them locked. Why did he lock anything over here? No one could even get into the room.

They looked just like the ones in the library, except taller than Rhonwyn. She frowned, pulled the library key out of her pocket, and stared at it.

It couldn't be that easy, surely.

The dense wood around every lock was severely scratched, gouges marking it as if someone had tried to break in. Who had done that? Had someone been in here before her? It didn't look as if the person had succeeded in accessing the cabinets, though. What had happened to that person?

Against all odds, the library key she'd stolen from Mistress Berwyn's room actually worked there, too, and she opened the left-most door of the cabinet. The first thing she saw was the point of a large sabre mounted at the back. She unlocked the other door of the cabinet.

The sabre's hilt was highly embellished – and familiar. This was the sabre depicted on the cover of that book in the library. She took it down and found it lighter than it looked. The blade didn't glow as it had in the picture.

She fiddled with a protrusion near where her thumb rested. When it flicked over, the sabre vibrated and a glow sprang forth, engulfing the blade. Rhonwyn jumped, nearly dropping the weapon. The switch sprang back and the glow ceased.

She tried it again and the glow reappeared. Magic. To maintain the glow, she had to keep her thumb down on the switch; if she let the pressure off, the glow would flicker out. It took great control to be able to hold the sabre with only one hand and keep enough pressure on the switch to keep the glow alive.

Once Rhonwyn had the knack of it, she cautiously brought the finger of her other hand up and touched the glow.

This time she did drop the sabre. Though the glow hadn't seemed hot, her finger felt as though it had been burnt. She shook it and put it in her mouth. Even in the dim light, she could see a mark on her skin. She went to the washroom to run water over it, biting her lower lip and hissing. It took some time for the pain to subside.

A magic blade. Could this be something that could hurt the king? This would be something to report to the Resistance.

She returned to the fallen sabre and picked it up. To learn more, she searched through the game pieces for one she knew wouldn't be missed, and placed it on the stone floor. She first pulled aside the rug over the spot, so it wouldn't catch alight.

She slowly brought the lit sabre down onto the piece and her eyes widened as, instead of bursting into flame, the piece fell in half before the blade even got near it.

Rhonwyn turned the glow off and touched one half of the playing piece again. It didn't burn or smoulder, so she placed her finger against the blade itself.

No pain. No heat. She slid her finger along its edge. It was blunt. So the thing, though beautiful, was useless without the magic.

She put it back on its mount. On the lower shelf was a rack of three identical objects. They had tubes moulded to be held in the hand, so Rhonwyn picked one up to inspect it. Even though made of metal, the thing was light.

Holding the tube by its grip positioned a switch near her index finger. Already nervous of switches from her last encounter, Rhonwyn though it best to assume the piece of metal above the switch was the part that would glow. A small, oddly-directed dagger, perhaps? So she first knelt on the turned over rug and placed the object next to the bits of the playing piece, and as far away from her head as possible, her elbow locked.

The switch required a lot more pressure to move. When it finally clicked over, Rhonwyn was blinded by a flash of lightning and tossed backwards, head over heels, landing on her knees again.

The backwards roll had knocked her head against the floor at great speed, so she spent some time blinking and gingerly rubbing the back of her head before she could see again.

She should perhaps leave the things in His Majesty's cabinet alone.

Surprisingly, the object was still in her hand. Warm. Returning to the turned-back section of mat, Rhonwyn's jaw dropped. The area where the playing piece had been was a circle of black and she could see no sign of its halves anywhere. The rock floor now had a depression in it. It, too, was warm.

The magic lightning from this thing had made a hole in rock.

Rhonwyn put the object back where it came from and locked the cabinet doors.

She panicked, however, when she saw how obvious the mark on the floor was. She flung the rug back and dragged it sideways to cover the entire black spot. But the King would detect the hole if he walked over it. She must fill it with something. Something flat and hard. She stared around the dim room. All she could see were games. And he would miss them, if that's what he did overnight.

She opened the other cabinet doors. More books … that were *flat* and *hard*. She went through them, looking for one to fill the hole and breathed a sigh when she found it. The rug was stiff enough to compensate for the rectangular book not entirely filling the round hole.

Rhonwyn walked over the area several times to make sure it didn't move and that it felt right. Her heart was still hammering.

She'd better get back.

17

Rhonwyn wore a completely different colour the next day – pink. Not only was it pretty, but the pants were a closer fit, which meant climbing in and out of windows would be easier. Not that she would be doing that today. She admired her reflection before flinging her arms out in a stretch.

Halfway through it, she jolted as she spotted the key on her side table. If she got caught with that, she would have no explanation to offer. She had to hide it. Where? She needed to be able to access it – she had to hand it over to the Resistance's contact at the concert tonight. It mustn't be in her room.

The clock outside chimed eight times. She turned towards the noise.

The clock.

She washed, dressed, and sauntered into the corridor, looking right and left. No one was in sight. Everyone was already at breakfast, perhaps. She stole over to the clock and examined it. A little hook held the wooden back shut. She flicked it open and glanced at the complicated insides before sliding the key behind the mechanism and out of sight.

She wandered out into the hallway, once again checking both ways. Smiling, she walked briskly to the dining hall, feeling lighter for having rid herself of the incriminating object. Thank goodness she wouldn't have it for long.

Felenya was excited about the concert to come and wouldn't

stop talking. Her friend had finally agreed to sing with her. Apparently, she was too nervous to eat and was in her room practising the songs to the walls.

Rhonwyn was ravenous after her stressful day yesterday and made up for it by scoffing down rather too much food for her own good. Fortunately breakfast was the least spicy meal of the day.

Felenya was off again afterwards to rehearse with, and reassure, her friend, and Rhonwyn went back to the library to read another Gymbal book. To avoid the afternoon slump, she tried a nap before lunch. It seemed to work, as Rhonwyn was alert and feeling almost confident when the king called for her late in the afternoon.

This time she was there before him and had the board set up and ready when he arrived. Of course, he didn't acknowledge this. He simply started the game.

When she used one of her newer strategies – gleaned from an idea from one of the books she'd read – she had the satisfaction of noting that Risick hesitated before making his next move. When she responded, a flicker of a frown disturbed his face before it set into its usual impassive glare.

Rhonwyn risked examining the king's eyes in short bursts as he pondered his options. She wondered what made them such an inhuman colour and what about his throat caused the jarring buzz. Did magic do that? And what of her friend ... was she happy with the king? Rhonwyn hoped she still giggled with mischief. Why hadn't she been at breakfast? How had the wedding gone? She didn't dare ask.

When it became obvious he'd lost, Risick grunted and stood to leave. He said only one word as he swept out the door, and Rhonwyn nearly missed it.

"Better."

Just before she headed to the concert that evening, Rhonwyn visited the clock outside her room to retrieve the key. She was keen to get this meeting over and done with so she could finally relax.

The concert had already begun when she arrived. The president and his retinue were there, including her contact. She avoided them and found a spot in the packed throne room, standing right at the back. Because she was back there – and looking for his movement – she alone noticed the captain of the president's guard edge out of his place and disappear into the darkness once the song had begun. Everyone else was focussed on the performance. Rhonwyn hoped this exchange wouldn't take long – she wanted to enjoy the singing.

Though she was keeping an eye out, the captain still startled her when he appeared on her left. His face stared stonily forward, and his lips barely moved. Felenya and her friend's voices were approaching a crescendo of pure sound.

"Anything?"

"Yes," she whispered, her eyes fixed on Felenya.

He took a breath and scanned the room before murmuring, "Fountain," and vanishing from her side.

How did he do that?

Rhonwyn's mind churned. She didn't want to leave. The music was extraordinary. The king was leaning back again, a smile on his face, his eyes closed, as the two women before him sang in exquisite harmony. Rhonwyn had never heard anything like it. Her father would have loved it.

But she had to go. Those nearby were engrossed, so she crept back into the shadows and eased open the door. At every intersection of the corridors, she expected to see a guard or Enforcer, but no one appeared. The only guards she'd seen had been when the king was around.

In her rush she got inexplicably lost in the palace for a time before she found an exterior door and dashed out into the night. She slowed until she could see well enough not to trip, then paced through the garden to the fountain.

He wasn't there. Was this a trick?

As the water slapped down, Rhonwyn circled the fountain,

the gravel crunching under her feet. She peered down each grass pathway. After one circuit, she strolled down one of the paths.

Where was he? Had he been caught? Perhaps she should go back inside. Drop the key in the garden.

A gust of wind caught the spray from the fountain and sent droplets of water over her. She darted away.

"Where are you going?" A voice suddenly from behind.

Rhonwyn clenched her jaw as she swung to face him, her heart lurching in fright. Where had he come from?

"What do you have?" he demanded.

Her throat was tight. "Do you have a name?"

He glared at her – much like the king did – before he answered. "No. Tell me what you have."

Rhonwyn tilted her head. "Why should I trust you, if you don't trust me?"

He clamped his teeth together. "Come on, woman!"

She simply looked at him, jaw set, eyebrow raised.

He huffed and shook his head. "Zaryc ma Gyn," he muttered.

"Well met, Zaryc." She nodded in formal greeting. "I broke into His Majesty's chamber last night."

His eyebrows shot up.

Feeling triumphant, Rhonwyn went on. "There's a magic sword in the cabinets there and three lightning-throwers." She'd made up the name on the spot. "The lightning-thrower threw me backwards when I pressed the switch, and left a hole in the stone floor."

His face twisted into concern. "You left evidence?"

"The rug covered the mark. It won't be seen." She was surprised at how confident she sounded. She was more angry than confident.

He pulled his head back. "You've done well."

She started listing all she knew: "He's there every night between midnight and six in the morning. Use the sitting room next to the library, climb out the window—"

He held up his hand and Rhonwyn stopped. Had he heard something? She looked around.

He continued to squint at her. "You can get back in?"

"Yes." She pulled out the key. "This is the key to the cabinets." She held it out, relieved to be rid of it.

Zaryc grabbed her by the shoulders, ignoring the key.

"You have to do it."

She blinked again. "Do what?"

He examined her face as he gave her quick-fire orders. "Get back in there. Get a lightning-thrower. Wait for him." He brought his face right up to hers, his voice lowering. "Kill him."

18

Rhonwyn felt her face slacken as her heart began to hammer.

"I can't do that. I'm just here to get information. I'm not a killer." She pushed his arm. "You do it."

He hissed at her, gripping her shoulders tighter. "I can't. You're the only one who can, Rhonwyn. You're the one who has access."

She gazed up at him, trembling. "I can't do that. I'm just a seamstress."

He took a sharp intake of breath before he released his hold and stepped back, turning away. "Then we are lost."

Rhonwyn's stomach dropped. "Surely ..." She stopped, remembering what Kephlen had said: '... *it'll be years before we can get someone inside again, if ever.*' Everyone they'd sent in before had been discovered and killed. She'd got further than them all.

Her throat tightened. "I just can't do that. I'm sorry. You'll have to think of something else." She felt herself backing away.

Zaryc faced her again, lifting his hands, and pleading, "Your access to him is all we have. You know what it's like outside. He must be stopped."

"We don't have to *kill* him," Rhonwyn insisted.

Zaryc's gaze drilled into her for a long time, as though he was waiting for her to see reason. Uncomfortable, she folded her arms and looked at the palace, beautifully lit for the evening.

"Rhonwyn," Zaryc said, stepping in front of her and leaning in, capturing her gaze. "If you won't kill him, we'll never be free. He's an evil man. Please, use what you know and get rid of him while you have the chance."

She refused to answer and angled her face away from him.

He finally sighed and glanced over his shoulder. "I need to get back or I'll be missed." He whirled towards the palace.

What was she supposed to do? Rhonwyn rushed to catch up to him. "Zaryc—"

He pushed her away. "We mustn't be seen together. Go through another entrance." He pointed off to the right and sped away.

His abrupt departure left her feeling lost and scared, the water still dancing high into the air behind her and slapping the surface of the pool as it landed. What had Zaryc expected? No one had told her this would be asked of her. She wouldn't have agreed to it if she'd known. Why hadn't the Resistance told her?

Well, they couldn't make her do it. She sighed and raked her fingers through her hair. Had getting herself trapped in the palace been pointless?

Rhonwyn trudged back to the throne room and the door she'd left by. She reached for the handle but stopped, her chest constricting as she heard the music inside.

Her world tilted.

Felenya was singing alone now and using her lowest notes.

> *Turn me like a boat to sail away from thee*
> *I'll be coming back again, so watch and wait for me*
> *Until I see thy face afore mine blessed eye*
> *I will not rest me easy till I'm moored by thy side*
>
> *The sooner I depart, the sooner I'll return*
> *And thou wilt laugh and dance and sing within*
> *my arms again*
> *Becalmed upon the sea, I'll think of only thee*

> *And pray for wind and waves to push me back*
> *to home early*

This was the song Rhonwyn's father had sung to lull her to sleep when she was young, or to comfort her if there'd been a storm. The last time she'd heard it, her father had been humming it intently, gazing into her eyes, his arms twisted behind him as he was arrested. The next time Rhonwyn had seen him had been during Announcements, when the king had torn his heart out for treason.

> *But if I never come into thine arms again*
> *Be sure to hold thy head up high, our love is not in vain*
> *My heart will be thy guide unto the bitter end*
> *And when the world has passed away we'll be*
> *together then*

Unable to breathe, Rhonwyn's body bent in the middle and shuddered. She would do anything to have her father's arms around her; she'd felt so safe. He was gone forever, though, and she was all alone, stuck in this beautiful, awful place.

Her imagination of him couldn't fill this dreadful loneliness.

She released the door handle as her throat closed shut. Covering her mouth, she leaned against the wall.

What was she going to do? She was trapped.

Rhonwyn soon gave up trying to control herself, pushed away from the wall, and stumbled back to her room, barely able to see where she was going.

19

"I'm worried about you, chook," Felenya said, bustling straight in the door without even knocking. It was late morning. Rhonwyn was dazed, and startled half out of the bed. Felenya gripped her upper arm and examined her face. "Are you not feeling well? My mum was a healer, you know. She was training me up when I was chosen for here."

"Oh no, I'm well." Rhonwyn dipped her head, confused by the affection Felenya was showing her. She dashed for the curtains and threw them and the windows open. The fresh air whooshed in and she realised just how stuffy it had become.

"Now, what is keeping you abed?" A frown marred Felenya's broad face, though she still seemed more concerned than angry.

Rhonwyn had been mired in memories and, feeling sorry for herself, had languished in her room. She'd wanted to hide from the world and wallow in her sadness. She'd wanted to stay in this safe place, with only the image of her papa in the room with her. She'd been pouring her heart out to him, fingering his button on the corner of her blanket when Felenya had walked in.

Rhonwyn took a deep breath. "It was that song you sang," she said, "Turn Me Like a Boat. My father used to sing it to me. I thought he'd made it up himself until you sang it last night."

"Ah no, that's an old, old ..." Felenya stopped, her face pained. "I'm sorry, my friend. I know what that feels like." She rubbed

Rhonwyn's back as they stood just inside the balcony doors, the light breeze cooling them.

"I'm just feeling a little sorry for myself this morning and thought it would be better to keep away."

Felenya nodded. "My mother's birthday was a few weeks ago and I stayed away from people then, too. Sometimes it's just best." She caught Rhonwyn's eye. "Not for too long, though. Why don't you come down to lunch now?"

Rhonwyn stood silent for a few moments, then smiled and nodded. "Yes, alright. Just let me get dressed."

The dining hall was empty, bar the servers. She wondered again where Kymra was. Once they'd selected their food and sat down, Felenya commented, "There'll be quite a few that don't come to lunch. The king's away until late tonight."

Rhonwyn stared at her. "I didn't know he did that." That would be a relief; he wouldn't be calling for her this afternoon. "Are we ever allowed to go out? I mean, could you ask to see your parents?" Perhaps she could go and ask Kephlen what to do.

Felenya shook her head gently and her eyes slid left and right. "No. The king wants us to stay in here. I did ask, once. I didn't get a good response."

Felenya was right – hardly anyone came to lunch and the two of them had a nice, quiet time. Rhonwyn tried tiny morsels of many of the dishes she hadn't tried before. The servers were attentive and Felenya didn't talk as much as usual. Rhonwyn eyed her with a slight frown.

At the end of lunch, Felenya pushed her chair back. "Well, I have to go now. I've got a meeting with the composers."

"Of course," replied Rhonwyn and then responded to Felenya's worried look. "I'll be fine. Thank you for your company. I need to go for a walk. I'll go and see the animals, actually. The monkeys are funny creatures."

It wouldn't be as much fun without Kymra, though.

"Good," said Felenya. "I must come and see them myself sometime. You have a lovely time and I'll meet you back here for the evening meal."

Rhonwyn visited the snake pit first. Deep, its walls sunk straight down. She imagined rather than saw bones and clothes lying at the bottom. It would be impossible for anyone to climb out. She wondered if the snakes could and shivered.

She wandered to the enormous, wrinkled animal with the long nose she'd been fascinated by last time. It stood quietly to one side, its remarkable, serpent-like appendage curling up and back as it lifted food to its mouth. The sign called it an elephant. Kymra had insisted that the king had ridden on it like you would a horse and that it was as gentle as a cow. Rhonwyn couldn't believe it. It could easily sit on you or just run you through with its tusks. As for riding it, you wouldn't be able to grip it with your knees – you would just slide off.

She tried to return to the monkey enclosure and the seat that overlooked it. An older woman already sat there though, her head down, so Rhonwyn moved on to the enclosures on the other side of the animal park. She circled around these before returning to the seat, hoping the woman would be gone.

She was still there. But something about her made Rhonwyn look again and then approach her, skin crawling.

It couldn't be. The woman's dull brown eyes were just visible between her tangled black hair. Rhonwyn had seen Kymra less than two days ago. Surely this couldn't be her bright, bubbly friend?

"Kymra?" she murmured.

The brown eyes rose at the sound of her name and flickered in recognition before dropping again. Rhonwyn's heart sank, her mouth dried up, and she joined the girl on the bench.

"What happened? Are you sick? What's wrong?" she whispered.

Kymra wouldn't look up and shook her head. Rhonwyn's heart squeezed.

"Do you need the king?"

Kymra flinched at the title and Rhonwyn looked around, swallowed and whispered, "Did he hurt you?"

Kymra's face crumpled then and she hid behind her hands. Rhonwyn wrapped her arm around the girl's shoulders. Kymra trembled and sobbed as she buried her head in Rhonwyn's chest. It took some time before she was calm enough to speak. Even then she whispered.

"I'm so ashamed."

"It's not what you thought, being the king's consort?"

Kymra shook her head. "He doesn't care for me at all. He didn't mean anything he said. He just …" She stopped and craned her neck, searching the area with furtive eyes. Rhonwyn could barely hear her next words. "I have to creep around and stay out of sight." She started crying again. "I can't tell my parents. I don't want them to see me. Don't tell them."

Rhonwyn's breath caught in her throat and she swallowed. "I'm so sorry, Kymra." She rubbed her friend's back as the girl sobbed silently against Rhonwyn's shoulder.

Kymra jerked out of Rhonwyn's embrace and looked around again, her red eyes wide. "You mustn't be seen with me. I'm no good for you. You should go," she whispered as she pushed at Rhonwyn.

Rhonwyn resisted. "Let me take you to your room. The king's outside the palace today. You're safe. Come on." She had to know where Kymra was so she could check on her and care for her. She coaxed her up and was shocked to find herself helping the girl to her feet. Kymra's face was tense and twisted, and she moved slowly and gingerly.

It took them ages to get to the nearest palace entrance. Just inside the door, the girl rattled out, "You can't come with me." She pressed on a wall panel and it popped open to reveal a hidden alcove with a corridor beyond.

Kymra said, "I used to think these secret passages were for something fun." She shook her head, her face a blank mask. "You mustn't see me again. If I see anyone he says he'll kill me …

and them." Her voice tripped. "Goodbye." She edged painfully into the alcove and pulled the door to, disappearing behind the invisible opening.

20

Rhonwyn excused herself after the meal and rushed back to her room. Once in the door, she stood and gazed at the state of it. The sheets on her bed were twisted, her clothes lay in piles on the floor. She'd been focussed entirely on herself this morning, wrapped up in her own little world.

How selfish. Poor Kymra was the one who was really suffering, along with all the people outside the palace. How could she not take this one, hard-fought-for opportunity to free Merynbyl from this evil man? Even if she died in the attempt, she should still try.

Rhonwyn paced her room from corner to corner, trying to think of everything she had to do and what she needed to succeed. Could she do it? Could she pull that switch on the lightning-thrower and kill the king? She wouldn't know until she was standing in front of him with the device. She would have to be quick or he would use his magic on her and she would lose her chance.

When the sun had sunk below the horizon and all its light was gone, Rhonwyn readied herself and waited for the hallway clock to strike eleven times. She slipped out to the clock, retrieved the key, and strode down to the lower sitting room. She hung the sign on the door, blinked, and took it off again. The king would see it on his way through and it might put him on his guard; she had to have every advantage possible.

She climbed out into the dark night and pressed the window closed with the still-sticky putty. The wind was stronger. Four times she ended up on her hands and knees, crawling, when a gust threatened to blow her off the roof of the corridor.

"You can do it, Rhonny," her father murmured in her ear. She didn't shoo him away.

The window at the other end lifted easily and she clambered in. Once past the second door, she stood and looked for somewhere to hide. The washroom, or under the games table? She shuffled through to the cabinets at the back, hands extended, too scared to light her lamp. It seemed darker tonight. The key flicked around easily again and she gasped.

The lightning-throwers were gone.

Rhonwyn's heart thumped against her chest as if it wanted to get out. Her face taut, her gaze drifted up to the sabre, the only weapon left. Should she leave now and come back later, hoping the lightning-throwers would reappear? Or should she use the sabre and do it now? She would have to be much closer to Risick to kill him. But at least she knew its lethal secret. If she got behind him, she would have even more of an advantage. If she didn't survive, at least Zaryc knew about the lightning-throwers.

A glance at the clock brought her deliberation to a close. Nearly midnight. The king would be here any minute.

Rhonwyn grabbed the sabre and closed the cabinet door. Whirling around, she studied the room again. She would hide behind the door and get him as soon as he came in, when he was least expecting it. She sprinted to the spot, stood in a half crouch, and tried to breathe as quietly as possible.

"It'll have to be as soon as he's cleared the door, love." This time, she was glad for her father's comforting voice, even though she knew he wasn't real.

Rhonwyn could feel her whole body trembling. Was she really a killer? Could she do this? She heard a low pounding –

was that Risick running? – and the first door rattled and opened. He seemed to get to the second door instantly and it too rattled and sprang open. Before she could move, Risick had cleared the door, shoved it to swing closed, and flung himself straight onto the sleeping pad.

Rhonwyn hadn't expected him to be moving so fast and was left standing there, staring at him, fully exposed to the room.

The king appeared to be asleep. He couldn't be, surely. Not that fast. However, if he was, she must take her advantage while she had it. At least his eyes were closed.

Starting forward, Rhonwyn flicked the switch on the sabre and raised it to strike. As she did so, he opened his eyes and sat up. He jolted when he saw her, his legs retracting. She tried to close the distance faster. If she was going to die, she would make a good attempt before she did.

Instead of raising his hands to perform magic, he threw himself to the side, arms lifted protectively, and cried out. He crashed to the floor and rolled to his hands and knees, scrambling away from her. She'd nearly been upon him. He couldn't go far crawling. She need only take two more steps to catch him.

Once again he behaved unexpectedly: rolling back to face her, he cried out again, "Please, no! Please don't hurt me!"

Something made her pause.

His voice.

He tried again. "Please! I haven't done anything." His voice was full of panic and bewilderment. But it had only one tone. He sounded like a normal man.

She braced to strike. "You're tricking me!" she yelled.

"No!" His face was crumpled in confusion, his hands lifted before him, palms out, eyes pleading.

His eyes. His brown eyes.

"What are you trying to do?" she cried, and – not wanting to lose her advantage – she drew the sabre back once more.

"No!" He cringed away and curled in on himself.

When the sabre came out from behind her and back into her field of vision, Rhonwyn saw she'd let the switch go in her confusion. The man was still cringing before her, even though the sabre couldn't hurt him at all.

He didn't know.

All the strength went out of her arms and she let the stroke slip to the side, landing with a clang on the stone floor.

"What's going on here?" she asked, breathless, drawing the sabre to her side. She couldn't kill someone if she wasn't sure he was the king.

"He sure looks like him, though," said her father, crouching next to the man on the floor.

The cowering man opened his eyes – his brown eyes – and stared at her. "I don't know," he murmured.

His accent was from the southern coast. The king didn't have that kind of accent.

She tipped the point of the unlit sabre at his throat. He flinched and his eyes widened. His fear seemed genuine. She could see sweat forming on his top lip.

"What's your name?"

"Dyfed ma Cothee." His voice quavered.

She blinked. "What are you doing here?" she demanded. This man couldn't be the king, he would have killed her by now.

His eyes roamed the room. "I live here."

She frowned. "But you just came in," she retorted, pointing at the door. "Where did you come from?"

"I did?" Seeing her frown, he began again, his hands raised. "Please understand: I just woke up, just before you attacked. I can feel I'm sweaty like I've been running and I was panting when I woke, but I don't remember anything before waking up, just now." He pointed at the bed. "I live in the night."

"What?"

"I only ever see the moon; I never see the sun," he explained. "Before it comes, I fall asleep; I can't stop myself. I've lived in the night for ... I don't know how long. My body seems older now. Much older. And you." At this he looked more closely at her. "You're the first person I've seen since I last saw the sun."

21

"I believe him," said her father, studying Dyfed.

"So do I," Rhonwyn replied.

"What?" Dyfed looked at her, his brows furrowed, eyes wide.

"That's impossible," she stuttered. "What you're saying doesn't make sense." She felt her face heating at her slip-up. It was like Dyfed had dropped out of the sky. She moved back and allowed him to stand, keeping the sabre lifted towards him. He behaved like it was a real threat and held his hands open in a gesture of surrender.

Even the way he moved, the way he stood, his whole bearing, told her this wasn't the king. Though, bar the eyes, he looked exactly the same.

She continued her interrogation, keeping her tone authoritative. "Where are you from?"

"We live on the southern coast, near the estuary, in Dymryd. My father has a farm not far from the grove of hardwood trees. He's the clan leader."

She tipped her head to the side. Clans. That's right, they used to have clans. Her family had been part of the Bonryd clan. They'd traded with the Dymryd clan at the annual gathering.

Rhonwyn tested him from the little she remembered. "What kind of farm did you have?"

His frown was brief. "We have a vineyard and horses," he said. Most of the Dymryd clan had grown grapes and their wines had been a valued commodity to trade for. He'd passed that test.

"Tell me what you know about King Risick," she demanded. She might as well get information if she could.

"Who?"

Rhonwyn's jaw dropped. Everyone knew who Risick was. She stared at Dyfed. He didn't seem to be faking his ignorance.

She wasn't the only one who was confused, however.

"There's a king?" he asked in return.

"Yes." She pointed at him. "He uses your body – during the day."

Dyfed pulled his head back, his brows descending. "What for?"

"To live in. He walks around in it. He's very different from you." She peered at him through the dimness. "How old are you?"

"I was seventeen summers when I last saw my family. I tried to keep a tally of the summers since then, but it kept disappearing. Is he the one who gives me the games to play? And writes the notes?"

Rhonwyn shook her head. "I don't know."

Dyfed looked at the sabre lifted towards him. "Are you going to kill me?"

"No." She returned the weapon to the cabinet. When she turned back, Dyfed was standing behind her, having followed her. He'd been peering at the contents. His closeness made her stiffen.

He didn't notice. "I've never been able to get in there," he said, his voice faint.

"Of course. It was you. I saw the gouges in the wood."

He nodded. "Are there more swords in the other ones?" He pointed at the cabinets alongside the one she'd just closed.

"No. All the rest are full of books in a magic language I don't understand."

"Books?"

She blinked. Of course, he wouldn't know the word; she'd only just learnt it herself.

Before she could explain, his frown deepened. "Magic?"

She sucked in a sudden breath.

"What's wrong?" Dyfed said, his worried eyes fixed on her face.

"What if he can tell I visited you? What if he remembers?" She felt her body trembling.

"Would that be bad?"

"Yes! You can't remember anything he does?"

He shook his head and peered around the room. "Can I light the lamps?"

She couldn't see why not. When she nodded, Dyfed circled the room using a taper he'd lit with a fire stick. So the light she'd seen from the king's chamber had been lit by Dyfed, not the king. And the games were for him, too. How long had he been stuck here? Since Risick had taken over? Twelve years was a long time.

Rhonwyn turned to find Dyfed again standing quite close to her. He was studying her face, one of the lamps in his hand. He smiled when she faced him. Seeing such a tentative, gentle, genuine smile on *that* face was unnerving. Without the evil-looking yellow eyes, his face was as handsome as she'd suspected it might be.

"It's been so long since I've seen another person," he whispered. "All I've seen is me – in the magic wall." He thumbed over his shoulder at the mirror without taking his eyes off her. He touched her face with his fingertips. "You're so pretty."

Rhonwyn felt blood rush to her cheeks. No one ever looked at her like that. When she instinctively pulled away, he drew his hand back and his face fell. He looked scared again.

"Sorry."

She blinked up at him. "It's alright," she said. "I'm still trying to understand what's happening here – with you and him." He was still standing close, their voices were barely above a murmur.

"The king," he said. "Can he do magic?"

"Can you?" Rhonwyn asked. That could be useful.

Dyfed spread his hand before his face and shook it, perhaps seeing if sparks would fly, like Domysh the faerie in the stories. He rubbed his thumb along his fingertips and shrugged. "I don't think so."

Rhonwyn sighed and suddenly felt the toll of the last few hours in her mind and body. All she wanted to do was go back to her room, curl up in her bed, and sleep until noon.

Dyfed took her elbow. "Are you alright?"

She took a deep breath and smiled up at him. "Yes, I'm just tired. It's been quite a day." The way she felt now, even if Risick did know she'd been there, she would be happy just to sleep, and wake to the guards dragging her out of bed.

Dyfed pulled over one of the chairs from the games table. He sat her down and asked, "Are you thirsty?"

She nodded. It felt like a long time since the evening meal.

Dyfed swiped up a cup that stood on the table. He filled it in the washroom and brought it back to her. He leaned towards her. "Is it his magic that makes the water comes out of the ... things ..." He waved his hand in the general direction of the washroom. "... in that room? Does magic bring the water from the streams to here?"

He knew nothing of the new things King Risick had brought with him. So much had changed since the king's arrival. More than she'd realised.

She finished gulping down the cool water before she answered.

"No. It's pipes," she said, and gestured with one hand. "They're long metal things that are hollow, like dried reeds. They can also bend, like saplings, and can go in all directions." She pointed towards the door. "There's a pipe that leads all the way from the palace to over here."

Dyfed's eyes widened. "There's a palace?"

"You didn't know?"

Dyfed shook his head. Despite being here for years he didn't even know the palace was there. Of course – all the windows faced away from it. Was this why they'd been placed that way?

"I want to see it." Suddenly Dyfed was as animated as he'd been when she was chasing him with the sabre. He ran to the door, shook it and ran back. "Can you let me out of here?" His lips were parted in anticipation.

Rhonwyn frowned. What would happen if she let him out? Other people might see him. If he didn't come back the next morning, what would happen? Would the king wake up wherever Dyfed was at some point in time? What magic was it that gave Risick control of Dyfed's body during the day?

Until she knew, almost anything would be a big risk.

Dyfed knelt before her and gripped her hand. "Please. Please. I want to go outside."

His actions were almost comical. The poor man had been stuck in this room for, how many years? He'd only ever seen this one place. And no people? He was a prisoner far worse off than she was.

"You can't stop yourself falling asleep?" she asked.

Wordless, he shook his head. He turned and pointed in the direction of the door. "That round thing with sticks above the door? The sticks move around. When the long stick points up and the short one down, that's when I fall asleep."

"Six o'clock," she murmured.

Dyfed stared at her. "Pardon?"

She explained. "That's a clock – a timekeeper. I know when the king will wake up. We'll have to be back before then, because I don't know how to stop you falling asleep either. And we have to stay out of sight. No one can see you, or there'll be questions the king won't be able to answer."

So Rhonwyn let Dyfed through the first door and watched his astonishment at just the small part of corridor between the two doors, looking back and forth from wall to wall. When he raced to the second door, she had to call him back and get him shuffling along the ledge towards the window.

"How can we get out this way?" he asked, as they both got on their knees to pass through the window onto the roof of the corridor.

"You'll see," she said, and pointed for him to go through the opening first. Dyfed was much taller than she was, so he had more difficulty.

"Be careful," she said as she held the window open for him. "It's a long way down on each side. Don't fall."

She tried to follow him out, but he stopped halfway through. Frowning, she scrambled around him enough to see, even in the dark, that his tanned face was pale and wide-eyed, his arms splayed out wide, hugging the roof of the corridor.

He'd seen the drop.

"Oh dear. Perhaps I should have warned you in stronger terms," said Rhonwyn.

Dyfed's voice was high and shaking as he echoed her original words to him. "It *is* a long way down."

She spoke in a low tone to reassure him. "It's alright. The roof is strong. You'll be fine. Just go slow and get up onto your hands and knees first. Don't look down." She gripped his arm. "I've walked across this roof three times." That was meant to reassure him, too.

Fortunately, the wind had died down.

"Why can't we use the proper floor?" he asked. He had his eyes screwed shut now and he was panting. Knowing he'd been up this high for so long and yet was afraid of heights was very strange. But, to be fair, anyone would be afraid of this height – it was only natural.

"I can't open the door down there," she said.

He peeked out between his eyelids. "You're brave." He eased himself up onto all fours.

"Don't think about … what's on each side." She went on quickly. "You could crawl if you want."

Dyfed gritted his teeth together. "If you can do it, so can I," he grunted. He placed his feet out wide and pushed up with his hands until he was almost there.

Rhonwyn got in front of him and stood to help him the rest of the way. He opened his eyes and fixed them on her face as he rose and stood to his full height.

They stood that way for a minute as he calmed, their hands clasped. Once Dyfed's fear had diminished all sorts of emotions washed over his face: curiosity, eagerness, determination. It seemed nothing was hidden. Of course, he'd had no one to hide from; he hadn't had to learn that skill. There were some emotions she couldn't identify, though one made her feel so warm she had to look away.

She dropped her eyes to his hands: slender, long fingers wrapped around her pallid, well-worn ones.

Rhonwyn inhaled and looked up again. "Are you ready?"

Rhonwyn led Dyfed – with one hand on her shoulder – across the roof and up into the sitting room. All the way, she heard him making sounds of wonder and astonishment, and not a few gasps of fear.

She remembered the first time she'd seen a building with more than one level. It had taken a while for her father to explain how the roof of one room was the floor of the one above, made more complicated by the fact their old floors at home had simply been the ground.

The first thing Risick had everyone working on – once he'd herded them together – was constructing the tall buildings that housed them. The women had been made to cook constantly to supply the needs of the men and boys – and some of the hardier women – as they worked through the days from sunrise until sunset. It had taken time for the workers to learn how to stay safe and keep the death toll down to only one or two per building. Every woman had fretted and prayed to the gods, hoping her husband, father, or son would be among the ones who came home at the end of the day.

Afterwards, the best workers had been taken away to work on the palace, but they'd never been seen again, even once construction had stopped. The community had still had its support systems back then and those women whose men had died or vanished had been helped, fed, and comforted by those around them. But that kind of structure didn't exist anymore. Day by day, year by year, everyone had been scared further into isolation. Rhonwyn hoped that damage could be undone. They would need a very wise leader indeed to bring the community through to healing. She hoped not all the Wise Ones had been murdered by Risick.

As the pair made their way through the dimly-lit palace, Rhonwyn continued to lead the way, walking into the corridors first, checking no one was there, then gesturing to Dyfed to join her. In the end, she saw only one person, and he was at a distance as he turned into a room and closed the door.

Dyfed could barely contain his excitement at all the new things he was seeing, and he asked so many questions. Rhonwyn finally had to tell him to wait until they got out the other side. She took him to the front entrance. He spent a long time staring at the building.

"It's so tall," he murmured, awed. Dyfed was more like an excited, curious boy than the stern, bitter, and angry man he usually was.

No, that wasn't fair; that was Risick – an entirely separate person; that was why he was so different.

He pointed at the base of the building. "How did we come up steps and yet here we are on the ground? Were we in a hole before?"

"Come around to the side and I'll show you where we were before."

They passed the fountain first and he stood and marvelled at the magic flinging the water high up into the air. This lifted his eyes to the stars and he stood for a long time, staring at them.

"I have missed them," he murmured. Such longing filled Dyfed's voice it brought a lump to Rhonwyn's throat. Her father had loved the stars, too.

As he continued to gaze upwards, she searched the grounds around them – as she had many times since they'd left the king's chambers – to make sure no one was there to see him.

Once again she wondered what she would say. Could they pull off pretending Dyfed was Risick? She studied the man before her, his smile wide, his attitude wondrous with his head flung back in pure abandon. His bearing contained no guile. He was completely open and trusting.

No, Dyfed was simply too different a person. Anyone would know he wasn't Risick. And Dyfed had never seen the king. He never would see him, so he couldn't possibly mimic him.

All at once, Rhonwyn's pulse began to pound in fear. She should never have brought him out.

"Come on, I'll show you and then we'd better get back." She scurried towards the wall at the top of the cliff.

She heard Dyfed stride after her, a note of surprise and resentment in his voice. "Why? We've only just got out here."

"If someone sees you …"

"But couldn't we pretend I'm the king?"

"No." She shook her head firmly. "That wouldn't work."

"Why not?"

How could she explain? But, no, that wasn't hard. "His eyes are yellow. And his voice has more than one tone. It sounds strange. You couldn't do that kind of voice. No one could."

"Yellow?"

They reached the stone wall. Rhonwyn was about to kneel to look through the hole again when she realised that Dyfed was probably tall enough to see over the wall. He was much taller than her.

"The room you live in is over there." She pointed.

Dyfed raised himself up on his toes, leaned against the wall, and peered into the darkness. The new moon emerged from the clouds again and provided enough light for Rhonwyn to see Dyfed's face change. His mouth dropped open and she could see his brown eyes flicking back and forth, the whites showing first on one side, then the other, contrasting with his dark skin. He had such a handsome face.

She felt her own face redden. She pulled her eyes away and

searched the grounds again. "We should go back."

"Who are you looking for?" he asked her, now frowning, his jaw set.

"Enforcers. Guards. Anyone, really. We can't have anyone see you." She grabbed his hand to tug him back towards the palace. But he wouldn't be pulled.

"Let's lie on the ground here and look at the stars," he suggested. "No one could see us down there."

Rhonwyn shook her head. "No, I don't think so." She tried to draw her hand out of his grasp, but he held on.

"Just for a little time," he pleaded. "I haven't seen the sky for so long."

She sighed and relented, letting him lead her to a wide lawn between flower beds. They lay down and took in the swathe of stars that crossed the dark sky. After a long pause, Dyfed lifted his arm to point. "There's the Archer." The note of pride in his own discovery and memory made Rhonwyn chuckle.

"Yes, and his arrow." She pointed in turn, her arm just crossing his, and he laughed and pointed further on, crossing his arm over hers.

"And there's the Deer of the Lord, forever ..." He faltered.

"... escaping the wounds of the hunter," she gently finished for him. "My father used to point them out to me all the time."

Dyfed turned his head to look at her in the dim light. "Mine too. But ..." Now he rose onto his elbow and leaned over her, his face close. "What happened to him? To my family? Why didn't they come and find me?" Rhonwyn heard the pain in his voice. She could only imagine what he'd been through, all alone for years. He must have felt abandoned to his fate.

"I don't know, Dyfed. Maybe they did. I'll try to find out for you, if you like. I can't make any promises, but ..." Her voice trailed off. She certainly couldn't make any promises. If the king found out she was asking after Dyfed's family, he would have some serious questions. "Your father's name is Cothee, right? What's your mother's name?" How could she get in touch with a Wise One who knew all the genealogies? She hadn't met one for years and they'd been the ones who knew all the generations, all the history.

"Syphryd."

That's right, the Dymryd clan had some funny names. Well, that would help, the names being so distinct.

"Cothee and Syphryd. Alright, I'll try to find out," she promised. For some reason, the pair of names stirred recognition within her, but she couldn't think why.

Dyfed now rested his head on his open hand and stared at her for a long time. "It's so strange. I've had so many things to say – to ask – for so long, and no one to say them to, but here you are, and I can't think what to ask first." His gaze dropped. "I suppose the most important would be how my family is, which you can't answer." He became silent once more, his eyes cast down.

"Lots of things have changed," Rhonwyn volunteered. Dyfed wouldn't recognise the world as it was now. "Most of us live in the city." That would be a new word for him. "That's just a name for a very big village. There are only a few people on farms, now, and the farms are really big and feed all the people in the city."

His forehead knotted together. "How can there be fewer people on the farms but they're making more food?"

Rhonwyn shrugged. "I don't know. I was a seamstress in the city. I made all the clothes for everyone."

Dyfed fingered his own clothes and then reached out and took the sleeve of her top between his thumb and forefinger. "You made these clothes? They're so odd-looking. But really soft."

"Oh, there are lots of seamstresses, so I didn't make these particular ones. But, yes, they are quite different, aren't they? I think they're a pattern that King Risick made up."

"The king makes clothes?" Dyfed screwed up his face.

Rhonwyn laughed. "No. He would have just told someone the pattern. He likes specific, very different things, I've noticed.

So different from anything I've ever seen. Even the design of the palace is strange."

Dyfed rolled over and looked at the building. Rhonwyn could see him nodding. He rolled back again and studied her face. He even tilted his head to put their faces on the same angle. He reached out, gently took her forearm, and rubbed her skin with his thumb. "Are you real?" he whispered, "or are you a dream?" His voice sounded strained and Rhonwyn thought she spied a glint in the corner of his eye. His hand slid down her arm and cradled her hand. His was bigger but more delicate, his fingers pointed and long.

She curled her fingers around his thumb. "I'm real," she reassured him.

She heard him swallow and he cleared his throat. "What about your family?" he asked.

Rhonwyn felt the emptiness inside her rear up to meet his. "I don't have a family," she said.

His brow wrinkled. "None?"

She tried to explain what life was like now. "Families are often split up and, anyway, my parents are dead."

Dyfed sighed and squeezed her hand. "How did they die?"

Rhonwyn briefly considered lying, but what was the point of that? Besides, it didn't feel right to lie to Dyfed.

"My mother died birthing my little brother, and the king killed my father," she said quietly.

She watched his jaw sink, his eyes widen. He released her hand and brought his own up in front of his face, perhaps looking for blood stains. It had a life of its own. His own body was a stranger to him.

"Is that why you were trying to kill me? Vengeance?" he asked.

"Partly, I suppose. But it's so much more. Risick controls us all with the grip of a rabid dog. His magic lets him see what everyone is doing all the time. The Resistance - a group trying to get rid of him - sent me into the palace. They told me I was here to get information, but when I figured out how to break into the king's chamber, they told me to kill him."

"But you haven't."

"No. Now I wonder if I could have. His magic protects him. Does it protect you?"

Dyfed again looked at his hand. "I feel the same as I ever did. I don't feel magical."

Rhonwyn searched the beds surrounding them and found one plant with thorns. She snapped a twig off and placed it against Dyfed's hand. Such a warm hand. She looked up at him, asking with her eyes if she could try to hurt him. He understood immediately and nodded. Before he could change his mind, she pulled the twig sideways across the back of his hand.

He winced and drew in his breath before lifting his hand so they could both see. Drops of blood formed a line there.

He lifted it to his mouth and sucked on the wound. "Well, you can definitely hurt me."

But Rhonwyn wanted to hurt Dyfed even less than she wanted to kill Risick. She would have to find a way to get Risick out of Dyfed's body without hurting Dyfed himself. How could she do that? Wouldn't she need a Wise One? There weren't any these days. But surely someone would have that information. Maybe.

She could only hope.

Dyfed lay back down on the grass and sighed. "It feels so good to be outside." His head tilted back, he smiled at the sky. He was such a lovely man.

Where had Risick come from, then? Had he been hiding in a bottle, or an enchanted cave somewhere? Perhaps someone had broken the bottle or rolled a stone away and let this evil spirit out. It had to be a spirit. One man's soul couldn't take over another's.

"What clan are you from?" asked Dyfed.

She blinked, the question unexpected. "Bonryd. But we don't have clans anymore. The king's pushed all the clans together and the state tells you where to go." She told him about Announcements.

He got up on his elbow again, frowning. "All the people get together once a day?"

"No, no. The panels show us." She shrugged. "It's magic. Wherever you are, you just look at the nearest panel and they all show the same pictures." She sat up, unsettled by the thought of Risick's all-seeing eyes. "We should get back."

This time Dyfed let her lead him towards the king's chamber. He stopped often to look at different things, though, so it took some time. Questions and answers were whispered back and forth. There didn't appear to be anyone around. Again, Rhonwyn wondered at the lack of security in the palace. She took Dyfed into the throne room on the way, and told him about Felenya and the singing she did for the king.

"If he likes music, can he really be that bad?" asked Dyfed.

She told him what had happened during the last Announcements she'd seen. The story made him gasp and go pale.

"Why are you in the palace now?" he asked as they walked down the steps to the lower floor.

"I won a Gymbal competition," she replied. "I'm now the King's Royal Gymbal Opponent." She was actually proud of that. Should she be?

Dyfed's eyebrows rose. "You must be really good then. I haven't played Gymbal for ages. No one to play against. But I used to be quite good." He gave her a lopsided smile.

"We could have a game."

"Ha!" He bent and slapped his thighs, altogether too loudly.

"Shh!" Rhonwyn held up her hands. "People are in these rooms," she hissed and indicated the line of doors on the right of the corridor.

Dyfed pressed his hand to his mouth. They scrambled forward and ran to the sitting room. But no one came out to investigate.

However, when they reached the window they had to climb

through, Dyfed balked and wouldn't go any further.

"Don't worry." Rhonwyn reassured him. "You won't fall."

He shook his head and folded his arms, leaning back. "I don't want to go back. I want to stay out here. I've been in that room for years." His jaw was set.

Rhonwyn felt a quiver of worry. She thought quickly. Pushing him wasn't going to help. She couldn't make Dyfed do anything he didn't want to. So she pulled a chair over to the windows and sat down. She would have to talk him around some way. She had some time at least.

Dyfed pulled up another chair to join her. They had a broad view of the valley beyond, lit only by faint moonlight.

"It's so amazing talking to someone." He leaned towards her. "But you are so nice, too."

Rhonwyn guffawed. "I tried to kill you!"

He threw up his hands and laughed too. "Well, it was exciting." His white teeth flashed in the moonlight.

She laughed out loud. It'd been a long time since she'd done that. She felt so free. What was it about Dyfed that made her feel so good?

She became serious. She had her own questions. "What's the last thing you remember before you were stuck in that room?"

Dyfed frowned. "Going to bed. We'd just finished a good day out in the vineyard picking the grapes. We had a wonderful meal together – me, my parents and my little sister, Nemalyn. We'd just been talking about where I could find a wife." He frowned and nodded, miles away.

Rhonwyn felt a surge of jealousy.

He went on, "And we had a visitor. We'd found him at the end of the day, wandering along the road next to our lavender field. He was an old man and he was upset and afraid. He'd been ill that day. We took him home and let him stay with us. He was very confused. He couldn't tell us where he was from – he couldn't remember. We let him sleep in the hayloft. We were going to take him to the local Wise One in the morning, poor fellow."

"And you just went to bed as usual?" Rhonwyn asked.

"Yes. Nothing else was strange."

For some reason his story sounded familiar, but Rhonwyn couldn't put her finger on the specifics. She sat and thought about it for a while, but nothing came to mind.

"What can we do?" Dyfed asked after a few minutes silence.

"What do you mean?"

"How can we get this other man out of my body? How can we get my life back? I want to see the sun." The thought animated him.

Rhonwyn leaned her chin on her hand, her elbow on the arm of her chair. "I don't know yet. I need to know more. But it's dangerous asking questions around here. I don't even know where to find the information we need. You're going to have to be patient."

Dyfed slammed his hands down on the chair's armrests, making her jump. His voice was loud. "I don't know if I can be. Now that I've been outside again and seen how beautiful it is – just as I remembered it – I don't want to go back in there." He leaned forward. "Can't I just run away? If I get far enough away, maybe his magic won't work." He half stood up. "If I start running now, I could go far. I'm a good runner."

Rhonwyn grabbed his arm, her mind racing. "Dyfed, I know you're frustrated, but if you run away, and Risick still wakes up in you – wherever you are – he'll know something's wrong. He'll use all his powers to find out what's happened and then he'll stop us."

Dyfed was about to argue, but she held up her finger. "But if he wakes up tomorrow and everything's the same as he expects it to be, then he won't know to start looking. That will give us time. If he starts looking, he'll tear the place apart until he knows." She looked up at Dyfed, still standing before her. "He might find out about me. And if he does, he'll kill me."

She watched her desperate tactic work as Dyfed's face

transformed into deep concern and he sank back into the chair. He was quiet a long time before he nodded slowly.

"Yes, I see." He reached to take her hand, squeezing it. "Will you come and visit me? And take me out? Every night? Please?"

"Yes, of course I will."

Rhonwyn was suddenly glad she hadn't shown Dyfed the code number for the door to the chamber. She would have to make sure he didn't see it, or he would be able to get out by himself.

She felt guilty for thinking such a thing. Dyfed was now her prisoner, too.

23

They spent the rest of the night in the sitting room, talking. Rhonwyn had to shake herself several times to stay awake. They talked about how the world used to be. For Dyfed the memories were fresher, for Rhonwyn ... she could barely remember.

But the more Dyfed talked, the more Rhonwyn recalled what it'd been like at home with her father. It made her realise anew how awful this Risick-created world was.

Was Risick some unheard-of demon that possessed people rather than animals? Would a Wise One be able to help, even if she could find one?

Finally, the two of them walked back along the roof of the corridor. Rhonwyn let Dyfed into the chamber and turned to go, her head sagging in exhaustion. But it seemed Dyfed wasn't ready for her to leave yet. He grabbed her and pulled her into a tight embrace.

"Thank you," he murmured into her hair. "Thank you so much. I never thought I would see anyone else, ever again."

Rhonwyn could smell his earthy tang. She held on as tightly as he did. Their meeting had comforted her just as much as it had him. Her father hadn't said a thing after the first shock of discovery.

She tensed. If Risick woke and found Rhonwyn in his arms ... she couldn't think of a more dangerous place to be. She pulled back and smiled up at Dyfed.

"I have to go now," she said.

He sighed heavily.

Rhonwyn kept hold of one of his hands and squeezed it. "I'll see you tomorrow night."

He smiled back, though it looked as if he was still questioning whether she was a dream.

"Bye," she said as she pulled the door shut. She shuffled as quickly as she could along the ledge and through the window.

The sun was coming up and the early morning light was far too revealing. She shook her head; she'd left this too late. She searched the windows above for a watching face before walking as fast as she dared along the ridge of the corridor. At the other end she clambered up and peered through the bottom of the window to check the sitting room was empty. She opened the window and climbed over the sill. Shutting the window behind her, she saw the two chairs she and Dyfed had been sitting in overnight. They sat on top of the trapdoor. She gasped aloud and rushed over to pull them away.

Just as she'd moved the second one, the shudder and grind of the opening of the trapdoor began. Her heart skipped a beat.

The king was at the bottom of the steps.

Rhonwyn sprinted to the door and flung herself through it. The corridor before her was long. Too long to make it before the king emerged from the sitting room. Spying the door to the library, she dashed through it and blundered through the dark room to hide behind the first shelf. She made it, just before she heard the sitting room door open and close.

Had Risick seen the library door swinging shut?

She froze, her eyes wide in the darkness, waiting and listening. But she heard only footsteps receding down the corridor. She sank onto her knees and covered her face, gasping for breath. That had been close. Far too close.

She waited a very long time before she had the courage to step out from behind the shelf, leave the library, and edge into the hallway. The king was nowhere in sight. She hoped he truly had no clue about the extraordinary night she'd just experienced. Rhonwyn made her way up to her room and collapsed on the bed without removing her clothes.

She woke just before lunch in a room that was stifling. She must open some windows when she returned from her night-time escapades. She hadn't had anywhere near enough rest; her eyes were bleary and crusted with sleep. She washed her face and freshened up as best as she could, dressed, and made her way to the dining room.

Felenya spied her the instant she entered. She was frantic, having not seen Rhonwyn at breakfast, and had been waiting for her to arrive.

"I was just about to come and find you," said Felenya, wagging her finger, once Rhonwyn had stuttered her excuse.

Thank goodness she hadn't.

Rhonwyn collected some food and then sat pondering as she chewed and Felenya chattered. If she was going to be keeping Dyfed company every night, she had to sleep sometime. And the afternoon was when the king required her for Gymbal. She couldn't have her friend knocking on her door every morning to check on her.

"Felenya," she began. "I'm probably not going to make it to breakfast most mornings now." When her friend fixed her with a quizzical look, she carried on, "I'm actually really enjoying being able to sleep in, in the morning. And it means I can be ready for the king in the afternoons, when he wants to play Gymbal. I tend to get sleepy, otherwise."

Felenya nodded and grimaced. "Yes, I often have an afternoon nap." She raised her eyebrow at Rhonwyn. "You'll let me know if you need me, though, won't you?"

Rhonwyn assured her she would.

After lunch, she took a fast walk around the entire edge of the palace grounds. She wanted to see exactly where the border was and whether it revealed any weakness. She could see none. All the gates were manned by at least six guards, all on constant alert. So Dyfed wouldn't have got far if he'd started running.

Her walk took her around the group of tall buildings on the city-side of the palace grounds. There were many more people in that area, too, bustling from place to place. She would have got lost in the streets between the buildings if she hadn't stuck to the wall.

She also spotted regular, waist-high posts just inside the border, whose yellow tops looked suspiciously like upside down king's-eyes – the first she'd seen since entering the palace grounds. She wondered what the king would make of her walk today.

How did he do that – know what everyone was doing through those things?

After more than an hour walking, Rhonwyn finally got back to the palace itself. As she passed along the corridor outside the throne room she spied, just ahead of her, part of the wall moving out and sideways.

Kymra. It had to be. Rhonwyn sped up to a run as she watched her friend emerge, the girl's shoulders slumped, her arms clutched about her. She turned in the other direction from Rhonwyn – she hadn't seen her – and crept along, deceptively fast. The door slid shut by itself.

The door Kymra was heading for was probably close by. Rhonwyn had to catch her quickly or she would be gone. So she waited to whisper, "Kymra!" until she was only a few yards away.

The girl flung a wild-eyed look over her shoulder as she surged away, but slowed when she saw Rhonwyn. She looked up and down the corridor, before she pressed another part of the wall, which slid aside to reveal an alcove. She ushered Rhonwyn through it to a tiny, dark room, lit only by a slit window at the end of a chimney-like hole in one corner. A thin pad lay on a low shelf, taking up almost the whole floor space. A faint odour of sweat and old milk lingered in the air.

Kymra sank down on the edge of the pad and Rhonwyn joined her.

Rhonwyn put her hand on Kymra's. "How are you?"

But Kymra's gaze was far away. She seemed dazed. "He was so strange just now." Her voice was barely above a whisper. "He grabbed me, shook me hard ..." As she said this, she grabbed Rhonwyn by the front of her clothing and pulled her close, though she still didn't seem to see her. "... and he said, 'How do you do it? How do you put up with all these ...'" She took one hand away and slapped the side of her own head three times, her face twisted in agony. "'... all these appetites?'" Her eyes were bulging from her face now. "He looked like he might eat me whole. Then he roared, pushed me away, and left."

As Kymra said the last few words, she released Rhonwyn and all the energy seemed to drain out of her at once. She deflated and her face became blank.

Shocked by her friend's actions, Rhonwyn slowly wrapped an arm around her; she didn't want to startle her. The girl's behaviour had somehow reminded her of what Rhymla had been like: enraged, confused, stupefied even. Where was Rhymla now? Rhonwyn hadn't seen her since that brief glimpse in the corridor.

Kymra, her breath growing more ragged, awakened to Rhonwyn's presence and sank forward, nestling her head into Rhonwyn's shoulder. She shuddered, her hands clenching and unclenching in her lap.

Rhonwyn fought to stay composed. This was awful. How could she leave Kymra in the hands of this monster? But what else could she do?

All at once, however, Kymra sat up and was scrabbling at her, her eyes wide. "You have to go. You have to go. You mustn't be here." She rose and began tugging and pushing Rhonwyn towards the door panel, a high-pitched keening noise leaking from her mouth with each effort she made. The poor girl wasn't in her right mind.

"I'm going. I'm going," she reassured Kymra.

Pulling her into a quick hug just inside the door, Rhonwyn

checked both ways before emerging into the hallway. The panel snapped shut behind her. She peered at the wall to see how to open it, but could see nothing but the regular design. She rested her hand against it, knowing Kymra was beyond, and aching for her young friend.

This should not be. Her sadness suddenly transformed to anger. Her jaw set, Rhonwyn swung around and marched off to Mistress Berwyn's office. She found the woman sitting alone at her desk, surrounded by piles of papyrus, writing furiously on one of them. Rhonwyn planted herself in front of her desk.

"Do you know what he's doing to her?" Rhonwyn demanded.

Mistress Berwyn didn't look up, but ceased her scribbling and froze in place.

"How could you let that happen?" Rhonwyn's voice came out in a hiss.

When Mistress Berwyn looked up she appeared older than before, her face drawn. It seemed she hadn't slept well either. Of course, Rhonwyn was being unfair; Mistress Berwyn hadn't had a choice either. And this made sense of her reaction to Kymra's practical joke. And her rules about clothes.

Rhonwyn leaned over the desk and pleaded with her in a low voice, "There must be something we can do. We have to get her out of there."

Mistress Berwyn swallowed hard. "You're not meant to have seen her." Her voice was barely audible and her eyes slid from side to side, checking the room. "You mustn't say anything to anyone." She fixed her with her gaze. "It does not end well."

Rhonwyn's stomach clenched. The familiar presence of her father re-emerged from his silence. He always came when she needed him.

"Please, Rhonwyn." The housekeeper snatched Rhonwyn's hand and gripped it. "We mustn't speak of this again. She'll suffer even more if we do."

Rhonwyn shook her head. "I can't see how it could be worse." She sighed and turned away, tearing her hand out of

Mistress Berwyn's grasp. Her throat was closing as she fled. She clattered up the nearest stairs to her room, but stopped outside the door, frowning.

She could hear Felenya singing. The sound echoed around the corridor. A thin woman, five doors down, had her head out her door and was peering up and down the hallway.

Rhonwyn could do with a chat with Felenya. She followed the sound of the voice singing the piece she'd heard during that first concert, the one with no words. Beautiful.

No wonder it was so loud, Felenya's door was wide open. She didn't usually leave it open, surely.

Rhonwyn stopped in the doorway. Felenya was in the centre of the room, a wad of papyrus stuffed under her arm as if she'd been interrupted as she was putting it away. Someone sprawled on the floor, half leaning on the wall in front of Felenya. Rhonwyn's stomach lurched. The king's eyes were shut. Had he collapsed?

Rhonwyn started forward. Should she call for help? Why was Felenya still singing?

Her friend spotted her as she entered. Her eyes went wide and she thrust her hand palm out to stop Rhonwyn coming farther. She kept singing as she gestured Rhonwyn should leave and close the door.

Rhonwyn complied but stood outside the door for a moment afterwards. What in the world was going on? Did the king usually do that – lie on the floor as Felenya sang to him?

Rhonwyn freshened up and headed to the games room. That way she would be ready for King Risick; he wouldn't have to wait for her at all.

But he was already there, pacing back and forth, when she arrived. She held her breath as she bowed. He didn't seem too irked, however. He simply sprawled in his regular chair and made the first move. Someone had already set the pieces up. Surely he hadn't done it himself? Rhonwyn sat and made her answering move.

Feeling inexplicably brave, she calmly commented, "At some point we should try me taking the first move. It will open up a whole different set of possibilities." She raised her eyebrow at him, her heart speeding up at the risk she was taking.

His look at her was intense and dangerous for a moment, but then the edges of his mouth turned up and his head jerked up before he returned to the contemplation of his next move.

That could have been a nod.

"Well done, Rhonny." Her father clapped his hand on her shoulder.

Rhonwyn had to swallow hard to make the imagined figure go away.

When Risick reached out his hand to move his piece, Rhonwyn saw the scratch on the back of it – the one she'd put there – and it made her heart squeeze in fear. What had he made of that this morning?

They had to be so careful.

Sometime later, Jarysha entered the room. Her eyes narrowed at Rhonwyn as she assumed her position off to the side. Of course. She would have been sent to find Rhonwyn, unaware she was already on her way. But Jarysha was soon engaged in serving food to the king. He was impatient, clicking his fingers repeatedly as he beckoned for the dishes to be brought to him.

And he never stopped eating, except to make a move. His feeding frenzy seemed even greater than at his regular meals. Had he not had lunch? Rhonwyn couldn't remember if she'd seen him in the dining room. Rhonwyn saw tiny crumbs of food sticking to the king's face, his clothes, and the Gymbal pieces, but she dared not say anything. She'd already taken her risk for the day and, if she wasn't mistaken, the man was becoming more agitated the longer he sat there, stuffing the crunchy, coloured morsels into his mouth.

Two men who'd been playing at the table behind the king made a hurried exit, one glancing nervously at their monarch as he left. Were they fleeing?

The king's leg began twitching intermittently and the tic grew over time until both legs were bobbing up and down like drumsticks on a tom-tom, only interrupted when he leaned forward to move his pieces. Not long after this began, he made a huge tactical mistake on the board. He didn't seem to realise at the time; he was grabbing for more snacks from the near-empty bowl Jarysha was holding. The girl had to use both hands or the thing would have ended up on the floor.

As it was, it ended up there anyway as – a few moves later – Risick suddenly realised what he'd done.

The bowl wasn't the last inanimate object to suffer violence. Once he'd batted the bowl from Jarysha's grasp, he leaned back and moaned in frustration, his fingers curled in the hair at his temples. More than one of his attendants edged away at the noise he made. Perhaps they knew what was coming.

Jarysha was wide-eyed and pale as she chased the bowl that was now careening under a table.

The king bent forward and, using both hands, flung the playing board and the table over to one side. The pieces flew in all directions. At least two shattered entirely. Rhonwyn only had time to lean as far away as she could, and several of the pieces bounced off her.

Risick leapt to his feet and stormed towards the nearest door, bellowing, "Wrestler! Bring me a wrestler!" His attendants scattered to do his will as the king disappeared.

What was wrong with the man?

Rhonwyn released the breath she was holding and looked at Jarysha. "Are you alright?" The girl nodded and flicked her a tiny smile before rising, brushing down her crumb-encrusted clothes, and heading off, the bowl in one hand.

Rhonwyn took a deep breath, righted the table, and collected the Gymbal pieces, her heart gradually returning to its normal pace. Once the pieces were in their usual places, she determined that one of them was missing and three were destroyed, their remains in a little pile next to the board. She scanned the floor again for the missing one but had no luck. What was she meant to do about replacements? She should've asked Jarysha before she'd left. She would have to chase her.

Rhonwyn hurried to Mistress Berwyn's office. Jarysha wasn't there and neither was Mistress Berwyn, but two workers were sorting linen at the work tables. She left a message with one of them and then went upstairs to visit Felenya. Perhaps she would know what was wrong with the king.

"Oh, yes, dear. It does happen sometimes." Felenya's nostrils flared. "I think he gets overwhelmed. He does have a whole kingdom to run, you know. Perhaps it's all the things he has on his mind. Stress. Frustration." She squeezed Rhonwyn's hand. "It can be frightening, I know. He's such an intense person. But, if you just do as he asks, as quickly as possible, he ..." She paused, looking lost. "Well, he will be grateful." She grimaced at Rhonwyn. "But that will come later." Her eyes dipped. "Much later."

She was making excuses for him.

Rhonwyn turned her hand to grip Felenya's. "Are *you* alright?" The king's visit seemed to have frightened Felenya more than had been apparent at the time.

"Oh yes." Her friend sighed. "But ..." the sparkle returned to her eyes, "I could do with a brisk walk, I think."

Rhonwyn laughed and the pair walked outside together. Rhonwyn led Felenya to the menagerie at her request. Felenya was unfamiliar with the place and her interest had been piqued when Rhonwyn had mentioned it previously.

"I don't go for many walks," Felenya commented as they stopped beside the monkey enclosure. She took a deep breath. "I think I should get out more."

"That's a good idea," said Rhonwyn. "You always seem to be working. The king asks a lot of you."

Felenya nodded. "He loves his music." She giggled at the tiny monkey which was peering at her through the bars, hanging upside down by its tail. "Hello you," she said, and wriggled her finger through the bars. She was rewarded when he gripped the tip of it briefly before scurrying along the branch above and clambering onto his mother.

Rhonwyn suddenly wanted to take the creature with her when she visited Dyfed tonight. He would love it. She drew a breath in when she realised she should be trying to keep the promise she'd made to Dyfed: to find out about his family.

She immediately asked Felenya, "Do you know if any Wise Ones are left? I'm trying to find out where someone's family is."

Felenya's head tilted as she thought about this. "I don't know." She turned away from the gangly monkeys and carried on along the path. "I'd forgotten about them."

"Yes, so had I," said Rhonwyn. She felt her eyebrows jerk up. "I wonder if Matu would know?"

"Who?"

"Matuthalyn. The librarian – the woman in the library," she explained, as Felenya's face had remained puckered in confusion.

"Oh yes," she said. "The lady with that funny thing in front of her eyes."

"Apparently it helps her see."

Rhonwyn didn't want to seem in too much of a hurry to get away from Felenya, so she stayed with her until they returned to the palace. Felenya's feet were hurting by then. So were Rhonwyn's.

As soon as her friend was happily ensconced in her favourite chair – her bare feet stretching and wriggling before the wide open window – Rhonwyn tore down to the library.

"Matu?" she began as soon as she walked in. "You remember the Wise Ones? They had all the generations memorised."

Matu assured her she did.

"Are there any left? Where would I go to find out where someone's family was?"

Matu froze and her eyes flicked to the door. Rhonwyn went on quickly. "I just want to see if they're still alive, not try to contact them or anything." Rhonwyn hoped this line of questioning wouldn't get her or Matu in trouble.

"Ah," said Matu, nodding. "Let me see what I can find out. That might be part of what the administrators do."

"Who? Where are they?"

"They're in the buildings near the city. There'll be someone who takes cares of records, I believe. I'll look into it."

Rhonwyn leaned on Matu's desk and lowered her voice. "Am I allowed to ask this kind of thing?"

Matu's face brightened, though her expression seemed forced. "I don't see why not, if you're just looking for information." However, as she said this, she eyed Rhonwyn, her brows creeping up. Rhonwyn got the impression that Matu didn't want to know anything more than that, for her own safety.

Turning around, Matuthalyn withdrew a clump of papyrus from high on the shelf behind her. Connected at one corner with a piece of string, it was rather dusty. Letting it fall on the desk before her, she said, "This might take a while."

It took her more than an hour, in fact, and Rhonwyn spent the time reading her current Gymbal book. Another strategy idea popped out at her and she managed to take some notes.

"Right," said Matu finally. "The person you need to talk to is Emylaza mi Lyngeth. She's in the records department."

Rhonwyn copied the information down on her sheet of notes. "Where's that?" she asked. Matu beckoned her to the desk.

On the back of the bound-together papyrus sheets was a map of the palace precinct, the buildings labelled with the departments housed in them. The department of records was right in the middle of the clump of buildings near the main palace gate. Rhonwyn would have walked past it on her way in.

She retrieved her piece of papyrus and drew a simple diagram she hoped would help her find it. She thanked Matu, who seemed very pleased with herself, and then hurried towards the door.

"You're welcome," said Matu, tapping all the sheets together and returning them to their place. "I wouldn't try visiting today, though, they'll be closing very soon."

Rhonwyn had already opened the door and felt her shoulders slump. She'd asked too late in the day. But, as she trudged back up to her room, she told herself she'd walked enough that day. She would go tomorrow. Early.

Disappointed she wouldn't have anything to tell Dyfed about his family that night, Rhonwyn sighed as she opened the balcony doors wide and let the breeze flow through her room. She reclined on the chair between the windows and pulled out the story book Matu had given her. She read one odd story after another about animals that wore clothes and could talk. In fact, they behaved very much like people. The stories reminded her of the teaching parables the storytellers used to tell the children when they visited the village.

She could take the book tonight, for Dyfed to read. The thought made her smile. She couldn't wait to see him again.

25

Rhonwyn stood waiting in the library for the king to pass the door. She'd crept through the darkness and felt her way past the first shelf. She'd found a small gap she could look through and spy on the door.

There.

Her stomach flopped over itself as his slender form silently glided by. She stood very still, listening, and heard the trapdoor opening. An unmistakable sound. How did the person in the room at this end of the corridor not hear those sounds? They must be curious about them, surely. But then curiosity wasn't exactly encouraged, was it? Perhaps they'd already investigated, only to find themselves face-to-face with the king. They wouldn't be curious again after that. Ever.

The trapdoor rumbled closed. She would wait a while yet.

Risick must know the body he used was vulnerable when he left it every night. That must be why he'd had his chamber built in the first place. No one could get near enough to Dyfed to know what was going on and Dyfed couldn't get out, not even if he broke a window – and they were so high he couldn't reach them anyway. The king was vulnerable now, but had no idea he was. This thought made Rhonwyn feel oddly powerful. An unfamiliar feeling. She shook her head.

The simplest way to get rid of Risick would be to kill Dyfed.

A queasiness overtook her. She couldn't do that. Even though her entire community was under this evil spirit's thumb, even with poor Kymra enduring ... *that*. Rhonwyn found her fist had clenched unconsciously. No, she couldn't do that. There had to be another way.

But she couldn't take too long to find out. How long was too long? And, if she couldn't find another way, how could she – alone – make this terrible decision? How could she bear this alone?

She must tell Zaryc. He was the only one she could tell, even though she didn't really like him. He was on her side and knew what was at stake. She would tell him during the next concert.

She checked the clock. Midnight. With a deep breath, Rhonwyn stepped out from her hiding place and entered the sitting room. Her eyes were already accustomed to the dark. Slipping through the window and down to the roof of the corridor didn't take as long, despite the terrifying precipice each side; she was getting used to it. And there was something to look forward to at the other end.

She walked through the night air, crouching several times to wait when the breeze became a gust. Ducking through the heavy window, she stood on the inner windowsill and took her shoes off for a better grip on the thin side ledge.

As she paused outside the chamber's door, putting her shoes on again, she heard a strange sound, like a high-pitched intake of breath.

What was that? Midnight had passed, hadn't it? Rhonwyn nodded. Of course it had. Surely the king would be gone and Dyfed would be back by now. Still nervous, she pressed the numbers and eased open the door.

Dyfed was kneeling on the floor, a few feet beyond the doorway, his face in his hands. A strangled sob escaped him.

"Dyfed?"

His eyes – those deep, brown eyes – appeared above his fingers as the door closed behind her. He sprang up and threw his arms around her, lifting her up. Tears dripped down his face.

"Oh, my friend," he cried, squeezing her breathless. The book fell from her hand as she grasped him for balance.

"What's wrong?" she asked.

He finally pulled away and held her face between his warm hands. "I thought you weren't coming. I thought I had dreamed you, that you were a vision. I thought I was all alone again." His voice broke and he pulled her against him again in an unbreakable grip.

"Oh, Dyfed. That's awful. Why?" Rhonwyn's voice was muffled in the folds of his clothing, against his muscled chest. She could hear his heart thumping against her ear.

"You took so long," he said. He held her away from him again, his face twisted. "Why did you take so long?"

She curled her hands up and grasped his elbows. "It takes time for me to get over the corridor, Dyfed. I can't let the king see me. I have to leave a bit of time."

Dyfed finally released her and put his hands on his hips. His head hung down and he shook it. "Of course. I wasn't thinking clearly." He frowned and thrust his fingers through his hair. "I feel so strange. This crazy feeling." He sighed and turned away. "It happens sometimes. Usually right after I've had a really bad night the night before."

"A bad night?"

His face reddened. "When I feel very sad or angry. I get so frustrated sometimes, I just ..." his eyes flicked to the floor "... have a bad night." She could sense so much he wasn't saying. "And then the next night, I feel so confused, I'm afraid for my sanity. But then the night after that, I'm alright."

Rhonwyn narrowed her eyes at him. "So, you're sad or angry one night, and then you're confused the next? Every time?"

He nodded and then threw up his hands. "But I wasn't sad last night. I was really, really happy. Crazy happy."

A thought struck Rhonwyn. She stepped towards Dyfed and took his arm to capture his attention. "Today ..." she began and then shook her head. "No ... yesterday, during the day, the king was acting very strangely. He was jumpy and really erratic. He threw the Gymbal board over when he realised he'd made a mistake."

Dyfed's eyebrows rose and then dipped in concern before she went on.

"He said something really odd to my friend." Her friend. Rhonwyn gritted her teeth. She couldn't tell Dyfed about Kymra – she didn't even want to put that into words. She moved on quickly. "He made my other friend sing to him, too, as he sat on the floor in front of her."

Dyfed was looking at her, his head tilted sideways.

"Felenya told me he's like that sometimes," added Rhonwyn. "And I wonder if those things are related. If your strong emotions trigger his strange behaviour. And then his strange behaviour makes you confused."

"Could be." He took a deep breath and wiped his face with both hands.

"Are you still confused?" she asked.

He nodded. "It usually lasts the whole night."

"Maybe we should stay in, then." Rhonwyn had secretly been hoping for some sort of excuse to keep Dyfed inside. She was so scared he would take off and ruin everything.

Dyfed's face dropped. "Do we have to?" He looked so dejected.

She must distract him. She gestured towards the table. "Let's have a game of Gymbal and decide after that."

He beamed at her, his face transformed. "Yes. Let's play." He strode over to the bed and reached underneath, withdrawing a case with a handle. "I asked for this at the beginning by writing on some papyrus. It took me ages to get the words down properly. He left a board for me with the pieces to play with, but ..." He shrugged. "I had no one to play against so, eventually, I put it away."

For a moment, Rhonwyn and Dyfed frowned at the grim predicament Dyfed had been in. But then Dyfed's face lit up with his infectious smile. Now he had someone to play against. The two of them cleared the table of its present contents, and Rhonwyn set the Gymbal board up while Dyfed lit the lamps.

"This is really old," said Rhonwyn fingering the Gymbal set. "I haven't seen one like this for years." The pieces were all hand-carved from a deep red wood.

Dyfed sprang up and retrieved the case again, opened it, and held up one corner of it for her to see. A name was engraved on the inside edge.

"Synfed!" Rhonwyn cried. "That was the king's first Gymbal opponent." She'd read that in the Gymbal history book only a day or so ago. In fact, Synfed was listed as the writer of that book – and most of the others. It hadn't been long after Synfed had been posted in that position that Gymbal boards had become available again, under Risick's rule. But the sets had all been drab-looking. Plain and all exactly the same. That was why she'd been so surprised at how elaborate the king's Gymbal board was. But this board reminded her of how the original sets had been – the ones her father had played on with her and the other people of their village during the long winter evenings.

There were two short disagreements over the rules as Rhonwyn and Dyfed played, but they were over quickly. Dyfed's memory had failed him, in his confused state, and he soon conceded that Rhonwyn's arguments made more sense than his. But it did make Rhonwyn wonder if the rules had changed since Dyfed had last played. Had the king had a part in that? How much sway had this wicked spirit had in her people's lives and traditions? What had they lost because of him?

She was assuming Risick was an evil spirit. What if he wasn't? What if it was some sort of disease?

Rhonwyn won the first game, but Dyfed was keen to play another. He seemed to have forgotten his desire to get outside – exactly as Rhonwyn had been hoping.

"I remember now," he said. "I remember it. It's been a long time. I want to play again," he insisted, slapping his palms on the table's surface. His enthusiasm made Rhonwyn giggle. She'd rediscovered the joy of the game too, playing opposite such an animated person. She'd forgotten how much fun it could be.

This was such a contrast to playing the king, who was so tense and silent. How did Risick take all the fun out of everything? Of course: fear.

She didn't mind playing again. She sat facing the door, and the clock, noticing between moves what a fortress the king had made – to keep Dyfed in, and everyone else out. But all Rhonwyn had needed to enter this fortress were four numbers. That was, indeed, a gap in his defences. She'd better not let that advantage slip away.

Dyfed had to hand over his general again the second time, but his game had been much better. He applauded her. "You're a very good player, Rhonwyn," he said. "No wonder you're the king's opponent."

She felt her neck grow warm as she smiled, her head on one side. "Thank you. Shall we play again?"

He tapped his forehead with his finger. "No. I think I have to have my mind working properly to beat you."

She giggled as they put the pieces back in the case and peered at the pile of other game pieces on the floor. They would have to restore the table to how it looked before. Risick couldn't be allowed to see that Dyfed had been playing a game with someone else.

"Rhonwyn?" Dyfed spoke quietly, his eyes anxious.

"Yes?" she replied, sliding the catches closed on the case.

He took the case from her and slid it back under the bed before he answered. His speech was hesitant. "Why don't you want me to go outside?"

Her face fell. She hadn't hidden her relief as well as she'd thought she had. "Oh, I'm so sorry." She shook her head and sighed. "I'm just afraid of what might happen if someone saw you, or if you decided not to come back." She spread her hands to indicate her feeling of powerlessness.

His brows descended as he sat back down. "You are so afraid of him."

Rhonwyn felt chagrined, absently shuffling the playing pieces around the table. If only she could be braver.

Dyfed's fingers twisted together as he pondered, then leaned forward, his elbows on his knees. "Would it help if I made an oath that I would come back here when you wanted me to? An oath on my honour?" He placed his hand on his chest. The gesture took her back to the time before Risick had taken power, when a person's honour had really meant something. You could trust the one who made an oath on their honour. This was no small thing Dyfed was offering. No one did that anymore.

"Well, yes, I suppose," Rhonwyn said.

"Then, I swear," he said. "I promise on my honour that I will return here when you want me to." Dyfed said this so seriously, his clear eyes looking directly into hers, his hand pressed to his heart, that Rhonwyn believed he truly would keep his promise. The poor man was desperate to get outside.

She smiled. "Thank you."

"Now ..." He sat up, rubbing his hands together. "What can we do about the other thing – people recognising me? Can I cover my face? Wear a mask?"

Rhonwyn frowned and nibbled at her bottom lip. "Well, we don't have a mask, but perhaps we could find something else to cover your face with. But we have to come up with an excuse for you to be wearing it."

"There didn't seem to be anyone around last night," he pointed out.

"No, but we can't count on that being true every night – there's too much at stake. The best thing I can think of is a bandage. Then we can cover enough of your face to stop them recognising you, but not make it look like you're hiding something."

The two of them looked around the room for something they

could use. As Rhonwyn checked the washroom, she heard a gasp of discovery from Dyfed.

"What about this?" he cried.

Rhonwyn returned to the main room. Dyfed was holding up the sleeping pad and fingering the material on it. He was proposing they tear off strips.

Rhonwyn shook her head. "I think that would be too obvious." Dyfed looked disappointed. "It looks like I'll need to go out and find something out in the—"

Dyfed began speaking before she finished, "Please, please don't go out without me." He grabbed her hands with both of his.

26

Once they'd got to the sitting room and clambered inside, she closed the window and grabbed Dyfed's arm, as he was already making for the door.

"We need to figure out what we're going to say to anyone who stops us. So ..." she pointed at him, "You are Dyfed." He peered at her askance. She spread her hands. "I can't think of any reason for us to lie about your name, and it makes it easier to remember. No one knows who you are." She became serious again, making up the story as she went. "You were visiting the palace last night to consult with one of the king's advisors and you fell and hit your head. You were knocked out and I only just found you. I'm taking you to the healer."

Dyfed nodded. "Am I allowed to talk?"

"Your voice is different to his, so yes, that should be fine. But don't say too much or you'll give away how little you know."

Dyfed nodded.

"Just hold your hands over your face until we get a bandage for you. This story is only going to work once. And we'll have to convince them not to accompany us to the healer, or it's all over." Dyfed attempted seriousness again, but couldn't quite manage to scrape all the smile off his face.

They made their way carefully up to Rhonwyn's room, encountering no one – luckily. Once inside, she found a piece of her old clothing, tore it up, and wrapped it around Dyfed's head, a diagonal piece covering part of his face. They would assert that the wound was on his forehead and that would have to do.

Once the bandage was on, Rhonwyn stepped back to inspect it. They needed to make it look more convincing.

"We need some blood," she muttered.

Dyfed held out his arm. "You can take some of mine, if you like," he said.

But Rhonwyn frowned, remembering the scratch on Risick's hand the previous day. "I don't think so," she said. "I don't want the King to suspect something is going on by seeing any more marks appear on his body. We'll have to use mine."

She found some small scissors in her washroom and, gritting her teeth, jabbed herself in the fleshy part of her hand. She smeared the result on the front edge of the rag around Dyfed's head before wrapping her hand in another. Hopefully, no one would look at Dyfed too closely. At least it would always be dark.

Dyfed had been thinking while she was gone and his tone was indignant as she worked. "I've found lots of marks on *my* body over the years and I've never known how they got there. Like this." He thrust his right arm out, his palm twisted upwards. "This appeared right at the beginning." A long, straight scar began just below his thumb and was as long as Dyfed's hand was wide.

"When it first appeared," he continued, "it was red and sore, with a bandage over it and what looked like sewing stitches crossing it, which disappeared a few days later. But it was the least of my troubles at the time, so I forgot until you said that."

Rhonwyn inspected the scar by the light of her lamp. It didn't look like an accident. Why would Risick cut his own wrist?

"Is this your room?" Dyfed asked abruptly. He'd moved on already.

"Yes, but only since last week," she replied, and stowed the remains of her old garment in the bottom of a drawer.

Dyfed discovered the doors out onto the balcony. He opened

them and stepped out. Rhonwyn followed him. She found him once again studying the stars, his lips turned up at each end. He was still able to be quite expressive, despite the cloth wound around his head.

"I'd forgotten how small the night sky can make me feel," he murmured.

Rhonwyn tilted her head towards him. "I kind of like that feeling, actually," she admitted.

Dyfed laughed. "Yes, I know what you mean. That stomach-sinking sensation." His eyes wide, he laid one palm upon another and then pulled them apart while he sucked in his breath.

She smiled. Yes, he did understand what she meant.

He grabbed her hand. "Where shall we go now?"

She paused, distracted by the warmth of his hand around hers. "Let's go to the other side of the garden and explore the woods." Rhonwyn could think of no safer place.

Her suggestion seemed to delight Dyfed. "Yes. Let's go."

Retaining his grip on her hand, he pulled her through her room, only allowing her to take charge again when they emerged into the hall and he didn't know which way to go. They moved quickly through the dim, empty corridors, out the doors at the front of the palace, and walked directly along the wide path through the centre of the garden and into the trees, where Rhonwyn could finally relax.

Not far into the wooded area, Rhonwyn randomly chose a path on the right and started down it before slowing. "I don't actually know my way around in here. We could get lost," she admitted.

"I like the sound of that," Dyfed cried. "Let's get lost." He surged forward, dragging her with him.

Rhonwyn shushed him and giggled at the same time. He made her feel just like a girl again – instead of a timid, cringing, impotent adult.

There were regular lamps burning alongside their path

which made the atmosphere magical, the leaves and boughs of the trees casting shadows, all moving in the breeze. Rhonwyn wondered who lit all these lamps. Whenever they came to a junction they took turns choosing which way they would go.

"Let's pretend," said Dyfed. "Let's pretend we're explorers. Far down beyond the southern marshes. Where no one has been before. And we know that up ahead," he pointed up the left hand path. "… is the treasure that Domysh the faerie stands guard over." His eyes were bright in anticipation.

Rhonwyn wasn't sure about this. "A treasure? I haven't heard that one."

"Oh, yes," Dyfed said as he released her hand so he could gesture with both of his, and his voice became hushed. "He stole it from the goddess of eternal fire, who lives deep within the ground beneath us. And now he is forever banished to the surface of the world."

Dyfed was facing her, staring into the space over her shoulder, his mouth open in a smile of wonder. Rhonwyn was mesmerised; he was so full of life.

"The gems are all colours and sizes," he went on. "Some are bigger than your head." He wrapped both his hands around her head and laughed. "And the biggest of all is the Lifestone." He was gazing into her eyes now. "It's got a fiery earth colour in the middle, but there's deep green and blue around the edges. It's beautiful. Whoever has it has the power to set people free."

With a jolt, Rhonwyn suddenly realised Dyfed was looking at her eyes and had been describing the colour of them. "You're making this up!"

He broke into a chuckle. "Of course I am. That's what stories are. Come on." He pulled her down the left path. It led upwards now, wending through the trees. At the next bend, Dyfed stopped and peered around the corner, then darted back and pushed her behind him. Her heart clenched in fear. Who was it in the path ahead?

He hissed. "It's Domysh! He's waiting in the path. We'll have to wait for him to look away."

Rhonwyn laughed, relieved, and was shushed by Dyfed. "What does he look like?" she whispered, playing along.

Dyfed gestured as he said, "He has a big, green head. Green like a river frog."

Rhonwyn covered her mouth to stifle her giggles. Dyfed dipped his head, his eyes bright with humour.

"And his knees go backwards, like a stork's," he added.

Rhonwyn's body was bending now, and shaking with mirth.

"He walks like this," said Dyfed, and he began waddling around Rhonwyn, his hands tucked under his armpits, his feet flying out to the side with each step.

She let out a loud shriek of laughter. Dyfed darted to her and clapped his hand over her mouth, grinning like a madman. He encircled her body with his other arm, backed them up to the bend and leant over to see around it. He gasped.

"Oh, no! He's heard us. We have to run."

Giggling, they ran back the way they'd come and then, skidding around the corner, took the other path at a sprint. But it wasn't long before they stopped and leant forwards on their knees, panting.

Dyfed spoke between gulps of air. "I can't run as far as I used to." He shook his head, frowning, and rubbed his side.

After a minute or so, Rhonwyn straightened and put her hands on her hips. "So, are we going to get this treasure, or not?"

Dyfed's head dropped between his knees and he roared with laughter. Recovering, he righted himself and indicated with a flourish of his arm they should continue. "We'll go the back way," he said, his eyebrows pumping.

Rhonwyn tittered. She hadn't felt this free in years.

This path was an even steeper climb and there were no longer any turnoffs. Within a few paces, the path began twisting back on itself in a series of switchbacks that went up and up. At one point they could see the palace behind them, through a gap in the trees. They stood side by side, gazing out over the grounds. There were lamps lit everywhere.

"This must be that hill I walked around," said Rhonwyn, glad for the break in their climb. She was doing a lot more physical activity than she used to.

Dyfed looked over all that was before him. "This king owns a lot of land. Perhaps that's how he became king." Without waiting for an answer, he turned and carried on climbing the hill. Rhonwyn followed.

The pinnacle surprised them with its suddenness. All at once they stood on an enormous, square plain. It had a low wall around it. They slowed as they crossed it for, the further across they went, the more sparkling lights appeared. Thousands of them, spread out over the plain.

Dyfed breathed, "The sky has fallen down!" His eyes were wide and his mouth had fallen open. Rhonwyn suddenly understood what he meant – it looked like the stars had fallen from the sky.

"No, Dyfed. What you're looking at is the city. Those are all the lights along the streets and in the windows." She moved closer to him and pointed at one of the high-rises. "Do you see the lines there?" She imagined it must be difficult to get the right perspective when you had no experience of what the buildings looked like during the day. "Those are lights above windows, all in a row, and row on top of row. Behind them are thousands of people sleeping in their beds. They'll wake up in the morning and go to work over there." She swung her arm to point towards the mine opening in the centre.

Dyfed blinked and shook his head before jutting it forward to squint again at what she pointed at. After a long moment, his head retracted. Frowning, he said in a faint voice, "You've turned my life upside down. This is a totally different world than I knew before. Where is my home?"

Rhonwyn gripped his shoulder. "It doesn't exist anymore, Dyfed. I'm sorry."

"Where are my family?"

"I don't know yet. I'm still looking. I'll tell you as soon as I find out."

She moved closer to the edge of the plain they stood on. The plain ended abruptly, beyond the low wall, and below was a grid of smaller buildings. Leaning out further, supporting herself on the sturdy wall, Rhonwyn was amazed to find they stood on the roof of the tallest building in the palace precinct. She could see the double wall that surrounded the palace grounds and pointed it out to Dyfed.

"If only we had wings," she murmured. But that wouldn't solve the problem of Dyfed's possession – or was it an illness?

Dyfed stared out over the city below, his liveliness muted now. He seemed to be contemplating something. He knelt on the ground next to the wall.

"Are you well?" Rhonwyn asked and joined him on the ground.

"I feel lost," he said. "I don't belong anywhere. I have no home. I've been dreaming for years ..." The thought stopped him for a moment. "I've been dreaming of getting out of *that room*," he jabbed his thumb back towards the palace "... going back home and just ... eating with my parents. Talking all evening about the crops in the vineyard, or who I could marry, or ... anything. Everything. Giggling with my sister, and then going to my bed, lying down ..." He stopped again, his face looking older than she'd ever seen, his eyes downcast. "And going to sleep. To sleep, to dream, and to know I would wake the next morning and see the sun again." His shoulders slumped and his voice became nearly inaudible. "I just want to go home."

Rhonwyn felt her heart squeezing. She rubbed Dyfed's back. "We'll figure something out. We'll work out how to get Risick out of you. Somehow. I'll do everything I can, I promise."

First Dyfed's eyes turned up to her, then the edges of his mouth curled upwards again. Now he looked more like himself.

27

In contrast to their approach, Rhonwyn and Dyfed's retreat from that high place was sombre and slow. First, they lay on top of the building and stared at the eternal stars above, the view better than ever. Dyfed continued to hold Rhonwyn's hand, which made her heart flip over.

On the way back, she took him through the menagerie, though there weren't many animals to be seen. The exception was a large cat, pacing back and forth in its cage. They spent quite some time watching it. At first, Rhonwyn tried to show Dyfed the maps and how small the area he'd known as their world was but, not only was it hard for him to see, he was spellbound by the movement of the predator within and couldn't concentrate on what she was saying.

"Sorry," he said once, "my mind is still not working very well." His smile was wry.

In the end, they sat on the bench opposite and their heads pivoted back and forth, following the lithe, striped feline's cooped up frustration. More than once, sitting there in the dark, they caught the eerie flash of light reflected from the creature's eyes as it looked towards them.

Dyfed murmured, "I know how you feel, you poor, beautiful creature."

The motion was hypnotic and Rhonwyn woke twice to find her head leaning on Dyfed's shoulder. When she jolted awake the second time, he chuckled low in his throat and circled his arm around her, drawing her close. Smiling, she leaned into him and dozed off again. He was so warm. He had to shake her awake.

"I think we'd better get back," he whispered. "The sky is starting to lighten."

Rhonwyn gasped. "Oh my goodness, yes. Quick."

They leapt up and Rhonwyn led him back to the king's chamber. Twice, she had to push Dyfed back and out of sight of early risers. But neither person took any notice of them. The second was rubbing his eyes as he turned into a corridor ahead.

Once Dyfed was securely within his isolated room, Rhonwyn turned to the door, yawning. Dyfed caught her arm.

"Do you have to go right away?" he asked.

Rhonwyn gave him a wan smile. "No, but I should go soon. I left far too late last time. It was light when I was crossing the corridor and someone could have seen me from the palace."

She could tell he understood the import of this, as his eyes widened in alarm and he turned her towards the door himself. "Then you should go, definitely," he said.

She laughed. "I have to take your bandage off first." Thanks the heavens she'd remembered before she left.

Dyfed grimaced and sat in a chair as she unwound the length of cloth. It had started to slip off, but Rhonwyn thought she knew a way to keep it on more effectively next time. She stuffed the bandage into her pocket.

"Well, I'd better go," she said, sighing. She turned towards the door. "See you tonight, Dyfed."

Dyfed sprang up from his chair and, just as he had the night before, grabbed her and hugged her fiercely. "Thank you, thank you, Rhonwyn. It was magical. I will be more patient the next time, before you arrive."

"You're a sweet, sweet man, Dyfed. Don't ever feel responsible for what Risick has done in your body. You're nothing like him." She paused, uncertain, before stretching up on her toes and kissing his cheek. "I've had a wonderful time with you, too. And now I have to wait all day to come back to you. It'll feel like forever."

His face broke into a broad smile as she turned away, waving over her shoulder.

Rhonwyn crossed the divide, slipped up to her room, and went straight to bed. They'd forgotten to close the balcony door, so it stayed cool until she woke gently to the sound of the hallway clock chiming eleven.

She lay there, eyes still closed, thinking about what had happened during the night. She remembered the texture of Dyfed's cheek, both smooth and rough beneath her lips, the heat of his body so close, the sight of his eye just inches from hers, his earthy, tangy smell. And all the laughter.

A drippy smile was plastered on her face. Wait. Where was this going? Was she in love with Dyfed? Well, that just made things worse, didn't it? The smile fell from her face.

Their time together last night had seemed very much like she imagined courting would have been – without a chaperone. Even her father's ghostly presence hadn't been felt. But Dyfed couldn't possibly be in love with her. She was plain and pathetic. He was only behaving so sweetly because she was the only person he'd seen in years. Vinegar would taste sweet to a thirsty man. She mustn't let herself get carried away by stupid fantasies. She had a job to do. At the very least, Rhonwyn had to get to the records department today. She shook herself and leapt out of bed.

Washed and dressed, she headed out, pausing to restudy the papyrus map she'd made yesterday. Pleased when the directions she'd written took her straight there, she stopped again in the street outside and re-read the name off the papyrus before she entered.

A woman sat behind a window just inside the double doors at the front of the tall building. "Peace to you," said Rhonwyn. "Could I speak to Emylaza mi Lyngeth, please?"

The woman, her face sour, referred to a piece of papyrus in front of her. "She's on the next floor down." She pointed at the stairs to Rhonwyn's right and sniffed. "Down to the end of the corridor. It's a blue door. You might have to call out, if she's in the shelves."

This was easier than Rhonwyn had expected. She descended the stairs and paced out the long corridor. Past the open blue door stood an empty desk, like Matu's, but surrounded by many more shelves than there were in the palace library.

Rhonwyn called, "Hello? Emylaza?"

"Be right with you," replied a voice from Rhonwyn's left. She heard footsteps and then a shapely, dark brown woman strode into view, carrying a large pile of books. When she reached the desk, she thumped the books down and looked expectantly up at Rhonwyn.

"How can I serve you?" she said.

Rhonwyn had thought carefully about what she would ask. "Peace to you. I'm trying to find out if some old friends of my family are still alive. Their names are Cothee and Syphryd. They are husband and wife. They belonged to the Dymryd clan and lived down on the southern coast, near the estuary."

Emylaza's eyes widened. "Well, that's a first." When she saw Rhonwyn's puzzled frown, she went on, "You've given me all the details I need to find them. Most people come in with little or no information and ask me to magically find people. Only the king can do magic." She drew in a breath. "Right." She headed off into the shelves. "The best place to look is the ledger for the Dymryd clan from when they were moved into the city."

When Emylaza returned, she was carrying a pile of papyrus secured on one edge like a book, but much larger, and its cover was two disconnected pieces of thick leather – one on the front, the other on the back. Instead of going behind her too-full desk again, she indicated with her head that Rhonwyn should follow as she walked around behind the door, where another desk stood. She plonked the ledger down and swung it open. She had to lean back to get the edge of it past her face.

Bending over the papyrus, she pointed at the top of the first page with her right index finger and then ran it down the page. "Cothee … Cothee … Cothee …" she murmured. Rhonwyn could see a grid of lines from side to side and from top to bottom on the page, with writing in between. Once her finger had reached the bottom of that page, Emylaza flipped over to the next, still chanting "Cothee." Though that occasionally changed to "Syphryd," at the same time as her finger paused in its slide down the papyrus.

Four pages in, she stopped. "Cothee!" Her finger slid to the side. "But his wife's name is Kupryna." She sighed, drew her finger back to the left-most column and carried on down the page.

Two pages later, she leaned back, her hands pressed into the middle of her back. "I do too much of this," she explained to Rhonwyn before resuming her search.

Emylaza got all the way to the end of the bundle of papyrus – with one more break to stretch – and did not find another Cothee.

"Well, that's all from that," she stated, looking up. "You're sure they belonged to the Dymryd clan?"

Rhonwyn frowned. "Yes, definitely." She thought for a moment. "Could Syphryd have arrived on her own?" Perhaps Dyfed's father had died. Rhonwyn wasn't looking forward to telling him that.

"No, I checked all the women who came by themselves," said Emylaza. "Sorry. If you're sure of those details then … I can't help you."

Rhonwyn clicked her tongue and looked away. "What would've happened to them, I wonder?"

Emylaza shrugged.

Rhonwyn thought she would risk another question. "What happened to the Wise Ones – the ones who used to memorise all the history and generations?"

Emylaza's face tensed and she spoke quickly. "We wrote down all the information they knew when they came into the city. We don't need Wise Ones when we can write everything down."

Her tone warned Rhonwyn not to push it any further, so she edged towards the door. "I understand. Thanks."

Emylaza relaxed. "Well that's such a shame, when you had all the right information." She heaved the ledger closed.

But her words gave Rhonwyn another idea and she turned back. "Oh, I forgot. They also had a daughter called Nemalyn. Would you mind looking for her, too?"

Emylaza nodded, unfazed, flipped the front of the ledger open, and started the whole process again. But this time she dragged her finger through the entire list of names without stopping once.

"Sorry," she said when she'd finished.

Rhonwyn sighed, thanked Emylaza and trudged to the main door. She still didn't have anything to tell Dyfed about his family. Where else could she go? She got lost in the streets between the tall buildings and was late for lunch. Felenya didn't seem to notice and immediately regaled Rhonwyn with something she'd heard about a new performer the king wanted to try out: a magician.

"A magician? Really? But only the king has magic," said Rhonwyn, startled by the news.

"Well, I've heard his is a different kind of magic that the king wants to see. He called it 'illusion' and he laughed, so perhaps it's not real magic like his," Felenya said.

Rhonwyn was inclined to think the king wanted to trick the magician to come to him so he could kill him. He wouldn't want any rivals. But that was none of her concern.

"When will the magician come?"

Felenya's eyes twinkled. "He'll be performing tonight, during the concert."

"You're singing again tonight?" asked Rhonwyn. Her friend

nodded.

As Felenya told her about her morning of rehearsals, the ones planned for the afternoon, and the possibility that she might see the magician perform during them, Rhonwyn remembered that this would give her another chance to talk to Zaryc. The thought irritated her; she would miss some of the concert again.

When Felenya left for her rehearsal after lunch, Rhonwyn went down to the library to ask Matuthalyn about history books. Perhaps that would give her a clue about where Dyfed's family was. But Matu wasn't there. Rhonwyn walked the length of the shelves to see if she could find it herself, but had no luck. So she took another Gymbal book to the desk and sat down with it.

A little while later, Matu returned. She knew nothing of books of Merynbyl's history.

"Emylaza told me the Wise Ones were asked for all their knowledge, so I thought it would have been written down somewhere," said Rhonwyn.

Matu's lips pursed. "Yes, it would have. Perhaps it could be listed under the legends." She showed Rhonwyn where the legends were on the shelves, and returned to her desk, leaving Rhonwyn to look through them herself.

Rhonwyn had barely opened the first book, however, when she heard the library door open. Moments later, she heard Matu gasp. She walked out of the shelves to investigate. As she rounded the corner she spied Matuthalyn curled up on the floor. King Risick stood before the librarian, his hands on his hips.

Rhonwyn dropped to her knees and tried to remember where everything went.

She knelt within a long silence before the king spoke. "You may rise."

As Rhonwyn stood, she found his focus upon her, which made her stomach clench. Were her eyes as wide as Matu's, who blinked like an owl as she stood waiting for the king to tell her what he wanted? He obviously didn't visit often.

The king was very still and his gaze pierced Rhonwyn. "What

brings you here?" he asked, his voice low. His cronies were lined up behind him, just inside the door.

Rhonwyn panicked for a moment. But no, she had a perfectly good reason to be there. She pointed to the book on the desk in front of him. "I come here to read about Gymbal tactics."

Risick eyes narrowed as he stared at the book she'd indicated. He flipped through it before grunting acknowledgement, though he still seemed somehow dissatisfied with her answer. He turned his attention to Matu's desk, then ran his eyes over the shelves behind it before pacing past each of the bookshelves. The two women froze in place and watched. What had brought him here?

He walked around the entire room, including along the back wall, where he tugged on one of the cupboard doors and found it locked. He returned to Matu, glaring. Rhonwyn heard the librarian's breathing stop entirely until Risick's gaze finally turned away.

He then stood looking at Rhonwyn, his hands clasped behind his back. She had the sudden, horrifying impression he was trying to read her mind. Could he? Did his magic go that far? What had provoked this? She hadn't done anything, that he would know of, to warrant this attention. Rhonwyn did her best to keep breathing.

Finally, Risick strode away. But, as he did, he lifted his finger over his shoulder and crooked it at her.

"Come with me, Rhonwyn," he said.

As she trailed along just behind the king, surrounded by his attendants, Rhonwyn racked her brain for anything that might have made him suspicious. Did he know she'd visited the records building that morning? Was he having her followed? Had it been the scratch on the back of his hand? But surely, if he was aware of her night-time activities, she would be dead already.

All she wanted to do was turn and run. But that wouldn't help, would it? She imagined he wouldn't need to spend any effort at all to catch her with his magic and, even if she could escape him, she still had the problem of getting past the walls. Besides, running would just make her look guilty. So Rhonwyn continued to follow Risick along the corridor and up the steps, her stomach folding itself, over and over. Her body was quivering so much she tripped over the last step to the main level.

She consoled herself with the thought that at least the king didn't draw out executions. Everyone seemed to die very quickly. Of course, those were only the ones she'd seen. Not all executions happened during Announcements.

Only when he entered the games room, sat in his regular place, and indicated that she should sit in hers, could Rhonwyn finally relax. The king's attendants took their usual places around him. But the king continued to stare at her, his eyes narrowed, even as he began to play. It made Rhonwyn so nervous she knocked over several of her pieces as she pulled her hand back from making her move.

As she righted her army captains, the king tilted his head to the side and asked, "Is something wrong?" His jaw was clenched.

Rhonwyn leaned back, and took a deep, shaky breath before saying, "I was going to ask you the same question."

One of his eyebrows rose as he studied her. He didn't answer, but seemed to relax and focus more on the game, much to Rhonwyn's relief.

Their game went on for hours and the advantage was held by both the king and Rhonwyn at different times. She was very soon immersed in rebutting his tactics and asserting her own to the exclusion of all other thoughts. The king was in good form today. But so was she.

Rhonwyn's neck stiffened from prolonged concentration on the Gymbal board. She rubbed it during her opponent's next move. But when her attention returned to the board, she was taken aback. Risick had done something totally unexpected.

She felt her brows descend. "Are you ..." she began, but then remembered to whom she was speaking. His move was technically within the rules, but seemed to leave his flank wide open to attack.

Well, attack she would then. She was astounded when her decimation of his forces over the next few rounds evoked no attempt at defence. Only when he moved his general – a piece that hardly ever moved – did she see the pattern he was creating. But it was too late by then.

She grimaced and made her last few attempts at regrouping before finally ceding the game.

"Nicely done, Your Majesty," she remarked as she handed over her general.

He eyed her with a self-satisfied smirk. At least this time she hadn't merely made a stupid mistake.

"I must get back to those books," she said and smiled, her

head tilted to one side.

Risick's smile was more genuine this time and he laughed, abruptly reminding her of Dyfed. That didn't happen very often. She looked down as the smile dropped from her face. Wicked spirit! She hoped she could figure out how to get rid of it. She had to get poor Dyfed out of his prison.

The king and his retinue left and Rhonwyn leant back in a long stretch, her eyes closed. She was startled by a young woman entering the games room to light the lamps, and finally noticed how dark it had become. How late was it? She must get to dinner. Her stomach chorussed its agreement.

Once the board had been cleared away, Rhonwyn hurried to the dining room where Felenya was waiting. However, Felenya was distracted, didn't eat much, and left early to prepare for the concert. Rhonwyn took her time at the table by herself and retreated to her room to relax before the concert.

She positioned herself at the back of the room and Zaryc materialised briefly at her side once the concert had begun in earnest. When he knew she had something to report he ordered her to meet him again at the fountain. She managed to slip out a side door without being seen – she thought.

She made her way through the palace and was just leaving by an outside door when she heard her name called. She stopped with a jolt.

Jarysha hurried up to her. "Are you well? Is there anything you need?" she asked. Rhonwyn saw the girl's face was slightly pink.

What could she say? Had the girl been following her? "No, I'm well, thank you," Rhonwyn said, her mind racing, but trying to keep her expression calm. "It was too smelly in there for me. If I don't get some fresh air I think I'll get a headache." She hoped that was a plausible explanation. To assist with the lie, she began fanning her face with her hand and panting.

The girl stood staring at her for moment. Did she not believe her? "Oh, good," she finally said, then half looked over her shoulder. "Well, let me know if you do need anything. Shall I fetch the healer for you?" She clasped her hands in front of her and instantly looked the part of an attentive helper.

Rhonwyn flapped a hand. "No, thank you. I'm feeling better already, just from the breeze here. I'm sure I'll feel better once I get outside." She took a deep breath and put on a strained smile.

Jarysha looked as if she would speak further, but Rhonwyn cut her off.

"I'll be fine. Now," Rhonwyn pointed at her, "don't let me keep you away from that lovely concert. You go back to it and please tell me later what I missed."

Jarysha gave her a stiff smile before retreating down the hallway. Rhonwyn noticed that the girl flicked a quick look back at her as she turned the corner. In the meantime, Rhonwyn stood leaning against the nearest wall and fanning her face to maintain the deception. She had to make sure Jarysha stopped following her.

When the girl was out of sight, Rhonwyn scampered out the door and sped along the path outside the palace. She didn't head directly for the fountain, in case she was still being observed. She wandered in the opposite direction for quite a while, entered the woods, and sprinted along the path just inside the trees to a place closer to the fountain. Here she caught her breath and looked around.

When she finally got to the appointed meeting place, she found Zaryc pacing back and forth, arms tightly folded. When he heard her footfall he spun to face her, his jaw clenched. He seemed ready to strike her, but relaxed when she held up her hands.

"Where have you been?" he demanded.

"Someone was following me."

He frowned. "Who?"

"My helper, Mistress Berwyn's assistant, Jarysha."

"The king must be suspicious of you," he said immediately. "Why haven't you killed him?"

"I can't," she began, and then quickly outlined what she'd discovered about Dyfed's plight. Zaryc looked more confounded with every word. This was not what he had been expecting.

"An evil spirit?" he asked, when she'd finished.

"Yes, I think so," she said, and went on quickly, before he could interrupt, "Do you know any Wise Ones who could drive it out of him?"

Zaryc shook his head, his forehead furrowed. "No. Risick killed them all," he said.

Rhonwyn gasped in horror. "Is there anyone who would know how?"

"Is he vulnerable when Dyfed is awake?"

That was not what Rhonwyn wanted to hear. "No."

"You're lying," Zaryc immediately replied.

Adamant, Rhonwyn jabbed a finger into his chest. "I am *not* killing him."

Zaryc grabbed her by the shoulders and shook her. "Then you condemn us all, including Dyfed. You must go against your selfish, emotional weakness and do what is good for all of Merynbyl. Sometimes individual sacrifices have to be made for the good of all."

She tried to wriggle out of his grip, but he just held her tighter.

"You're hurting me!" she cried.

He finally let her go. "Pardon me, Rhonwyn, but we're desperate. You're the only hope we have. I know it will be hard, but it's the only way."

"You don't know that," she countered.

"We don't have time to look beyond this option. Somehow you've made him suspicious of you. He's having you followed. Spied on. Please act, before he ..." Zaryc stopped, and pressed his thin lips together.

"Before he kills me?" she finished.

Suddenly, her father was nearby, raking his fingers through his hair. She hadn't seen him for a while.

Zaryc grunted and nodded, a sour look on his face.

Deep within, Rhonwyn knew he was right. All of the people of Merynbyl were trapped in misery. And she couldn't deny that Jarysha's actions that evening had shown that somehow Risick had found out what she was doing.

"Alright," she whispered.

Zaryc's eyes brightened and she held up her hands to forestall his reaction.

"A compromise," she said.

She went on before he could speak, "One more day and we'll both look for someone who could drive the demon out, if it's a demon. If we find nothing ..."

Her heart lurched. Could she kill Dyfed? Contemplating killing an evil king was one thing, but planning to kill her friend another entirely.

"You'll kill him?" Zaryc interrupted her reverie.

Trapped in his gaze, she could only nod. She couldn't say it out loud.

"You will have our eternal gratitude. You'll be a hero!"

"Go away," Rhonwyn blurted, and pushed him from her, bile rising up her throat. She retreated to the far side of the fountain, her arms wrapped around her as she swallowed down the tears.

She didn't *want* to be a hero. She simply wanted not to be alone anymore. In the last few nights she'd had a taste of true companionship, the joy of connection, possibly even love. And now she was going to have to end that in the worst way possible.

Zaryc's voice startled her. He was right behind her. "I'll try to find a Wise One. I promise you." His voice was low, his words precise. He meant it.

And he was gone.

29

No one noticed Rhonwyn's return. Everyone's eyes were fixed upon the man on stage. What had he done to command their attention so? He stood in the middle of the stage and was wordlessly waving his arms about and showing the audience how empty his long shirt sleeves were.

What was he doing that for?

He circled his hands over and over, whirling them around each other, like he was rolling a ball of yarn. He snatched a small white cloth from the front pocket of his shirt and now the audience could see one hand with the cloth distinctly from the other hand. And then, somehow, the cloth turned into a white bird, perched on the man's motionless finger, its wings shivering and lifting as it gained its balance.

Rhonwyn gasped.

She wasn't the only one to do so. A cry of astonishment rose from all those watching, and then another as a second white bird appeared next to the first. Was this man a god? Rhonwyn had never seen such a thing before. She glanced at the king to see what his reaction was to a rival magician.

He was laughing.

Rhonwyn's mouth dropped open. Why wasn't the king threatened – or even amazed – by the magician? Could he do this too? Was this man possessed by another evil spirit? But his eyes were normal; nothing like Risick's unnaturally coloured ones.

The man put the two birds in a cage on a table next to him. He picked up a candle, lit it, and dangled another piece of cloth over it. The cloth burst into flame and the flames turned into a fluttering red bird.

Another gasp.

The magician grabbed a clear glass of water next to the cage and held it up for all to see, the red bird wobbling on its perch in the other hand. The man looked at the king and offered the glass to him. The king nodded.

But, as the man walked towards the king, he stumbled. The glass flew out of his hand and those in its path screamed and ducked in the anticipation of the cold water about to hit them. But instead, as the magician recovered his feet, a bright blue bird shot out over the audience, flew a circuit of the room alongside the red bird that had been propelled into the air, and all the way back to the magician's waiting hand.

Over the gasps and stunned applause, the king could be heard, laughing and clapping at the mysterious creation of birds. The magician bowed his head to receive the king's appreciation before putting the birds in the cage, next to the white ones. With a flick of his hand, he shook out of thin air a much larger piece of cloth and settled this over the cage of birds, hiding the entire thing from sight.

The buzzing room settled into attentive quiet. What would he create next?

He stood behind the cage and grasped its back corners. When he lifted, the cage seemed to collapse in on itself. But now something else was under there. Something another shape entirely. It lacked sharp metal corners, and had soft, rounded edges. As he slid the cloth up and over where the cage once was, the form became more distinct, the cloth hugging its surface. And then he drew it off completely.

A little girl in white, red, and blue sat curled up on the table, facing the audience.

He'd created a girl!

After a moment's shocked silence, pandemonium ensued. Among screams and cries, some knelt to worship the magician, others rushed forward to touch him, while a few, their faces pale, turned in fear and tried to flee. The man, his jaw set, grabbed the newly-minted girl and pulled her off to the side.

Frozen to the spot, Rhonwyn saw the king laugh, frown, stand, and then shout.

"Stop! Stop!" His command rose over the din. "Calm down." And so he went on, trying to reassure his subjects and restore order.

The guards stationed behind the king had not joined in the panic. They stormed into the melee and pushed people back from the stage, enjoining everyone to listen to the king. Other guards appeared behind the crowd – as if this eventuality had been anticipated – and prevented anyone from escaping the room.

When peace was restored, the king gestured for everyone to sit. There were frightened sobs and mutters of awe as he stepped from his throne and onto the stage.

"This man is not a god," the king explained, the buzz of his two-toned voice ringing through the room. "He is a performer. He entertains by making people see illusions. He has not created this girl." The girl had stepped forward, just behind the magician. "She's his daughter. I met her before the show. She was hiding somewhere – I don't know where." At this he sniggered. "He's made you think you've seen something you haven't really seen." He held up one of his hands and waved it before them. "He's caught your attention with one action." He held the other hand down and away on the other side of himself, and wriggled his fingers as the other hand waved. "So that he could make something else happen where you weren't looking." His face became stern and his gaze circled the room, daring anyone to challenge him. "You will not fear him," he ordered, his voice hard. "You will not worship him. He is just a man." He turned to the magician and his face relaxed into a smile. "A very clever man."

The magician smiled and tilted his head to the king, then edged closer.

The king looked back at his rapt audience. "You will see him perform here again." He held up his finger with a grin. "And if anyone can tell me how he does any of his tricks, you'll get a prize."

Then he stalked away, leaving the magician looking oddly disappointed.

The befuddled crowd flowed out the doors, the chatter gaining in volume the further away they got.

Rhonwyn, blinking, wandered back to her own room, utterly distracted by what she'd just seen. She prepared herself for bed before remembering she had something else to do that night.

The bandage was in her pocket, and she'd retrieved the key from the clock, when she set out just before midnight. The clocks chimed twelve as she descended the steps to the lower floor. Knowing the king would be asleep by now, she went straight through the sitting room and over the corridor-bridge. After entering the antechamber, she stood for a moment at the inside door, listening.

"Rhonwyn?" Dyfed's voice floated through the thick wood.

She opened the door and was again lifted from her feet in a hug. "Hello, my friend." She could hear the joy in his voice.

When he released her, she grabbed hold of his hand and squeezed it.

"I didn't find any information about your family," she said. "There doesn't seem to be any record of them anywhere."

His face became serious. "The Wise One didn't know them? Did you ask the right Wise One?"

"There aren't any Wise Ones," she explained. "They're all dead. Everything's written down now. The woman went through all the Dymryd clan who were brought into the city. None of your family were there. I'm sorry, Dyfed. If I push any more, it could be dangerous."

Dyfed frowned, but then waved his hand. "Don't worry. When I'm free of this Risick spirit, I'll find them myself."

When I'm free …

Rhonwyn's stomach squeezed.

"Where shall we go tonight?" Dyfed asked. He didn't seem to have noticed her mood. He was bouncing on his toes.

"You're definitely feeling well enough?"

He nodded forcefully. "I feel very well. I could probably beat you in Gymbal, but I want to go outside first."

This made her laugh. "Then we shall go outside," she said.

She first wrapped the bandage around his head as he sat and chattered. She took her time, making sure it was tight, and feeling the shape of his head as she did so; his soft, curly hair and the warmth of his beautiful brown skin under her hands.

This might be the last night they had together. How could she do this? Rhonwyn shivered and swallowed hard. Perhaps she couldn't. Would she have to get Zaryc in here somehow?

"Before we go, I need to check something," she mumbled when she'd finished the bandage, the blood stain in just the right place.

His warm brown eyes sparkled as he beamed up at her. He'd lit the lamps before she'd arrived.

Her face warmed as she headed for the cabinets at the back. She unlocked the one on the far left. The sabre hung there. But still no lightning-throwers. She would have to stab Dyfed at close range. Did she have the strength? She frowned and locked the cabinet again. She pasted a smile on her face as she went back to Dyfed. He was standing again, rubbing his hands together, just like her father used to.

"I can't think of anywhere new to go," she remarked.

They passed through the inner door.

"We could go back into the woods again, or visit the big cat, or climb that square hill," said Dyfed.

They shuffled along the ledge to the window.

"That was the best view of the night sky I've ever seen," said

Rhonwyn. "I vote for visiting that."

Dyfed grinned in agreement.

Then they could lie there, next to each other, and hold hands in the dark. Rhonwyn sighed. This was going to be the worst week of her life.

The wind was more boisterous than usual as they crossed. Several times they had to sit down and wait for the gusts to die down. Dyfed sat with his eyes closed, holding her hand. He wasn't as accustomed to the height as she had become.

Rhonwyn felt a sudden, intense cold welling up from within. That's how she could do it. She could lead him out here and ... push him off.

30

They circled the edge of the garden, hand in hand, heading for the woods again. They would explore its other side tonight before heading up the 'square hill' as Dyfed had referred to it.

Rhonwyn delighted in the fact that Dyfed seemed to love the night sky as much as she did. This was something close to her heart, but had been hidden for years while she was shut away in the tenements. Now she was sharing it once again with someone as alive as she remembered her father being. She'd forgotten so much about her father. Or simply thrust her memories away to lessen the pain.

Perhaps that's why she liked Dyfed – because he was so like her father and shared his ability to really see Rhonwyn. Dyfed saw things in her that no one had even noticed since her father had died. She hadn't realised how enlivening it felt to be truly recognised and appreciated by someone. Her heart sank. She'd better enjoy it while she could. Even if she managed to free Dyfed, he wouldn't be interested in Rhonwyn once he had his pick of women.

There were fewer torches on this side and it was darker amidst the tall trees. Rhonwyn was grateful for this as she was having difficulty stopping her tears flowing along with her maudlin thoughts. She would have to pull herself together before they got to the torch-lit places.

They came to a lighter patch of ground beside the track, with a pitch-black centre to it. They stopped and Rhonwyn stared at it for a full minute before she realised what it was.

"That's the snake pit," she said, her voice quavering.

Dyfed turned his head to look at her and she could imagine his baffled expression. As she was trying to hide her tearful eyes, she kept them directed forward as she told him, in as few words as possible, what the snake pit was for. His grip on her hand intensified.

They didn't stay long. As they walked on, Dyfed was uncommonly quiet. When they emerged out into the garden again – there seemed to be an unspoken agreement between them that they should leave that part of the woods as soon as possible – Dyfed relaxed again. Rhonwyn had recovered her equilibrium and hoped her face didn't betray her recent lack of control.

"My father is a very clever man," Dyfed stated softly as he allowed Rhonwyn to precede him through a narrow gaps between flowerbeds. "He spent two years, before he married my mother, walking the land around the southern coast, working for various vintners and trying to learn as much as he could about how to grow vines to make wine from them. He learned from all the best and then he brought that knowledge home and prepared the land. He only built the most rudimentary house for us to live in. He was determined that he would improve the house only when the vineyard was going well."

He paused in his story as they crossed the central path. The area was covered in ferns.

"I wonder if he's built that dream house yet?" he murmured.

Rhonwyn didn't want to ruin the moment by pointing out that Dyfed's father wouldn't have been allowed to stay on his land. There wouldn't be a house.

After a short pause, Dyfed shook his head and they entered the torch-lit path. "He only started making a profit from the vineyard ten years after he married my mother. But word got about quickly that his skins of wine were far and away the best in Merynbyl. Then the other vintners were coming to *him* to learn."

Rhonwyn could hear a smile in his voice. "He told me all about what he was going to do with the house. In fact, he was going to build another one, in a different part of our land, up on a hill with a view over the river. We would simply live in the current house until the new one was built."

When they had a choice, Dyfed and Rhonwyn chose the path that went upwards, unless one of them happened to remember which way they'd gone the night before.

"I was so proud of my father. I wanted to be just like him." Dyfed had his face turned away from her and his voice seemed shaky. He became silent again as they started up the zig-zag path in earnest. Rhonwyn felt honoured Dyfed trusted her enough to confess such a thing.

Once they reached the top they stood for a while, side by side, and took in the city-constellation below. Dyfed asked Rhonwyn to explain the layout again and what everything was for. However, as he'd never seen it, he couldn't comprehend it all.

"What is this boros you speak of?" he asked.

"It's something in the rocks beneath us. Men are sent into big holes in the ground to dig it up, then it's separated from the stone around it in the workhouses. Then he stores it in big, barn-like buildings. It took years to set everything up before they could start digging."

"What is it used for?" Dyfed's face was scrunched in his effort to understand.

But Rhonwyn shook her head. "I don't know. It's just sitting there, in the barns."

Dyfed sighed. "Is the king utterly mad, then? How does this benefit the people? How does it benefit him?"

"I don't know," she confessed.

"Have people tried to ask him? To make him explain?"

The idea of 'making' Risick do anything was laughable.

"He tells us there are things we don't understand," she said. "In fact," and now her voice became animated, "he seems to think we're stupid." She released Dyfed's hand and waved hers about. "He treats us like we're children, not old enough to know grown-up things."

"But you're all so afraid of him that you have to keep doing what he says," he stated.

Rhonwyn sighed heavily in answer. "He just gets everything he wants. And we get nothing." Of course, Dyfed was one of the ones who wasn't getting what he wanted either. Rhonwyn hoped with all her heart that Zaryc would somehow find someone who could evict Risick from Dyfed's body. There *must* be some spiritual knowledge left somewhere. Or healing that would help.

Dyfed drew her towards the centre of the flat area before they sat down and stretched out under the stars. As she stared up at those mysterious, beautiful lights that had always been there, Rhonwyn relaxed. Some things never changed.

She began sharing her own story. Even her voice sounded small beneath the vastness of the heavens. "My father taught me to take notice of everything around me."

Dyfed tilted his head to listen.

"He said that to observe the animals, the seasons, the sun ... everything, was to be truly part of the land, of the world. That the earth, the water, and the sky were things we all had in common, and they would keep us united and at peace with each other."

"He sounds like a very wise man," said Dyfed.

Rhonwyn smiled. "He was." She wished Dyfed could have met him. Her heart squeezed. "He was brave, too. He joined together with others in the Resistance to try to get rid of Risick, even though the king was able to find out what they were doing, and executed them when he found them."

"How did Risick became so powerful?"

"I don't know. He seemed to come out of nowhere."

Rhonwyn tilted her head back and was about to go on, but instead stiffened and gasped, staring at the sky.

31

A larger light in the sky – closer to the horizon and behind them – had caught Rhonwyn's eye. To see it better, she had to tilt her head back even further.

She pointed. "What's that?" She'd never seen anything like it before.

"I don't know," Dyfed replied, his voice animated.

It wasn't her imagination, then. They both sat up and swivelled around.

"It's got colours in it." Rhonwyn couldn't believe it. "Can you see them? Blue, green—"

They gasped as the star sprouted a tail, brightened to a blazing white, and then separated into many smaller, tailed stars before their eyes.

"It's moving," Dyfed cried. "All the colours, yes, I see them. What is it?"

She shook her head, speechless.

The coloured streaks of light seemed to be getting bigger – moving closer as they passed. It looked like a whole constellation moving in concert. They surged up and over the pair of mortals, though they made no sound. Tiny lights that seemed like sparks broke from the main group and spun away, only to dissolve into nothingness.

Dyfed and Rhonwyn sank onto their backs once more to keep it in sight, and Rhonwyn lifted her hand and held it up against the passing mob of stars – or angels. They and their tails barely spanned half the length of her hand, from thumb to little finger, though they seemed so large in her eyes.

"Are there seven?" Rhonwyn murmured as she lowered her hand again.

"Nine," Dyfed stated. One then split into two. "Ten!"

They kept their eyes pinned to the extraordinary display for several minutes. Rhonwyn felt Dyfed's hand slip around hers as they lay there. They daren't even look at one another for fear of missing a single moment, their heads inching backwards to follow the arc of movement.

Rhonwyn murmured, "This time, the stars *are* falling from the sky – like you said last night, about the city." Had Dyfed's words made it happen? Was he a Wise One himself?

The flying stars continued to split up, but the smaller ones were disappearing – becoming smaller and smaller until they fizzled out. The largest burned bright white on its leading edge, changing through green, blue, and a faint purple before thinning to a granular tail.

Finally there were only three moving stars left, then two, then the smaller one surged in brilliance briefly before disappearing, leaving its mate to burn a while longer before finally succumbing to the blackness.

Were they more evil spirits coming to take over other people's bodies? Rhonwyn shivered.

"Is it a sign? An omen? A portent of disaster?" Dyfed's voice was low and breathy.

That's right – the Wise Ones had always said that signs in the sky mirrored what was happening on the ground. Perhaps they should be afraid.

Rhonwyn said, "My father told me he'd seen falling stars, long, long ago, when he was out late looking for a sheep that wandered off. He'd first thought they were cinders from a fire, but then he realised they were moving too fast. He was so distracted he nearly allowed the sheep to get past him."

Dyfed had propped himself up on his elbow to listen, and his outline was pitch black against the sky beyond: a friendly horizon. "Faster than cinders? I don't think these things," he pointed up, "were the same as what he saw. Too slow."

"Yes, you're right, that doesn't sound the same, does it?"

Had they seen something new entirely? What did that mean? Were angels about to visit them? Perhaps they could help get rid of Risick.

They lay for some time, keeping watch for any other extraordinary signs in the heavens.

Rhonwyn awoke to Dyfed's chuckle. He was watching her now, instead of the sky.

"What?" she mumbled, rubbing the back of her hand against her mouth. Had she been drooling?

"You were ... you were purring."

"Hah! That's a very polite word for snoring."

He objected, "No, it was a purr, not a snore. It sounded very sweet."

Rhonwyn scoffed and sat up. "We'd better go. If I fall asleep again—"

"I would wake you in time. I swear," he promised, unperturbed. He didn't seem to want to leave.

"Let's go down to the fountain," she said. Perhaps that would distract him.

He chuckled and became suddenly animated. "I'll beat you."

He sprang up, sprinted over to the head of the path, and disappeared. Rhonwyn scrambled to her feet and hurried after him.

If he was found on his own, what would she do? Perhaps she could just leave him to it. He would be safe. They would think he was the king. But surely the main risk would be the king finding out about 'his' body being out at night.

She could only just hear Dyfed scuttling down the path, skidding on every sharp corner. She rushed after him. At least it was downhill. Once she'd got to the flat she pounded through the woods, but could no longer hear him.

When she emerged from the woods she stopped near the fountain and scanned the area for movement. Nothing. Where was he? Rhonwyn hoped he hadn't done anything stupid.

She weaved along the grassy paths between the flowerbeds towards the fountain. The sweet smell of an unknown bloom filled her nostrils as she passed, but she didn't stop. She had to find him. Rhonwyn was just rounding a circular bed of delicately petalled irises when a hand clamped around her ankle.

She yelped.

"Shhhhh!" Dyfed was giggling, lying flat between two side beds.

She crouched and thumped his shoulder. This just made him laugh all the more, which made it hard for her to stay annoyed.

He jumped up. "Let's get back." He began strolling away.

Shaking her head, Rhonwyn caught up to him, took him by the elbow, and turned him in the right direction. Once inside, Rhonwyn found the closest clock – a quarter past four. They had plenty of time.

"We could have a short game of Gymbal," she whispered.

"Why are there so many of those?" Dyfed was pointing at the clock.

Rhonwyn shrugged. "I don't know."

They didn't see a soul as they made their way to the sitting room, out the window, and straight across the pale bridge to the room perched on the finger of rock. Not a breath of wind this time. Dyfed drew the Gymbal set out from under the sleeping pad and set it up as Rhonwyn went to use the washroom.

When she returned, she sat down in her place only to find a light pink flower lying on the table in front of her. She looked at Dyfed as heat radiated up her neck. He gave her a crooked smile. Was his face red, too?

"It's not a bribe to let me win," he said.
"Ha! Like I would!"

32

Leaving Dyfed that morning was so difficult. Would this be the last time Rhonwyn saw him? Before she had to kill him? The thought kept turning over in her mind. She shuddered. She *had* to find a better way. Killing him couldn't be the only answer.

"What's wrong?" Dyfed squeezed her hand, concern in his eyes.

He must have seen her shiver. She scrambled for an excuse. "I'm tired and a bit cold."

Dyfed leapt up from the table and grabbed her wrap. She'd left it on the sleeping pad when she'd come in. He returned and draped it about her shoulders. Her heart squirmed. She was betraying him while he was treating her like this. How could she do it?

They'd played the short game of Gymbal – the version Rhonwyn and her father had made up for when she had to go to bed soon, but still wanted to play.

As he sat down again, Dyfed flung his hands up. "Even with all my mind working, you still beat me."

Rhonwyn tittered.

"Teach me how the clock works." He sounded distracted. What was he thinking?

Rhonwyn recited what Kymra had told her as she studied his face, trying to see if there were any hints.

"So, I go to sleep at six ah clock—"

"Six *oh*-clock," Rhonwyn corrected him and then set him a test. "So, what's the time now?"

"The small pointer is on five and the long one on three. The long one tells you parts of the hour. So, it's quarter ... past ... five ...?"

"Exactly. Very good," said Rhonwyn.

"What if the long one is pointing at the four?"

"Um ..." This was still new to her, too. "That's twenty minutes past five."

She frowned; she should get back to her room. She stood up and looked around.

"We must put this away before I go," she said and bent to sweep the Gymbal pieces together.

They put the pieces and the board where they belonged and Rhonwyn stowed the cupboard key in the case before Dyfed slid it under the bed.

"Well, I'll see you tomorrow night." She made for the door as she couldn't meet his eyes. "I'll keep looking for information on your family and how to get Risick out of you."

Dyfed turned her back and gave her a goodbye hug. He seemed to be about to say something more, but Rhonwyn couldn't bear how trusting he was of her, so she bustled out, pretending not to notice. She clicked the door shut behind her, leaned against it, and heaved a sigh.

"Bye, Rhonwyn," he called, from just the other side. His voice sounded thin and forlorn through the locked door.

Rhonwyn covered her mouth, swallowed, and then, without responding, made her way along the ledge, through the window, and out onto the corridor's roof. She had to stop once as she traversed it, tears blinding her and making the few lights shining from the palace smear across her vision.

She had clambered into the sitting room and latched the window before she realised the other window was wide open. Rhonwyn stood stock still. Had she left it open herself? No, she hadn't even gone near it for a couple of days now. Was there someone in here?

"Hello?" A bleary voice came out of the darkness on her right. Rhonwyn jumped, her tongue tied.

"Who's that?" A woman's voice.

Someone was sitting in that chair. Rhonwyn's heart leapt up her throat. She stood watching as legs descended to the floor and whoever it was leant towards her.

"Rhymla?" she blurted out.

"Rhonwyn?" The voice was too young to be Rhymla's.

Rhonwyn could breathe again. "Kymra, you scared me. What are you doing here?"

Kymra rose, but said nothing. Her eyes glinted in the growing light outside. The back of Rhonwyn's neck prickled. She shivered again. "Are you well?" she asked, stepping towards Kymra.

Kymra's head sank. Of course she wasn't well, how could Rhonwyn ask that?

"You should be in bed." Rhonwyn curled her arm around Kymra and led her out and along the corridor. She made no sound at all. At the top of the stairs, Rhonwyn realised she didn't know where to take Kymra – she still had no idea where her room was – but she pressed the biddable girl towards Mistress Berwyn's rooms. Surely she would know.

Her room was shut tight, however, and Rhonwyn's knocking roused no answer. Perhaps Berwyn had been with her lover overnight. She would take her to her own rooms – Kymra could sleep there until she was needed.

At least Kymra was moving more easily than the last time Rhonwyn had seen her. They drifted up the steps and met no one before they entered Rhonwyn's room. Drifting indeed – Kymra's state of mind lent an unreal air to the situation. Rhonwyn's own sleep-deprived mind didn't help. It took very little to coax Kymra to lie down and submit to being wrapped in bedclothes. Perhaps she'd been sleepwalking.

Rhonwyn stared at the sleeping girl for some time before she realised she didn't have time to stand around doing nothing.

She had to find some way to free Dyfed. She freshened up, changed her clothes, and hurried to the library – the one place she might find her answer.

Beginning at one end of the first shelf, she picked through all the subjects, determined to see if there were any that might give her the right information.

))) ● (((

"What are you doing here so early?" Matu found Rhonwyn standing at the desk, going through a pile of books. "I saw the lamps on."

Of course Matu would have her room on this corridor. Was hers the one next to the sitting room?

"I woke up really early," lied Rhonwyn, "and I was thinking about some of the other things the Wise Ones used to do. Are there any books about spiritual things?"

But Matu wasn't listening. Her attention was fixed on the chair. Her face paled. All Rhonwyn saw was her own wrap, swaying back and forth in a breeze from somewhere.

"What's wrong?"

Matuthalyn's face was taut as she turned it to Rhonwyn. "Last time there was a breeze through here, the w … window …" Her voice stuttered to a halt and her head swung around to stare at the door. When she gasped and hurried through to the sitting room, Rhonwyn scurried after her.

Once there, Matu stopped and clamped her hands over her mouth. "Oh, no! Not again," she moaned.

"What?"

The only thing out of place was the open window. Rhonwyn had forgotten to close it when Kymra had captured her attention. She skirted Matu's stationary form and darted towards it as it banged in the breeze. If it wasn't closed soon, it would smash.

"Is there anyone down there?" cried Matu, her voice

quavering.

Rhonwyn stopped, her hand on the window frame. "Down where?"

Rhonwyn stuck her head out, looked down, and regretted it. The drop was so much easier to ignore when it was dark. She pulled her head back in, gulping. "The only thing out there is a cliff. The ground is a long way down."

"And there's no one down there?"

Rhonwyn shook her head, frowning. "No."

Matu drew in a breath her shoulders releasing downwards. "Oh, thank goodness."

"Why would ..." And then suddenly Rhonwyn understood. "Did someone fall?" Her grip on the windowsill tightened.

"She broke the window, when I tried to stop her, she just flung herself out." Matuthalyn's hands were over her mouth and her voice had become a strangled squeal.

Rhonwyn skin crawled. This was the window Rhymla had called *hers*. And she'd been sitting in the chair opposite it, angry and drunk. Had it been Rhymla who'd thrown herself out?

"How horrible."

And now Matu looked over her shoulder at the open sitting room door and stepped towards Rhonwyn with her hands outstretched. "I wasn't supposed to tell anyone. Please, please don't say I told you," she whispered.

"Of course, of course. Don't worry Matu, I won't," Rhonwyn said. "But, who was it?"

Her face still wrinkled with worry, Matu shrugged. "I don't know. I'd never seen her before. She didn't look very ..." Her eyes flicked to the side. "She didn't look very well. Or happy."

Rhonwyn closed the window, her imagination filling in the blanks of what would happen to someone who fell from that height. Her head turned of its own accord towards the chair Rhymla had been hiding in.

Rhonwyn suddenly felt like she'd been hit in the stomach. *Kymra!*

She ignored Matu's cries of concern as she sprinted back along the corridor, up the steps and all the way to her bedroom.

Her bed was empty. Panic blocking her throat, Rhonwyn checked the balcony Kymra had first shown her less than a week ago and, holding firmly to the ledge, peered over.

The distant floor of the valley was shadowy, but clearly no body lay there.

Rhonwyn rested her forehead on the ledge and took great gasps of air. Her stomach untwisted and let her know in no uncertain terms that it needed to eat.

)⟩◗●◖⟨(

"I thought you weren't coming to breakfast anymore," said Felenya.

Rhonwyn shook her head as she sat, plonking her full plate down before her. "I woke up early this morning," she muttered.

Felenya beamed. "Wasn't last night amazing?"

How did she know about last night? Of course. Felenya was talking about the magician.

Rhonwyn said, "Yes. That was incredible. Did it frighten you?"

Felenya nodded, her expression serious. "Yes, it was disturbing at the time. But I've thought about what the king said, and he knows what he's talking about."

Rhonwyn bent her head to eat. Many incredible things had happened last night. She could barely keep them clear from one another. The magician, the stars flying overhead. She needed sleep.

"It's all everyone's talking about. How do you think he did it?" Felenya's eyes were bright.

"I have no idea," said Rhonwyn. Her mouth twisted. That wasn't the first time she'd said that in the last day.

"Are you alright? You look a little frazzled," asked Felenya.

"I didn't sleep very well. My brain's not working." She gave Felenya a wry smile.

"You could go back to bed after breakfast." Felenya began to look mischievous. "But then you would miss out on meeting the magician."

"Meeting him?"

"He's going to visit me later this morning," Felenya whispered, casting her eyes about her. Rhonwyn had never heard her speak so quietly.

It would be interesting to meet someone like that. And it was always possible he had the kind of magic that could help the Resistance get rid of Risick. He might know how to get the evil spirit out of Dyfed. What if she could recruit him?

"Can I come and meet him, too?" She had to ask. She had to try everything to save Dyfed.

Felenya nodded before holding one finger in front of her lips.

The two made their way back to Felenya's apartments after breakfast and sat down with a pot of tea Felenya had picked up from the kitchens.

"He shouldn't be long. We can talk in the meantime. Tell me how you're finding the palace," said the singer.

Rhonwyn leaned back into the enormous couch just inside Felenya's open windows. They looked out over part of the garden, and an unknown, musky scent was making its way inside.

"Well, it's taking some getting used to, but I've discovered some lovely friends." She patted Felenya's knee, which elicited a grin. "And Kymra. Do you know her?"

Felenya grimaced and shook her head. "There are too many people in the palace for me to know them all." She sipped at her hot tea.

"She's a lovely girl. Her parents work in the stables. She was assisting Mistress Berwyn, but she was ..." Rhonwyn rubbed her mouth. "She was selected for another job and I don't see her as much now, which is sad. I didn't have many friends outside the palace."

She hoped Kymra wasn't back down in the sitting room

contemplating the precipice.

"I'm so glad you've found friends here. I know you've been exploring." Felenya's eyes dropped to her drink. "You know you need to be careful, don't you? Not everyone is friendly. Mainly because they're afraid." This last bit was said so quietly, Rhonwyn could barely hear it.

This observation sobered Rhonwyn further. What if she *had* been followed? What if everything was blown? If her friend had noticed her snooping around, what would someone notice who was motivated to protect their safe place here, near the king? The main thing was getting Merynbyl free from Risick. That was the priority of the Resistance: making a safe and free future for the coming generations, not any single person's safety. Zaryc was right about that.

Rhonwyn had to make sure what she'd discovered wasn't lost if she was caught.

She turned and looked her friend in the eye.

"Can I trust you, Felenya?"

33

"Are you going to tell anyone?" Rhonwyn asked. She grabbed at Felenya's tea – precariously close to tipping over into her lap.

Felenya's face was pale, her eyes bulging. "An evil spirit?"

"Do you know any Wise Ones that survived, or someone else who might know about that kind of thing?" asked Rhonwyn.

Felenya's head wagged from side to side for a long time before she said, "No. I haven't seen any Wise Ones for years." As if waking from a dream, she took a deep breath and put her hand on Rhonwyn's, her expression stern. "I'm sorry I can't help you. And no, I won't tell anyone."

Being able to speak about this with someone was such a relief.

"What about the magician?"

"Oh, yes." Felenya blinked. "He'll be coming any minute."

"I mean, could he know something about driving a demon out?"

Felenya gasped. "Of course. He might. You could ask."

Rhonwyn chewed on her lip. "Could I really? He seems very friendly with the king, so I'm not sure I can trust him."

Felenya's face dropped. "Oh dear. You're right."

Someone knocked on the door. "That'll be him now." Felenya answered the door and ushered both the magician and his daughter inside, then introduced them to Rhonwyn, who'd risen and moved halfway to the door as well.

"This is Talsen ma Gruryn and his daughter Brytta."

Rhonwyn nodded. "Nice to meet you."

Talsen nodded but barely looked at Rhonwyn.

He was more interested in Felenya. "Dear lady, your singing last night was exquisite." He took her by the arm and led her to the settee, where they sat chatting about music, her singing, and the pieces composed within the palace. He claimed he was a musician of sorts, too.

Brytta seemed quite accustomed to being left to her own devices.

"Well met," said Rhonwyn. "Did you enjoy Felenya's singing, too?"

The girl's face puckered. "It was lovely."

Rhonwyn leaned close to her and whispered, "Can I ask you how you got to be sitting on that table last night?"

"You can ask, but I'm sorry, I can't say. Please don't take offence."

Rhonwyn chuckled. "I understand. Worth a try."

She and Brytta trailed Felenya and Talsen to the window and sat down. The sun was much higher in the sky now and the room was bright. Felenya had sat in the single padded chair beside the window, facing the room. Rhonwyn sat next to Talsen on the couch, and Brytta took another single chair on the other side of the window.

Felenya was describing how the composers taught the musicians their pieces. As she spoke, Talsen reached towards her and took something out of her ear. Felenya stuttered to a stop.

"Why do you keep this in here?" he asked, holding it up.

Felenya's mouth dropped open. He was holding the tiny reed flute that Rhonwyn had seen sitting on a table near Felenya's door. How had that got into Felenya's ear?

Rhonwyn's friend used her hand to investigate her ear, her voice was uncertain. "I don't, usually."

"Well, it's just as ridiculous as keeping this in here," said

Talsen as he whipped a pack of fire sticks out of her other ear.

Rhonwyn laughed in disbelief. She should've told Dyfed about the magician last night. He would have loved it. If only he could come to a performance. She couldn't believe it was just a trick.

Felenya felt her other ear. "How did you do that?" she breathed.

Talsen simply grinned before his face became earnest. "Do you meet with the king often, then?" he asked, setting the objects on the side table.

Felenya's eyes fluttered. "I see him every two or three days." She leaned back, well out of Talsen's reach. "He invites me to join him late in the morning to catch up with the other musicians and the composers."

"That often? What privileges you have. He values you deeply, then," gushed Talsen, leaning forward and touching his hand to her knee.

Felenya giggled and fanned her face with a hand. She was blushing and had glanced at her knee after he'd touched it.

"Well, he's a very interesting man. So clever." She pointed. "Rhonwyn sees him even more than I do. She's his Gymbal Opponent."

Talsen swivelled to face Rhonwyn, and her heart lurched at the overwhelming attention he now poured upon her. He hadn't seemed to be interested at all before.

"Really?" he said. "Is that so? I love a game of Gymbal myself. Is he any good?"

Rhonwyn couldn't help but edge away from Talsen a little. "Yes, he's very talented. I really have to focus to beat him."

"You do beat him, though?"

All eyes were on Rhonwyn now and she squirmed. "Yes. But not all the time," she said. If only they would look away.

Talsen leaned in. "Do you think he would mind if I watched?"

Rhonwyn's eyebrows rose. "I don't think so. The people who are with him do all the time."

Talsen rubbed his hands together, his gaze distant. "Then I will ask."

"Do you ..." Rhonwyn began in the sudden break, then changed tack, her words tumbling over each other. "Were you ever a Wise One? Do you have spiritual knowledge?" This was as specific as she dared get.

Talsen fixed her with his gaze and sneered at her. "No, my magic isn't a spiritual force." It sounded as if others had asked that question before and he didn't think much of it. "When do you play?" he asked.

"What does *he* want?" her father asked, peering at Talsen. The stress had brought him out again.

Hush, Papa!

Rhonwyn had to think for a second. Talsen seemed to be fixated on her playing Gymbal with the king. "Usually in the late afternoon. He sends someone to find me when he wants to play," she explained.

At this, Talsen sprang to his feet. "Then I must go and find out if I am allowed to join you." He moved towards the door.

"Don't you want to wait? I have some refreshments coming," Felenya called, half standing, confusion written all over her face.

"Of course. I'll be right back. Brytta, wait for me here," he called out. And he was gone.

Rhonwyn said, "Goodness! He's like a summer storm."

They all chuckled, Brytta's laugh accompanied by a sidelong look at the door and a blush.

Felenya graced the girl with one of her most winning smiles. "Are you learning to do magic? Do you have the gift, too?"

As the girl answered, Rhonwyn suddenly felt time slipping away from her. She'd found out Talsen couldn't help, and his behaviour had made her suspicious of him, so she must continue her search for knowledge. She didn't have much day left.

She jumped up. "Thank you so much, Felenya, for the lovely

conversation. It's always delightful talking with you, but I have things I need to do. Sorry."

Felenya's eyes were wide again. Talsen wasn't the only one jumping from subject to subject.

"That's fine, dear. I'll see you at lunch," she managed.

Rhonwyn tore down to the library and returned to where she'd left off – the pile of books on the central desk. Fortunately Matu had left them there. The librarian mentioned – pointedly – that she would have put them away at the end of the day if Rhonwyn hadn't returned by then. She seemed very protective of her charges.

Rhonwyn apologised, and sat down to go through the books as quickly as possible. She had many more shelves to check by the end of the day.

When she met Felenya at lunchtime, she found her friend still baffled by the magician. He had returned and focussed his attention on her once again. Rhonwyn now knew how intense that was. Just before lunch, he'd flitted off to see if he could get a seat closer to the king for the meal. When Rhonwyn looked to see if he'd succeeded, all she saw was the king, alone, inhaling as much lunch as possible into that slender body. How did he do it? And did Dyfed ever end up with a stomach ache as a result?

On her way back to the library, she stopped at Mistress Berwyn's room to let Jarysha know where she would be. The girl thanked her sincerely before she rushed off to her next task. Everyone was busy.

Rhonwyn wasn't summoned that afternoon, for which she was thankful as she rifled through book after book to see if she could find the lost spiritual knowledge. Nothing turned up. A headache began to throb behind her right eye. Matu tried to help as she seemed to sense Rhonwyn's desperation, though was frustrated when Rhonwyn couldn't reveal more details about what she was looking for.

Only half a shelf remained by the time Rhonwyn made her way up to the dining room again, her head tender. She rubbed her neck and sighed as she sat down at a table after standing for hours.

"How do you fare?" asked Felenya. She wore a slight frown and seemed to be holding her breath.

Rhonwyn gave her a wry grin. "It's been a busy afternoon."

Felenya filled in the silence. "Well, I busied myself with rehearsals. I haven't seen Talsen at all." She sniffed and shrugged. "Ah well. I suppose I'll never find out how he does it."

"Do you really want to know?" Rhonwyn asked.

Felenya gave her a sly look. "Well, the king doesn't offer rewards every day, you know."

Rhonwyn smiled. The food was helping the headache, thank the heavens.

She got back to the library straight after dinner. Matu did not join her – she was meeting a friend. Rhonwyn was pleasantly surprised to hear Matuthalyn *had* friends.

Finally she'd flicked through the last book in the last section of the last shelf – to no avail. She flopped into a chair and rested her head in her hands. What was she going to do?

An hour later, Jarysha found her and shook her awake.

"The king wants to play Gymbal," she said, her face pinched. Rhonwyn must look a sight.

"Really? Now?" Rhonwyn ran her fingers through her hair and cleared her throat.

"Yes. But I'm sure we could stop by your washroom for you to wake yourself up. It helped that I tried here first – you have a bit of extra time," said Jarysha.

Rhonwyn put the lamp out and scurried after Jarysha. After she'd freshened up, they went downstairs and arrived outside the games room door just as Talsen, Brytta, and Felenya walked up. What were they doing here? Talsen was wearing a bulky robe, totally unsuitable for the warm evening. He must be roasting.

He looked at Rhonwyn, his gaze intense. "Are you going to play the king now?"

"Yes," Rhonwyn replied, her hands clenching.

Talsen turned to his daughter. "Go back to our rooms and go to bed." The order was abrupt.

"But ..." stuttered Brytta. Her eyes widened and she gazed at her father, frozen in place.

His jaw stiff, he seized her shoulder. "Off you go." He pecked her on the cheek and turned her away.

"Good night, Papa." Strangely, the girl looked as if she was going to cry, her head craning over her shoulder several times as she departed.

Talsen ignored her. Instead, he gave Rhonwyn a grim smile, opened the door for her, and then followed her inside. Jarysha was left to trail behind and Talsen seemed to have forgotten Felenya entirely. She had joined them, though her face was tense and she was uncharacteristically quiet.

They all bowed low before Risick. Once he'd permitted them to stand, the king, reclining in his usual chair, gave Talsen and Felenya a keen look. "You would like an opportunity to observe?"

Talsen bowed his head. "Yes, Your Majesty, if that would be acceptable." He seemed abruptly cowed by the king's presence. But he changed so much from minute to minute. Was this another act?

The king narrowed his eyes and nodded. "You may." He pointed to a spot behind Rhonwyn's chair for them to stand.

Rhonwyn sat down. She mustn't let this extra audience distract her. She took long, deep breaths and waited for Risick to start the game. After a few seconds, he flicked his fingers at her.

"You start," he commanded her. He'd remembered her suggestion.

She leaned forward and began with her most unconventional move. The king stared at the board for quite some time as if he were checking that her move wasn't illegal, before he leaned back and chuckled.

"Good. Something new," he said.

He adapted quickly and they were soon trading blows to one another's scouts and armies. Rhonwyn found she was riding a second wind.

"Do you play Gymbal, magician?" the king asked absently as he placed half his centurions on the left flank of Rhonwyn's main cavalry.

"When I can, Your Majesty," replied Talsen. "I imagine I don't have your level of skill, however." He had edged forward and was bending over to see the pattern of pieces on the board.

"No, of course you don't," said Risick, his voice dry. "Perhaps we should play sometime, nevertheless."

"I would be honoured, Your Majesty." Talsen's eyes were sparkling, his jaw set. He bowed low and somehow, when he rose, ended up beside the table, between the two players.

The king grunted. He was still studying the board. "You have a mixed accent, magician. What region are you from?" He made his move.

"Termyl, Your Majesty."

"Termyl? Your accent has southern sounds, hasn't it?" said Risick.

The magician was unfazed. "Yes, Your Majesty. I was born in Termyl, but my sister married a man from the south. I lived with them for some time and picked up the accent."

The king nodded. "Where did you get your skill of illusion?" He removed some of Rhonwyn's soldiers and progressed his own into the space remaining.

"I'll tell you – if you'll tell me where you got your magic skills."

Rhonwyn's jaw dropped and her eyes swivelled towards him. One side of Talsen's mouth had risen in a smirk. How could he talk to the king like that? The man suddenly seemed to have no fear.

The king laughed and looked at Rhonwyn, his eyebrow raised. Her move.

Talsen went on, his relaxed air a little stiff now. Somehow he'd moved closer to the king and his attention had turned from the board to Risick himself. "My sister inspired me." His voice was low and he spoke quickly. "She inspires me still. She died just as you appeared. You might remember the incident – a whole family murdered in their home?" His face was set like flint, glaring at the king. Rhonwyn couldn't take her eyes off him. His visage had changed so completely since he'd walked into the room. And that family's murder. The details made her insides go cold. She recognised it. The back of her neck prickled.

The king huffed and clicked his fingers at Rhonwyn to draw her attention. He didn't seem aware of, or concerned with, Talsen's proximity, or his changed attitude. "No, I don't remember that," he murmured.

Rhonwyn had to concentrate on the game. But Talsen's next words rocked her back in her chair.

"Her name was Syphryd, her husband was called Cothee. I don't know how you did it, but it had to be you." Talsen was sneering at Risick now. "And now it all stops." A lit fire stick materialised in his hand and Rhonwyn saw a string dangling forth from the front of his robe, its other end disappearing inside, next to his chest.

But Risick was glowering at Rhonwyn, for she had gasped loudly at the names.

Cothee and Syphryd!

"I thought so." Risick's tone was one of confirmation, his look stony.

Talsen lit the end of the piece of string, which began sparking strangely. The sparks moved up its length, eating the string as it went. What *was* that? Talsen's expression was grim as he moved as close to the king as possible.

Risick, not moving his gaze from Rhonwyn, raised his left

hand and pinched his index finger and thumb together in the air. The string stopped sparking. Talsen's eyes bulged out and his face paled. At the same time, Risick raised his right hand and clenched it.

Rhonwyn could no longer breathe.

34

Rhonwyn grabbed at her throat while trying vainly to suck air into her lungs. She couldn't find anything to fight against. The blockage seemed to be within, her own breathing tube closing up.

The king's hand maintained its pinching gesture as he stood, a sneer on his face.

"Seize the magician," he ordered, not taking his eyes off Rhonwyn.

Two of Risick's burly retainers moved to take Talsen captive. Realising his game was up – whatever game that was – Talsen took one step back and threw both of his hands down in a sudden movement. Light flashed and billowing smoke engulfed him. The bodyguards halted and shielded their faces, temporarily blinded. This gave Talsen just enough time to slip between them and ram his way through the games room door. The guards gave chase as the king growled.

Felenya's hands were over her mouth as she stared at Rhonwyn, who found she'd risen from her seat. The room was beginning to fade and there were spots of light swimming in her vision as she pawed at her neck uselessly. She felt herself dissolving.

She could hear faint music, her ears strained for the words:

> *And when the world has passed away ...*
> *we'll be together then*

Papa?

The world faded to grey and dimmed relentlessly until all was black.

She returned slowly, her single focus to draw in all the air she could manage to gulp. Her throat was open. Nothing else mattered in that moment.

Why wasn't she dead?

The tile floor was hard and cold beneath her. She was stretched out, having collapsed upon passing out. Light slowly leaked into her vision and sounds started making sense. That whimpering – was that Felenya?

She heard a furious shout. "Give me those. Find him." The two-toned voice created shrieking harmonics.

The colours of the tiles came into focus as Rhonwyn's breathing became easier. Her hair was seized, her head pulled back. Sulphur eyes, narrow and furious.

"You stupid girl," Risick snarled.

He yanked Rhonwyn towards the door. She tried to regain her footing but was unable to keep up. Her limbs flailed in the empty air as Risick stalked along the corridor.

"Leave me!" the king cried, just before he lugged Rhonwyn down a long set of stairs. Her shins and knees clattered against the sharp edges of each step, gouges of flesh taken with strikes of sharp stone. As Risick hauled her along the corridor, she heard a door open ahead only to snap closed again a moment later, the occupant withdrawing in haste.

Of course no one would help her. No one would be so foolish.

Rhonwyn tried to twist out of his grip, but could not free herself. Risick simply rattled her until she straightened up. While she was facing backwards, she saw streaks of blood lining the floor behind them. She was so occupied with her struggle, she only realised where they were going when they arrived in the sitting room, next to the library. Risick dragged her to the wall, pressed the numbers, and took a firmer hold of her hair, making her whimper. He drew her face close to his and leered as the trapdoor droned open.

Rhonwyn could feel the wide-eyed look of horror on her face.

What time was it? Please let it be midnight.

She was grateful for the less-sharp steps down to the bridge. As he strode over the span, however, a cramp seared through her neck. She cried out in pain, once again stumbling over her own feet to try to release the pressure.

The king laughed.

He dragged her through the two doors and slammed them behind him before throwing her on the floor.

"I won't give you the tour. You already seem to have visited," he said and swept his hand up into the air.

How did he know?

The games table flipped over, flinging its contents in every direction. With his magic, Risick positioned the table on its edge, the legs facing away from the door as Rhonwyn shook uncontrollably on the floor.

Risick snatched her hand as she rubbed her neck, and yanked her to the table. At the same time, he drew a rattling metal object from his pocket and snapped it around her wrist. It looked to Rhonwyn like the metal had passed through her flesh and bone to encircle her arm. The other end he fastened somehow to one edge of the table, up high.

When he tried to grab her other wrist, she wriggled and squirmed with all her might. The king simply stood back and cuffed her head twice, the second blow smashing her temple against the hard wood of the table. It left her stunned, and he snatched her hand and fastened it to the other side of the table. Now he had her stretched out across the width of the heavy table, standing upright. He could do anything to her. She closed her eyes and hung her head, trying to shrink into herself as he circled the room, lighting the lamps.

"You people are so ridiculously dull-witted," he said, returning to stand before her. "Did you really think I wouldn't figure out what you were doing? You blunder about my palace doing incredibly suspicious things and then you go and leave this in here." He held up a book.

Rhonwyn swallowed and peered at it, trying to read the title. She took too long. Risick's hand whipped out and slapped her across the face, snapping her head to one side.

"*Stories for Children?*" he yelled. He waggled the story book in front of her and used it to rap her over the head. "Did you think I wouldn't wonder how a book from the library got into my chamber?" He paced back and forth and tossed the book away.

That was why he'd visited the library yesterday morning.

"Did you think I wouldn't wonder why the *real* winner of the Gymbal competition was poisoned so you would get in here instead?"

Poisoned? Yern was poisoned? Who would have done that?

The Resistance. Who else? How could they?

"Did you think I wouldn't notice you walking the perimeter of my grounds? Were you looking for a way out? Imbecile."

He grabbed her face and crushed it between his fingers and thumb as he drew close. His evil eyes burned into her.

"How did you get in?" He spoke through clenched teeth, his voice almost a growl.

"You don't know?" she blurted out.

He shoved her back against the table top, and punched her in the stomach. As she gasped for breath and bent over as far as her bonds would allow, he stepped away and sighed.

"That kind of smart mouth will not make your final hours very pleasant, will it? How much, exactly, do you want to suffer?" He stood looking at her, his feet spread, his arms crossed over his chest.

Rhonwyn began coughing and then tried to stop, for the pain was incredible. She groaned instead.

"How did you get in?" he asked again.

If she told him, there would be no chance of Merynbyl ever getting rid of him. She had to keep her mouth shut. Perhaps Felenya could tell Zaryc and they could somehow get someone else in. To kill poor, dear Dyfed.

Anger overrode her fear. "May the gods drag you to hell, you evil spirit," she croaked. Could the gods hear her?

He spat out a laugh. "You people are so backward." He turned away, shaking his head. "Superstitious mumbo jumbo."

What was he talking about?

"Get out of that body, you despicable ..." she stuttered. She didn't know the right words to expel the demon from Dyfed's body. "You have no right to it. Dyfed is by far a better man than you could ever be." Her body was wracked with another coughing fit. She drew one of her knees up as far as she could to relieve the pain.

"Fancy the boy, do you?" Risick leaned towards her, a mocking grin on his face.

Rhonwyn straightened and spat at him. The gob of bloody mucus landed on his cheek.

His eyes widened in rage as the smile fell off his face. He wiped it off and backhanded her, pounding her head against the table again. She lost consciousness. When she came to, her shoulders shrieking in agony, he was searching the room. It seemed to yield nothing as he eventually threw up his hands.

"That's right, I didn't want to leave anything sharp in here, did I?" He seemed to be laughing at himself.

Blood was dripping from Rhonwyn's nose and her eye was swelling so much she could barely see out of it. She raised her head and glared at him, catching a glimpse of the clock above the door.

"Hah!" Her laugh sounded almost like a sob. "It's nearly midnight."

His nostrils flared as he stepped up to her again. He jabbed her in the stomach, this time with stiff fingers, making her wince and wriggle away. He seized her face again.

"Were you working with the magician? He was ready to blow you up, did you know that? Well, the man's got guts."

'Blow her up'? What did that mean?

"I have to give you credit, too. You got much further than I thought you would. You know when I have to sleep, do you?" He pursed his lips and checked the clock.

He had less than five minutes.

Risick glared at her. "You're not going to tell me, of course. And I don't have time to make you." He pointed at her and sneered. "Yet."

He brought his hands out in front of him, stretched out his fingers and glared at them, an expression of distaste on his face.

"How do you stand it?" he cried. "All these sensations? All the time?" His eyes were wide, manic. "The hunger, the thirst, the lust, the urges," he yelled in her face. "How do you put up with it?" He staggered away and bent over double. "I can't bear it!" he screamed at the top of his voice. He began scratching, tearing at his own head, and then rubbing his hands down his thighs.

Rhonwyn stiffened at his display of insanity.

He shuddered to a halt, panting. "The best thing," he said, and cleared his throat. "The best thing your lover can do is put you out of your misery." He straightened and approached Rhonwyn once again. "Because when I wake up, I'm going to make you beg me to kill you. Let's see if the boy has the courage to murder his sweetheart, eh?"

His face twisted, Risick found a piece of papyrus. He wiped his finger under Rhonwyn's nose, laid the papyrus against the table top, and wrote in her blood. He placed the note on the floor in front of her, checked the clock, then lay down on the sleeping pad.

"See you in the morning," he drawled.

Risick's whole body sagged into unconsciousness, his head lolling back to centre.

He stayed that way for barely half a minute. Rhonwyn was expecting to see the dark spirit leave Dyfed's body, some indication of the change, but she could see nothing. Risick, however, was gone. Of course, she'd seen this once before, when she'd come in to murder him with the sabre.

Dyfed took a long breath as he woke, stretched and yawned. She saw his eyelashes flick open and blink a few times at the ceiling before he sat up and rolled his shoulders.

His eyes wide, he scrambled up and ran to her. His hands shook, positioned around her face, but not touching her. She could feel the warmth radiating from them. The hands that had just hit her.

"What does it say?" she said, her voice faint in her own ears. She nodded her head towards the note on the floor.

Dyfed was standing on it.

He looked down, frowning, and picked it up. He stared at it for some time; she could see his struggle to read it. His face drawn, he finally looked back at Rhonwyn.

He could only whisper, "'*This is what happens when you try to escape. Shall I kill her, or will you?*'" Stricken, Dyfed dropped the note and covered his mouth with his hands. "What have I done?"

"Nothing. You've done nothing," insisted Rhonwyn. "He's the one who's done all the wrong." Her shoulder spasmed. "Would you untie me, please?" She spoke through gritted teeth.

"Yes, of course." Dyfed fingered the metal bracelets and rattled them back and forth.

"Can you slip your hand out of it?" he asked.

Rhonwyn tried but the bracelet was too tight. How had he got it on? "What about the other end of it?"

Dyfed ducked his head around the back, but quickly returned. "It's the same. It's around the metal part of the table. I don't think I can untie you. I'm so sorry." He returned and gently cradled her face in his warm hands.

He grimaced at the state of her and dashed to the washroom,

coming back with the towel. He'd soaked it in water and he dabbed her face with it and then pressed it to her eye to cool the swelling.

"What else can I do?" he asked.

Rhonwyn looked up at his worried brown eyes. "Forgive me?"

He huffed a dry laugh. "What for? Making my life liveable again? Giving me joy and a view of the world – of the stars?" He pressed his cheek against her less-battered one. "There's nothing to forgive," he whispered in her ear.

He stood back, surveyed her position, then collected a chair. She couldn't quite sit down on it, so he hefted the pad of the bed over and slid in it behind her. She was as comfortable as she was going to get, with her arms spread-eagled as they were. Her shoulders were aching.

Dyfed brought another chair and sat with her, knee to knee.

"What happened?"

35

Rhonwyn spoke in whispers, halting to gain her breath. She had to stop completely once, her voice refusing to cooperate until Dyfed fetched her a cup of water. He held it to her lips and mopped her face again. She found herself trembling.

Dyfed's forehead furrowed above his grey face. "He wants me to kill you," he whispered.

Her shuddering was getting worse; she was cold.

"It would be better," she answered, looking away.

Dyfed's eyes widened. "You don't really believe that, do you?"

She fixed him with a look from her one good eye. "Dyfed. When he wakes up in the morning, he's going to hurt me until I tell him what he wants to know. I can't risk that. More people will die – because of me."

Dyfed dropped his head into his hands and became silent. He shook his head. "I can't, Rhonwyn, I can't do that. I'm sorry," he muttered.

She knew exactly how he felt.

"I know. It's alright, Dyfed. Hopefully he'll kill me before he can get me to tell. He's got a terrible temper. If I make him angry enough, he'll just …" She didn't bother finishing.

Dyfed surged to his feet and slunk away, his head bent low. "I'm such a coward!"

"No, Dyfed. That's not true," said Rhonwyn, before she coughed again. The movement jolted her body and a cramp started up in her left shoulder. The muscle spasmed until she cried out in pain.

Dyfed ran to her. He rubbed her shoulder with his hand then stopped.

"You're shivering," he said.

He sat back down and wrapped his arms around her, resting his face against her shoulder. He breathed warm air onto it as she groaned.

The warmth that he created helped, and her muscles slowly relaxed until the cramp was only a dull ache. Her shaking continued, however.

Dyfed pulled back. There were tears on his face. "I have to make you comfortable somehow." He stood again and studied her position, the table, and the room, with his lips pressed together, then took an edge of the sleeping pad in one hand and the chair in the other.

"Can you stand?"

Rhonwyn rose on unsteady legs. Her shins were crusted with blood.

Dyfed pulled the chair out from beneath her and supported her against the surface of the table as she inched her feet backwards. The sleeping pad was still between her and the table top.

"I'm going to pull you and the table forward," he said, "and then I'm going to tip the table back onto its feet, so you can lie down. I think you'll be more comfortable that way."

She nodded dully.

Dyfed did exactly that, his arms stretched out, gripping the edges of the table top just below where Rhonwyn was chained, his lean body pressed up to hers. Then he went around to the other side of the table and heaved the top legs down, being careful to set her down softly.

He perched on the edge of the table and leaned over her. "Is that better?"

She wriggled a bit on the mattress and nodded. "Thank you."

It had taken much of the pressure off her contorted shoulders.

He retrieved the pillow and blanket from the bed for her, but still she shivered. So Dyfed climbed up on the table, lay down next to her and offered his arm for her to lean her head on. Once she was settled, he wrapped his other arm around her waist. He was facing her and his body heat radiated into her side. He pulled the blanket around them both.

Despite her bruised body and soul, Rhonwyn's heart squeezed and her stomach fluttered. Dyfed was so close, she could feel his warm breath on the side of her neck and her ear. She nestled her face closer, their noses brushing.

She'd never been this close to a man before. If only she'd met Dyfed years ago, before Risick had come. She would have asked her father to arrange a marriage to him. But she wouldn't have been of marriageable age back then.

What they were doing would not have been allowed during courting. Rhonwyn almost laughed at the idea. With her chained to the table, that was a ridiculous thought.

She tilted her face towards him and Dyfed gave her a lopsided smile. His eyes searched her face, constantly checking, his head resting on the end of the pillow. He was so, *so* different to Risick that she had no difficulty having him near her, though his body had been the one to injure hers in the first place.

"I had no idea," he whispered.

"About what?" she replied, her brow wrinkling. The words were no more than a breath and yet Dyfed heard them, he was that close.

"How much I needed people in my life." He held her tighter. "I feel alive again, finally. There's a reason to exist just because you're here. There's a reason to be sane."

Rhonwyn felt her face warming. She could only nod. She'd felt that alive-ness, too. At least she'd had the chance to know that feeling once before she …

She couldn't finish the thought and focussed back on him. All she saw was kindness and gentleness. He was a true, noble man. He was where she would want to be. Always.

If only she could stay.

Dyfed eased his hand out from under the blanket and brought it to her face. First, he cupped her cheek in his palm, the edge of his thumb brushing her nose, a feather-touch.

Rhonwyn stayed very still, her breathing quickening. She'd completely forgotten her bruises.

Using his fingertips, he drew a line down the curve of her face, oh so gently. When he reached her chin, his thumb stroked her lower lip from the fullness in the middle to the corner of her mouth.

He leaned over the last handbreadth and pressed his lips to hers. The touch was so light, all she felt initially – once she'd closed her eyes – was the tingle of proximity, the heat of him. The pressure grew gradually, each touch exploring a different part of her lips, gingerly avoiding the broken skin. It tickled in fact, but in such a pleasurable way that she wished it wouldn't end. His kisses were so chaste, she felt like the most fragile of creatures being cared for by the most honourable of guardians.

Dyfed pulled back, carefully placing his hand around her waist again. He stayed close and so, upon opening her eyes, his face filled her field of sight.

"Rhonwyn," he sighed. His sad brown eyes drank her in.

The warmth Rhonwyn felt within blossomed into a smile, answered by another smile.

The worm of reality couldn't be ignored for long, however, and the ache of her shoulders and face drawled its horrific truth. She did her best to ignore it. They had hours yet.

How kind of him to make me feel so special before the end.

Sore and exhausted, but warm from Dyfed's nearness, she closed her eyes, snuggled in as best she could and managed to drift off.

She jolted awake again as he withdrew his arm from under her head.

"Sorry," he mumbled and rearranged the blanket over her.

He slid to a sitting position on the edge of the table and massaged his upper arm. Rhonwyn dozed a little longer, but forced herself to rally when she realised Dyfed had been sitting there a long time. She shouldn't just sleep her last night away.

"Dyfed," she began. She had something difficult to tell him.

He tilted his head towards her.

"Your parents and sister." She took a deep breath. "They're dead, Dyfed. I'm so sorry." She wished she could hold his hand, or something, to comfort him.

His face sagged as he closed his eyes.

"I thought I recognised your parents' names when you told me," she continued. "I couldn't remember where I'd heard them before until the magician mentioned them last night." She swallowed. "Years ago, your closest neighbours found them in your home. Someone had murdered the whole family, except the son had gone missing. Everyone assumed he'd killed them, that he'd gone mad, but he was never found. The story shocked us all. It happened just before Risick appeared." Her voice trailed off.

Tears were coursing down Dyfed's face.

"Oh, Dyfed." Rhonwyn did all she could think to do: she twisted her lower body onto its side and laid her legs against Dyfed's back, despite the strain that put on her shoulders.

Dyfed took a shaky breath as he thrust his fingers through his hair. He nodded to himself. "Thank you, Rhonwyn. Thank you for telling me." His voice broke. He cleared his throat. "That makes this easier."

Rhonwyn frowned, her own tears dripping onto the table.

Dyfed slipped off the table and retrieved the Gymbal set from under the bed. He placed it on the end of the table and opened it. Rhonwyn had eased onto her back again.

"I don't think I'm quite up to a game right now," Rhonwyn

quipped, her throat tight.

Dyfed guffawed, his veneer of humour thin. He leant over her and brandished something thin and black before her face.

"You left the key last night," he said.

How would access to the cabinets help?

Dyfed pocketed the key and stretched out on the table once more, laying his head down on the pillow, face to face with her. His palm warmed her, wrapped around her chin and face. His thumb caressed her skin.

"I wish I could have seen you in the sunshine," he murmured.

He stretched over and kissed her lightly on her forehead, her nose, her cheek, avoiding the swollen tissue and broken skin. He lingered on her lips, his eyes closed, before he smiled gently.

"Thank you, Rhonwyn, my angel," he whispered. "You brought light to my life here, at the end." He kissed her once more before standing up again.

A coldness yawned within Rhonwyn. Why was he saying goodbye?

He turned, grim determination on his face. "It's not much of a life, anyway, is it? It's not much to give away. I might as well make something of it."

Fluttering panic rose up within Rhonwyn's chest. She suddenly knew what he was going to do.

"Dyfed, no!" She struggled against her bonds, though she knew they were unbreakable, as he walked to the back of the chamber. "Please don't leave me!" Rhonwyn begged him. How else could she stop him? What else could she say? This was what she'd been ordered to do, but had been unable to bring herself to obey. He was doing the right thing. She knew it, but she couldn't bear it.

As he unlocked the cabinet door, Dyfed spoke calmly. "You'll be alright. When he doesn't show up in the morning, they'll break in. They'll find you and set you free." He'd thought of everything.

Rhonwyn sobbed. "Please!"

He circled her once more, striding over to the shelf where the sleeping pad had lain. The sabre clutched in his hand, he faced her one final time and bowed formally.

"Goodbye, Rhonwyn. Be well and happy."

She forced herself to dampen her crying, dragged herself up to a sitting position on the table, and bowed as best she could. He deserved no less.

"Dear Dyfed ..." Her voice broke. "You are the best and most honourable of men. Thank you. I will not let this be in vain. I swear to you on my honour."

He stood, swallowing several times before clamping his teeth together and settling the handle of the sabre in a corner on the far side of the shelf. He knelt on the sleeping ledge and propped the tip of the sabre against his chest.

Dyfed's breathing was ragged and shallow. He shuffled his knees back on the ledge, drew in one more breath and threw himself onto the sabre.

Rhonwyn gasped at the same time he did.

Instead of piercing him directly, though, the sabre only went in partway before getting stuck. He groaned in pain and his arms flexed vainly, trying to pull it further in, before he toppled sideways and fell onto the floor.

"Dyfed!" Rhonwyn cried.

The sabre wavered back and forth once before it tipped over with a squelch of wet flesh. Blood oozed from Dyfed's chest and pooled on the floor.

"Rhonwyn," he gasped before his head sagged to the side and his body became limp.

Rhonwyn drew her knees up, pressed her face into her lap and cried. Merynbyl would be free, that was what everyone wanted, what everyone needed, but this man, right now, he hadn't deserved this.

Rhonwyn wanted to be close to Dyfed again, so she threw herself from side to side, using her weight to rock the table. It took a few tries, but when she used the weight of her legs over the edge, the table finally crashed to its side again, briefly crushing her fingers under its edge.

She couldn't get any closer than that, however. The table was simply too heavy to drag. Pulling it only made it fall on top of her and she only just managed to push it back to an upright position. So she was forced to lie a body length away and talk to Dyfed from there, to keep his soul company until it departed forever.

At least his face was pointed towards her. His handsome face.

"Dyfed ma Cothee," she said, her voice shaking. "Your family would be proud of you for such bravery. You've freed the whole of Merynbyl. I'll tell your Uncle Talsen what a courageous nephew he had."

She'd forgotten to tell Dyfed she'd met his uncle. She hoped the magician had managed to evade the king's guards.

"Papa, this is Dyfed ma Cothee. He is a good man. Guide him to the other side. Dyfed, this is my father, Hywel." The image of her father in her mind was now sitting, cross-legged, next to Dyfed's body, his head bowed, his hat off.

"I'm so glad I met you, Dyfed. You made me feel so ... not alone anymore. Thank you." Her throat closed up.

Clearing it, she sang, her voice scratchy. Though no Wise One was here, Dyfed deserved a decent goodbye. This was the only song she could think of.

> *Turn me like a boat to sail away from thee*
> *I'll be coming back again, so watch and wait for me*
> *Until I see thy face—*

Dyfed's face moved. Rhonwyn froze, her stomach curling. "Dyfed?"

His face distorted this time, his jaw jutting forward and to the side and Rhonwyn watched, horrified, as something thick and viscous slithered out of his mouth.

The ooze sat before Dyfed's face. Blood? No, this was darker than blood – and it moved as a whole. Like an enormous slug, charcoal grey and slimy, it squirmed to the edge of the room and glided up the wall, undulating as it went.

Rhonwyn couldn't take her eyes off it. Was it changing colour? It had been dark, but seemed to be getting lighter as it glissaded up the wall. The thing slowed as it reached the ceiling and began creeping out into the centre of the room. At one point in its oozing progress, part of it flopped down and hung suspended for several seconds. The thing seemed to have to exert itself to draw that section back before it continued across the ceiling.

It finally seemed to have stopped. Rhonwyn's eyes were fixed on it, directly overhead. Had it lost its power? It must have, because it fell towards her, slapping down on her suspended left forearm. She shrieked and rattled her arm. The thing wouldn't budge. It felt like a sick dog's nose, warm and clammy. She swivelled around on the floor and pulled her head as far away from it as she could. The thing oozed along her arm, towards her face, covered with dust from its journey around the room. But as it came, it exuded moisture and the dust fell off with it. By the time it reached her shoulder, it was clean, but smaller.

Rhonwyn screamed.

She threw herself back and forth, not caring if her joints dislocated. She tried to scrape it off with her chin, but that only attached it to her face.

Out of her mind with panic, Rhonwyn clamped her mouth shut and shook her head as it crawled past her lips and towards her nose. She twisted herself around and tried to rub her face against the table, but she just couldn't reach.

She felt it slither into her nose. Soon she felt it down the back of her throat. She retched, trying to force it out through her mouth again, where she could bite it, but it held on.

The pain began. Rhonwyn could taste blood in her mouth. The thing must be burrowing into her flesh somewhere. She could do nothing. The pain in her neck changed as the creature forced its way through her body. She twitched uncontrollably, her hands flexing, opening and closing, seemingly by themselves. Tears coursed down her cheeks as her body shuddered. The room around her changed colour and she shivered before everything went black and she knew no more.

36

Rhonwyn started awake, panting heavily. Where was she? She sat up and looked around. She was still in the king's chamber, though the lamps were out again. When had they gone out?

She wasn't chained to the table and that was back where it belonged. She lay on the sleeping pad. Her face was tender still, with broken skin, but it was clean. Her right wrist hurt as well. She could feel a cut on it. From the chains, perhaps.

Rhonwyn needed to see. She fumbled her way over to the table where a lamp stood next to a pack of fire sticks. She lit the lamp, held it up and surveyed the room. Game pieces were strewn across the table top, the cabinet was shut again and there, under where her feet had just been, was a dry red stain on the floor.

Rhonwyn's breath caught in her throat, the image of Dyfed's body vivid in her mind. Tears rose up in her eyes. She brushed them away. Blinking, she found a taper and lit all the rest of the lamps in the room, so she could see better. Then she returned to the sleeping pad. The stain was smeared and had a point on one side, like something had been dragged out of it. An irregular line of blood led to the door.

The door. Lifting her eyes she discovered it was just after midnight.

Midnight. Rhonwyn's stomach dropped and her hands shook so much she had to set the lamp she was carrying down.

She examined herself. Her right wrist had a long, straight cut in it, with short, black lines cutting across. It looked like her skin had been sewn together. Just like the scar on Dyfed's wrist.

What had Risick done to her? She swallowed, feeling the rawness in her throat where that thing had burrowed into her. Where was it? Was it eating her? She felt her neck to see if it had left her body somewhere, then picked up the lamp again and stood in front of the mirror.

The first thing she noticed was the clothes she was wearing. Silky and fitting, they were perfectly tailored – and that strangely alien design. Pulling the top's front opening to each side, she found bruises on the skin underneath. From Risick's rough handling of her, she presumed. She couldn't see any opening the slug might have come out of. Except her mouth, of course. She inspected her lip, which was a dark purple colour. The swelling had gone down.

Rhonwyn spun around and looked again at the door. She was accustomed to being able to leave. Could she still? She strode to the door and pushed the numbers on the glowing square. 8 – 4 – 2 – 6. The door didn't open. Had she pushed them incorrectly, in her haste? She tried again, slower. Nothing. She pushed the numbers in a different order and then rattled the heavy wooden barrier, the noise echoing around the room and, she could hear, around the chamber outside.

She couldn't get out. Had the Risick demon now possessed her? Is that what that slug had been – the demon? A parasite? Was she never going to get out of there?

That was it, wasn't it? That was how it was.

Her breath shuddering in her throat, Rhonwyn paced the room, trying to push down panic, trying to think clearly. She'd circled the room twice before she spoke.

"Papa, I'm the puppet of the evil one now. He ... it's in me, and doing evil things," she said, her voice echoing off the walls. "Is there a queen now in Merynbyl? Who have I killed? What can I do?" She pressed her hands against her mouth. Had she killed someone she knew? Felenya? Kymra? Berwyn? Talsen? Her whole body was tense with the thought. A sob echoed off the walls.

"Papa, I can't let that continue. I know what's going on. I can't let this demon get away with it." She knew this was the only time the demon was vulnerable – when she was awake. "I have to do what Dyfed did, don't I?" Another sacrifice to this wicked thing. But this time, it wouldn't be able to find another vessel. There would be no one close enough.

The sabre wasn't on the floor, where she'd seen it last. Rhonwyn ran to the cabinet at the back. Locked. She checked every cabinet door. None opened to her tugging. She scoured the room for something to cut herself with. Everything was far too blunt.

She gazed up at the windows, high in the back wall of the chamber. Nothing in the room was tall enough for her to stand upon to reach them – and throw herself out.

"Papa, how do I do this?" she asked the air.

She prowled over to the sleeping pad and knelt to check under it.

"Rhonwyn." The voice rang about the room.

Springing to her feet, Rhonwyn felt the stiffness of her muscles from last night's ordeal. She cast her eyes about the room.

"Who's there?" she called.

The washroom. She hadn't been in there yet. No one was in there, but Rhonwyn stood staring at the basin. Could she drown herself in that? She tried to imagine standing and putting her face in there. When she choked on the water, surely she would pull away instinctively. That wouldn't work.

As she passed through the doorway to the main room, the voice sounded again.

"Rhonwyn."

She froze and her eyes scanned the room. She couldn't see anywhere a person could hide in here. Was she losing her mind? Hearing voices? Was her father finally talking back?

Perhaps that wouldn't be so bad.

"Papa?" she tried.

No reply. Had it come from the room outside the door? She approached the door again, leaned her ear against it and called out, "Hello? Anyone there?"

After a long silence, she whirled and struck out around the room again, circling it several times.

"Look, don't just say my name. That doesn't tell me anything," she shouted. She made another circuit of the room, looking for anything she could use to end her own life.

"If you're going to say something, make it useful and give me an idea, will you?"

Rhonwyn changed direction before she could make herself dizzy. As she did, she caught sight of someone on the other side of the room. A man, tall and broad, his hair straw-coloured.

She froze, staring at him. No. Not a man. Her own face in the mirror. The fright, however, left her shaking again. Where had the image of that man come from? She didn't know anyone who looked like that, his hair such an unnatural colour.

Taking a deep breath, she continued pacing the room, searching for something to kill herself with. She had to find some—

"Rhonwyn, listen."

"Dyfed?" Rhonwyn stopped again. It had sounded so much like his voice.

No answer. She put her hands over her ears. "Stop it!" she ordered as she walked forwards again. But when she took her hands down, another voice sounded.

"Rhonwyn!" It had a strange accent. And there were others.

"Rhonwyn!" A woman's voice. Not hers.

"Look in the mirror, Rhonwyn," a completely different voice urged her.

"Look!" Was that a child's voice? So high and thin.

"Don't be afraid."

She was losing her mind. Hearing voices.

"No, you're not crazy, Rhonwyn. Look in the mirror." Another voice, another accent.

Trembling, she stepped around the edge of the room to the mirror and looked into it. She felt her face go slack.

A woman looked back at her, her skin near black. She was short and voluptuous. She held out her hands.

"Don't be afraid, Rhonwyn." Her voice was like silk.

Rhonwyn's stomach churned hard as the woman went on.

"My name is Dressida," she said softly. "I am one of the people the Risick worm has used in the past."

'Risick worm'?

"I am one of many," the woman said. "Most were aware and agreed to the worm entering them."

Rhonwyn's eyes widened. "Why would they agree to this?"

The dark woman's lips pressed together before she spoke. "We were deceived." She glanced down. "We were told this would benefit us. That the worms would work towards all our good. That their experience and wisdom would benefit our societies. That they were wise and benevolent." She looked at Rhonwyn again. "Now we know they lied. They made our societies better – for a while – then took over our worlds and arranged them to dig up a mineral they wanted. They destroyed our worlds for its riches and made our people slaves to do this."

Rhonwyn couldn't take it all in. "'Worms' you said? More than one?"

The woman nodded.

Rhonwyn thought some more. "Do you mean boros? Is that what we've been digging it up for?"

"Yes." The woman's dark brows descended. "There is so much more we need to tell you. And we don't even know it all clearly. Our memories are hidden ... confused." She tilted her head. "Rhonwyn, we don't have time to tell you the whole story in this way." Her hand indicated between the two of them: Rhonwyn and the reflection of a stranger in the mirror. "We need to do this quickly. We cannot process all this information without using your mind to do it. Will you help us?"

Rhonwyn didn't understand what Dressida was asking of her. The other woman seemed to know without Rhonwyn saying a word. She spoke again. "I know you don't understand. You will have to trust us."

Rhonwyn jolted – had the woman read her mind? – and suddenly saw herself briefly in the mirror, instead of Dressida. But the other woman's image returned immediately.

Dressida's eyes flicked down. "Ah, yes, perhaps that's a good idea," she said, as if she were speaking to another, invisible person. Her eyes rose again to Rhonwyn's. "You should speak to someone you know."

The image of Dressida in the mirror faded away and Rhonwyn's image took its place, but only briefly, as the form of a slender, brown-skinned man appeared. He gave her a crooked smile and his eyes sparkled.

"Dyfed," Rhonwyn whispered, before her throat closed up.

"Peace to you, my lovely Rhonwyn. Yes, I am in here too. All my memories and my soul remain. But it's too confusing. We have barely room to sense each other in here." His look was sober. "It sounds like it will be difficult, Rhonwyn, for you to do this, but I want you to do it freely – by choice. There is a chance that, if we work together, all of us in here might be able to stop Risick. But, if not, we will help you stop him ..." He paused briefly, his eyes dropping. "... that *other* way." At this his smile fell away and his forehead wrinkled.

That *other* way – where she killed herself.

Rhonwyn took some time to think as she gazed at her dead friend's face. She'd thought she would never see him again. What had Risick done with Dyfed's body?

She looked hopefully at the mirror. "Papa?" Could she see him in the mirror, as she had the others?

As if in response to this thought, Dyfed shook his head. "He's not here, Rhonwyn. I'm sorry."

She closed her eyes, fighting tears. What would her father have done? He would have done the right thing. Whatever it took to help Merynbyl. If she stayed as she was, she would never escape and more people would suffer, and she would be even more alone than she already had been. Her heart squeezed. She must try.

Rhonwyn opened her eyes. "Well, I can't do anything with just me." Her voice shook, though she was doing her best to be brave. "So I might as well join you all." She gave Dyfed's image in the mirror a tiny smile. "What do I do?"

Dyfed gazed into her eyes. "So brave. I'm so proud of you, Rhonwyn. I wish I could have got to know you better."

Through Rhonwyn's tight control, tears threatened again.

With their eyes locked together, Dyfed lifted his hand and pressed it to the mirror and they were palm to palm.

If only ...

She took a deep breath.

As their hands lowered, the image of Dyfed dissolved and Dressida's returned, her eyes averted briefly, as if she were giving the two of them as much privacy as she could manage. She pressed her lips together before she raised her head and spoke.

"Rhonwyn, we're not sure what this will do to you. It's only ever been the host," she pressed her hand to her breast, "and the Risick, involved. And we can only hope that doing this will not wake it from its sleep." She bit her top lip.

Rhonwyn frowned.

"As you've noticed, we can make you see things. I'm going to give you a box. You'll take it from me. It's a mechanism to ..." She stopped and exhaled. "I'm explaining too much. We need to get on with this." She pointed at Rhonwyn. "You'll open the box and then ..." She paused and shrugged. "... and then we don't know."

Before Rhonwyn could ask any more questions, Dressida turned to the side and reached her hands beyond the edge of the mirror, so Rhonwyn couldn't see them. When Dressida's hands drew back into Rhonwyn's field of view, they held an elaborate box, exotically decorated with alien-looking symbols and shapes. Dressida held it out to her.

Fear of the unknown hit Rhonwyn in a rush. What would this do to her? If Dressida didn't know, would it be safe? Safe? When was the last time Rhonwyn had chosen the safe path? She laughed at herself. She was in an impossible situation. She had to act.

One last time, she looked up at Dressida's face, patiently waiting for her to take the box she held out. This peace, this patience, helped her decide. She took the box that somehow passed through the mirror to her. Rhonwyn could feel it in her hands. Heavy, the carvings on it dug into her fingers. The creamy scent of butter mixed with resin filled her nose. This seemed so real, how could this be an illusion?

She looked up. Dressida had disappeared. It was just her own face in the mirror now, the forehead creased, the eyes wide.

The voices were silent. She'd been left to her own choice.

Mellorwood. That was what she could smell. Mellorwood? Rhonwyn had never even heard of mellorwood. Where had that word come from?

Desta. Mellorwood came from Desta.

The universe struck Rhonwyn in the back of the head.

Images, smells, sensations, words. One after another after another after another. And then all at once.

Rhonwyn felt as if her head was exploding: from a tiny mote, into the vast emptiness of space, bending back on itself and spinning. Spinning stars in a disc. A galaxy. What's a galaxy? That ... that's a galaxy. A thousand galaxies. A thousand voices, all speaking in other languages. All shouting at her. Rhonwyn tried to close her ears to it, but she had no hands ... no ears. And none of the voices made sense.

But in time – whatever that was – words came loaded with meaning, then more meaning when strung together with other words. Totally alien words, alien languages, alien ways of thinking. Their meaning so heavy, so immense, she felt her heart torn, writhing in pain.

Thoughts ... identities now loomed in her mind, all-consuming. She wasn't Rhonwyn anymore, she was D'far, from G'tolen. He loved music and mathematics. His sister had been a dancer.

Mirsla, she was now. Daddy had her doll. He wouldn't give it back until she apologised. No ... that was an older memory ... she was an ambassador to the far country now.

A flying craft of unknown origin descended into the rich, green field before him. Jengenadan was about to welcome the first visitors from another planet. No one could ignore him now.

Memory after memory, identity after identity, flashed through Rhonwyn's consciousness, flinging her aside, forcing her to give up her place. She didn't exist anymore. What was her name? Where was she from? She felt herself shrivel under the onslaught of ideas, memories, and identities. Her own memories shredded apart, mixed with others' memories until she couldn't distinguish hers from theirs.

"Stop!"

The shout rang around her. Who's voice was that? She didn't have a voice. Was it real? Or was that another memory belonging to ... who?

One memory fought its way to the centre, fierce in its singularity. But the word 'singularity' diverted it. The weight of this word spun the memory off track again.

Singularity ... a point at which a function takes an infinite ... an oddity ... a black hole ...

"Stop! You're hurting her!" the voice cried out again.

Sitting on a rock by the estuary, he rubbed the seeds carefully between his palms and ate them, one by one. The first taste was the salt from his fingers, and then the creaminess of the seeds came through, permeating his mouth. His teeth shattered them and spread the fragments all around: against his cheeks, lips, tongue, the roof of his mouth. He swallowed and felt them slip down his throat and further. His stomach was aching with hunger. A good hunger. He was looking forward to the evening meal.

It had been a long day. He'd worked hard. He and his father had been picking all day, just like yesterday. His fingers were stained purple. But the harvest was done now. All done. He allowed himself to feel the satisfaction of accomplishment.

Remember this feeling.

The last seed got stuck between his teeth so he used first

his tongue, then his fingernail, to push it out again and then chewed as he flicked the husks out over the wide, sparkling, rippling water. The sun would go down soon and his parents would expect him back home. But in the meantime, he could relax.

He lowered his dusty feet into the river water flowing around the warm boulder beneath him. *Ah, so cool, so soothing.* He took a deep breath of sweet, fresh air, moist and crisp.

A faint, high voice sounded behind him, barely heard over the rushing water around him.

"Dyfed!" She called again.

He turned his head and smiled.

"Nemalyn!" He felt the stretch of well-used muscles as he raised his hand to wave her over. As his sister picked her way from rock to rock to reach him, he bent forward, filled his hands with cold water, and splashed it over his head and another handful down his neck.

But he stayed bent over, looking into the water, waiting until the dripping from his hair stopped, until the surface calmed enough to see his reflection.

Instead, the river showed him a pretty woman, brown hair, hazel eyes, long neck. He smiled at her, the familiar feelings of affection and desire filling him.

"Rhonwyn, it's alright," he said, reaching towards the water. "I remember who you are."

Suddenly, Rhonwyn knew where she was, who she was, and what was happening. She was flat out on the hard floor, having collapsed under the strain of all those people, all that knowledge, all those memories, sensations and emotions. She was still trembling as she pushed herself up to a sitting position, breathing hard.

How long had she been there? She looked at the clock over

the door. Five o'clock.

*The fool **would** divide days up into the hours of **his** original planet! He should've just used—*

Hush!

As these thoughts passed through her mind, Rhonwyn froze in place, her mind spinning. They'd been other people. In her mind. One had been a scientist – a physicist. She sensed the compassion of multiple people, just beneath the surface, as they restrained themselves. Each was capable of taking her place, but they held back their knowledge, opinions and personalities. Instead, they allowed her reign of her own body. She blinked. Risick had occupied twenty-five previous hosts before he'd come to Merynbyl.

In a trans-galactic space vehicle.

She blinked again. There were other planets and other peoples. Other languages. *That* was what the 'magic writing' had been in the hidden books. Not magic, just another language. Which she could now read.

Five o'clock. Her body jolted.

The Risick worm didn't seem to have woken up from its hibernation, despite the kerfuffle within Rhonwyn's consciousness. Good. But they had less than an hour to prepare for the battle that would ensue when it woke up. With no guarantee they would win.

I would say about fifty-five percent possibility of success.

A laugh bubbled out of Rhonwyn's chest.

I'm glad you think it's funny.

I hate to point this out, said another voice, *but the fright we gave Rhonwyn has caused her body some distress. We need to clean up.*

Rhonwyn checked herself. Yes, she'd lost control while the transfer had been wracking her mind. Perfectly normal. She just needed to change her clothes.

She chuckled. Look how calm she was. 'Perfectly normal.' Anything but!

Rhonwyn, there are usually some clothes over there. Dyfed's memories directed her swimming attention to an unwalled closet in the corner of the room. Yes, Risick had often brought clean clothing with him when he'd come over for the night.

Not 'him' – 'it.'

Picky, picky!

As Rhonwyn rose and walked cautiously over to the closet, she asked a question.

"If that was what it was like having all of you – friendly souls – make yourselves known, how bad is it going to be when Risick wakes up?"

A short pause, then Rhonwyn had to stand still as the voices came bubbling up, overwhelming her mind.

She has a point. It's not going to be pleasant.

We have no idea what it's going to be like. Or if we can do anything at all.

We can do it. We just have to do it together.

It's going to be a struggle, Rhonwyn. One voice pushed its way forward. *But it shouldn't be as confusing. It should be clear who is who.*

You're not alone.

As she changed her clothes and cleaned herself, Rhonwyn faced away from the mirror. Some within her would scoff at that, but this was *her* body and some of her recent cultural norms still held strong. The idea of 'cultural norm' was still a new concept to her, somehow lifting her out of her own self and people group and letting her see them – and herself – from a distance. But the love and concern for her people was still there. A strange contradiction to hold within her.

She straightened her collar. When Dyfed had seen her in the strong memory he'd used to buoy her back to the surface, she'd experienced those feelings with him: affection, desire. Dyfed really had loved her. He hadn't been pretending, or desperately taking the only option. He'd really thought she was pretty. She'd seen herself through his eyes.

Her heart ached.

I'm here, Rhonwyn.

She had all his memories, now. She saw all the time they'd spent in the freedom of outside and how good that had felt to him. And further back. Much further back: The old man who'd arrived that last day – Mulyn. He'd had the Risick worm in him, too, because he was here. He'd thought he was sick. He'd gone blind and then deaf and his body had done strange things, against his will, though all his capacities had returned quickly afterwards.

Knowledge from another host who'd been a doctor emerged then: the worm had been burrowing further into the man's brain stem and taking over more and more parts of his nervous system. As it had been unfamiliar with the new species, it'd taken longer than usual, and had meant experimentation was necessary.

The thought made Rhonwyn cringe.

The fact that Risick was willing to permanently damage its host is an indicator that its priorities aren't what they used to be.

Actually, Rhonwyn, your memories of Risick's actions shed more light on what might have been going on, said another voice. *Its actions seem to indicate it was overwhelmed with the sensations from the new species. I don't think what it experienced was normal. Perhaps it's your people's physiology, or maybe the Risick worm itself is unwell.*

Rhonwyn recalled what Risick had said to her when she'd been bound to the table: 'How do you stand it? All these sensations? All the time?' The same thing Kymra had witnessed.

What I was doing to Kymra …! This voice was strained, guilty.

Dyfed, that wasn't you. You mustn't blame yourself. Risick was in control then.

"No, Dyfed," Rhonwyn agreed with … whoever had spoken then. "You would never do that." He must have seen what had happened to Kymra from Rhonwyn's own memories. How awful to find out that Risick had used his body to do that to someone.

The only memories they didn't have were Risick's. Would they get access to those when – if – they won the struggle? And that struggle: now she knew what it entailed and how unlikely their success was.

She looked down at her wrist. "Does anyone know why this scar is here? It looks like an implant." Knowledge from the healer had again emerged. Rhonwyn noticed she was speaking differently. She was even using words from languages she didn't know. Well ... she *hadn't* known, a few hours ago. But no one knew about the scar except Dyfed, from his own experience with it.

Rhonwyn felt her lips purse and she positioned herself before the mirror. "I would like to see you all," she said, and waited. That caused some consternation within her, which made her dizzy.

Rhonwyn, we do look quite different from you.

You know, I think she can handle it.

She knows everything. What difference does it make? She'll figure it out anyway.

That's quite a nice idea, actually, Rhonwyn. But ... you know me already.

Dressida appeared in the mirror and smiled. Then the white-blond man appeared and waved, raising an eyebrow. Rhonwyn had never seen anyone with hair that colour. But, in the end, he and Dressida were the most normal-looking hosts Risick had had, apart from Dyfed and Mulyn, the old man. One host had antennae. One had blue skin. One was half her height. One walked on four legs. But she knew them all by name when she saw them and she had all their memories, knew all those they'd loved.

Once she'd seen them all, her own likeness emerged again. But she was left feeling nauseous.

I don't think we'll be able to maintain this. I think, for Rhonwyn's sanity, we'll have to go back to sleep. Once she doesn't need us, that is.

We'll have to decide later. It's nearly six o'clock.

Rhonwyn's heart squeezed in fright. Time had marched on more quickly than she would have liked.

Brace yourselves and be alert. Most of us have been asleep for many years, whereas the Risick has been awake and alert much more. Don't expect this to be easy. It might not even happen today.

She lay down on the sleeping pad as there was a short period of unconsciousness between host and inhabitor.

Rhonwyn felt no drowsiness. The darkness simply dragged her under.

38

Rhonwyn struggled to surface in the ocean of silent darkness. There was nothing to surface *to*.

Had she been asleep? She could see nothing, hear nothing. She could only sense movement. Not even her own movement, which disoriented her further.

No, wait. It *was* her own movement. She could sense warm breath through her nostrils, her neck turning, her hand lifting. A rush and she was sitting upright. No light. No sound. Someone else moving her body. She was helpless. Panic overwhelmed her. Rhonwyn's alarm brought a presence. Comforting, soothing – a wordless exchange.

She calmed enough to become curious. Who was this other presence? Another different presence made itself known and directed warmth and affection at her. Someone loved her.

Papa?

Both presences immediately encircled her and urged silence ... no words ... stillness ... *danger*.

Rhonwyn now sensed more identities, hovering, searching, working at something.

Sound began to leak through. The rustle of clothing, the rush of air. Her throat was cleared, and the noise reverberated around her. Over these things she had no control.

What was happening? Her body stood. Walked. She could hear her feet landing and feel the movement. The sound had direction now. It was *below*. Now her breathing sounded different. It was bouncing off something very near to her.

In an explosion of light, her face appeared in the mirror, right up close, the bruised cheek tilted towards it, the eyes squinting to the side, inspecting. A deep breath and her fingers were thrust through her hair, combing it back. Someone else was controlling her hands. Who?

Just as her hands dropped, Rhonwyn caught sight of an oddity: one of her eyes was its usual hazel, the other was sulphur yellow. The details of their plight hit her.

But Risick might see the oddity, too. Alarm and urgent adjustment occurred around her, the presences – with relief she recognised Dressida and Dyfed – negotiating swift, immediate change with those others in there with them.

The hazel eye changed to yellow just as her whole body froze, her eyelids wide. Back and forth the eyes flicked. Right eye. Left eye. Had they changed it in time?

Rhonwyn's eyes narrowed with a frown before a huff escaped her nose. "Crazy." A two-toned voice emerged from Rhonwyn's throat. The harmonic buzz sounded even stranger from inside.

Her mouth had formed the words. She'd felt the movement, heard the sound, but Rhonwyn had *not* said that. Her head tilted to one side, pondering thoughts unheard.

The double voice spoke again, musing. "I must kill Felenya today."

Felenya!

No!

And Rhonwyn's mouth repeated it aloud, "No!" Her shout echoed through the room. This time, the voice had no double-buzz. She had moved her own mouth with her fear for her friend.

Her body whirled around, her eyes scanning the room. Risick thought it was someone else's voice. Just as she had.

Dressida and Dyfed blanketed Rhonwyn with reassurance and, again, the pressing need for caution. She tamped down her fear for Felenya.

Her body carried them all into the washroom and looked around before its shoulders dropped back down. Her head shook.

"Okay, Risick, old ..." An amused breath drew in. "... girl." A chuckle. "Don't go losing your mind now," her mouth said aloud. The buzz was back. "There's only a few months to go. You've just got to hold on till then. Just a little while longer."

After a thoughtful pause, Rhonwyn felt a surge of what could only be referred to as lust flow through her before she perceived an internal voice. Dim, but growing stronger. Another presence, but removed from them all.

Unaware of them.

... and that's what I can use that redundant wrestler for. Hmmm, that should be fun.

Her body stepped towards the exit.

Though Rhonwyn herself was confused about Risick's intent, more than one of her internal companions had understood Risick's thought and reacted with fury. All went black and Rhonwyn's body became limp and collapsed to the floor while Risick's consciousness was silenced. She and her cohorts, however, retained their awareness.

More urgent reshuffling, and sight, sound and sense were restored. These shifts happened so fast. She had to pay close attention. The others seemed to have more knowledge of this.

Her body had landed on its hands and knees on the mat.

Did I lose consciousness? Risick's alien presence had reawakened and was now alarmed and confused.

Rhonwyn's head was swivelled up and her narrowed eyes directed at the door. She was merely a passenger in her own body, which jumped to its feet and made its way towards the cabinets in the back. All the silent passengers were carried along with it.

Blacking out – that's not good.

It seemed they could only hear Risick's most deliberate or near-verbal thoughts, whereas – as the consciousness in control – Risick would 'hear' even the slightest thought of theirs. That's why they had to be 'silent'.

They approached the wall next to the cabinet.

"Panel open," the double voice rang out.

A small square hidden in the wall retracted and slid to the side, revealing two keys. Rhonwyn's hand picked up one of them.

"Panel close."

I'll need to kill Berwyn, too.

Rhonwyn's horror at this, combined with that of the others in there with her, seemed to shut down her body again. Her physical form sagged towards the floor, the dominant personality losing control.

So that's what it was: they needed to control their emotions as they worked or it overrode Risick's control of her body – which was giving away their presence.

This time they restored function almost instantly. Rhonwyn wasn't sure how they were doing it, but somehow she was involved.

On her knees once more, her eyes searched the floor – her hand had dropped the key in the short period of unconsciousness. The search ended at the edge of the rug, which was turned up a little.

It must have fallen under there.

When her hand flipped the corner of the rug back, her lungs sucked in a breath.

This view was familiar to Rhonwyn, but not to Risick. Along with the key, there on the floor underneath the rug, was a semicircle of coal black. A blue corner peeked out from under the mat. Her hands pushed the mat further back to reveal the book Rhonwyn had used to conceal the hole she'd made.

"What?" The double-toned voice this time.

Rhonwyn could feel the blood draining away from her face, disconnected from any emotion she was conscious of. Risick must be realising she'd figured out how the firearms worked –

how close he'd come to being defeated.

"Dammit, Risick, pull yourself together."

She felt her teeth clench as she reached up and opened the cabinet, remaining on her knees. Her eyes moved over the shelves of books.

It's not here.

A growl escaped her before her hand snatched the key from the open cabinet door and she scrambled to her feet. At the door, her finger pressed the usual number into the keyboard before pausing. She felt her head shake before a new number was jabbed in. Her hand wrenched the door open, and she jogged over the bridge, opened the trapdoor, and sped through to the library.

At Matu's desk, she lit the lamp, swiped it up and hurried down to the back of the room. Her hands opened the cabinet and yanked out the largest book there. Her body paused, lingering over the image on the cover, the sulphur eyes standing out from the silhouetted figure holding the sabre.

I'll need to clean that. Stupid boy.

The book had only just opened when a breathless voice sounded behind her.

"Rhonwyn! What in all the gods' names are you doing? How did you get in there?"

Her body swung around. Matu stood there in her nightwear, a horrified expression on her face. But when she saw Rhonwyn's eyes, her face paled. She seemed to shrink.

"Go away," growled Risick's double voice and Rhonwyn's body turned back to the open cabinets.

"Can I help Your Majesty?" Matu squeaked and Rhonwyn heard a thud.

Rhonwyn's body looked back. Matu was bowing. From Rhonwyn's throat came a roar she would never have thought she could make – feral and furious. Her hand extended and pinched the empty air in front of her.

Matu jolted up, her face distorted, her hands pawing at

her throat.

This time the shutdown was deliberate, all the stowaways working in concert. They waited until Rhonwyn's body lay prone and the door had banged shut – the sound of the librarian's footsteps retreating at a run.

When they released control to Risick again, Rhonwyn's body lost no time. It sprang up with the book, slammed the cupboard closed, and grabbed the key out of it. They flew through the library and sitting room, stabbed the code in and stood, fingertips tapping on the book, as the trapdoor ground open.

"Come on!"

Her body sprinted over the bridge and slammed its way through the two doors before leaning on the rear of the inside door and breathing a sigh of relief.

In the meantime, Rhonwyn, Dressida, Dyfed and the rest of her companions were working to wrestle back complete control of the body, *without* making it collapse. All they had presently was an all-or-nothing switch. Time was running short. If Risick found some way of stopping them with that book, they wouldn't get another chance. Surely that was why he'd fetched the thing.

Her body sat at the table, next to the lamp, and flicked through the back of the book, one finger running down the illegible words inside. None of the previous hosts could read it. Her hands rifled through several sections before a fist thumped the table. It seemed Risick hadn't found the answer yet.

Good.

The stowaways were still working frantically when the room faded into darkness. But this time, Risick remained conscious, though he seemed in a sudden panic. Rhonwyn's hand was thrust out until it came in contact with the lamp, which scorched the back of it before it jerked away. The room faded back into view through her widened eyes.

They had control of her sight. They must pretend Risick still had it while they got the rest.

It wasn't long before the next faculty was secured and, in the transfer, silence seemed to attack Rhonwyn's ears. Her body rushed to its feet, panting, rubbing her ears with her hands.

Rhonwyn and her friends allowed the noise of the world to leak back. He mustn't know. Not yet. If only they could do this more surreptitiously.

But Risick spoke. "That's not possible."

And suddenly, Risick was in there with them, like a nightmare come to life. Impotent horror gripped them. He hadn't found them yet, but they could sense his powerful presence searching for them. They seemed insubstantial next to his monstrous reality. They were ghosts in comparison. No wonder they'd had to remain concealed. Rhonwyn felt as flimsy as the discarded shell of a snail.

But Rhonwyn sensed one of her companions separating themselves. Dressida. Rhonwyn could feel her pulling away. How she did it was impossible to grasp, but the feeling of separation was unmistakable.

Dressida spoke to their opponent.

Risick. What you have done is wrong. I can't allow you to continue.

They could all sense Dressida's apprehension. Was she mad? What was she doing?

Rhonwyn felt her body tense around them, her hands curling into fists. Risick could hear her. Dressida had attracted Risick's attention. He'd stopped his search. They sensed him exploring Dressida's consciousness. Hers alone.

Dressida? What are you doing here? You're dead.

His inner voice by itself seemed able to disintegrate them as it rippled through their souls like a storm.

Rhonwyn's body turned towards the mirror and the burning yellow eyes glared at them while she, Dyfed and the others frantically tried to complete their mission while he was distracted.

Dressida spoke again, her presence and voice tiny compared to Risick's.

No, I'm still here. I was merely sleeping. Your evil woke me and I'm going to stop you.

They felt a wave of amusement, and a sneer crossed the image of Rhonwyn's face in the mirror.

I don't think so. You can't touch me.

He seemed so very certain. Was there something they didn't know? Some other ability they weren't aware of? As they fumbled for control in the dark, they were astonished to feel Dressida's presence surge towards Risick and attack him. The effect was like an insect stinging an enormous predator.

Though he would have barely felt it, Risick's amusement turned to rage in an instant. He lashed out and his strike was infinitely more effective than hers. Dressida's soul cried out.

You can't!

Risick reached out lazily once more, with a single dreadful action, and the stowaways all froze in horror.

Dressida was gone.

I think you'll find I can.

Risick fixed the mirror with a haughty, contemptuous look.

Rhonwyn had never seen her face make such an expression. She felt the touch of true terror; this creature could dispose of them with a breath.

39

The remaining hosts' emotions seemed obvious to Rhonwyn – loud even, for she wasn't the only one panicking – but Risick didn't seem to sense them. How was that possible?

Was that what Dressida had done? With her one attack?

The stowaways began to calm down, despite the confusion. They had another chance and Dressida had given it to them.

Risick used Rhonwyn's finger to flip shut the book he'd been referencing, and he returned it to the cabinet. Whistling, he slipped the key into his pocket and sauntered back to the mirror to check his appearance. But what he saw wiped the smile from his face.

Rhonwyn and her cohorts saw it too: her eyes flashing one colour after another. Blue, brown, yellow, hazel, red, green, purple. The colours flickered in and out, over and over.

They'd found the solution. They were in control.

Abruptly, their perspective changed, all their wills combined and, working in concert, they expanded beyond the sum of them. Now they were capable of taking Risick down. In fact, they'd already begun. Playing to their advantage, one canny female had hidden several essential memories and abilities. Risick wouldn't be aware of the lack until he tried to draw on them. The rest followed her example, quickly disconnecting Risick from his lifelines as he paused in shock.

The pause was his downfall.

They sensed his consciousness scrambling, finding parts of itself missing. Abilities and capacities – and control – had slipped from his grasp. Now it was he who grew frantic.

Sensing his weakness and fuelled by fear – and fury at Dressida's sacrifice – the unified hosts tore into Risick's soul like dogs at a carcass.

As Risick diminished, Rhonwyn's face went slack in the mirror, the horror plain.

"Help!"

One final gasp in the worm's strangled double-tone.

"I don't want my eyes to look like this," Rhonwyn blurted out, noting her voice sounded normal – no extra harmonics. Thank the heavens.

The sulphur colour persisted, however, as her new friends returned control of her body to her, part by part, memory by memory, sense by sense. She felt it all except the worm itself. It remained wrapped around her spinal column, a repository of memories, but two fewer souls – Risick and Dressida were gone.

She'd been able to watch the last part of the process, her eyes cycling through the eye colours of Risick's previous hosts, slower and slower. In the end, it landed on sulphur and stayed there. This was not how she wanted to look for the rest of her life.

We're not sure how to change it. You might have to live with it.

The disorientation had increased. As the voices, with all their personality behind them, assumed and released control of her mind just to say something, her head swam and she was forced to stop moving.

That is why we have to go back to sleep.

"Well, I don't want you going for the moment," said Rhonwyn. "I still need you."

We've been examining Risick's memories. It is not good news.

Rhonwyn's stomach sank. She'd been aware of activity in the back of her mind, but had no access to it. It'd been like being conscious of having a dream, but not being able to remember any details.

Your planet is in danger of being overrun. You are the only person who has the knowledge to stop them. You'll have to take charge. Better sit down.

She took that advice. Rhonwyn's brows descended as a trickle of memory – Risick's memories – began to enter her mind, turning into a river and then a flood. Not as bad as the previous hosts all swarming her at once, but not pleasant.

Not much of what Risick had done was pleasant. And he ... it ... had lived a very long time. What she was receiving this time was memory only. No personality or emotion accompanied it. They – Rhonwyn, Dyfed and all the previous hosts, aside from Dressida – had torn Risick's consciousness to pieces like a pack of animals. Rhonwyn wasn't sure how she felt about that. It had been so violent, angry and wild. But now she saw what horrific things Risick had done with his life, their actions were easier to justify. Unfortunately, she could now remember her father's death in detail. At close range. She shut that memory down straight away; that would upset her and she had much to do.

Look how cold she could be now!

Rhonwyn stood, took a deep breath and headed for the door. The number sprang to mind – one of Risick's empty memories. She pulled the door open, glanced at the clock above, and stopped.

"What happens at midnight?" she asked.

But there was no answer. No one knew. This was not within anyone's experience, not even Risick's.

I suppose we'll find out tonight.

Rhonwyn staggered, flinging her arms out for support.

Hush!

As she strode over the bridge to the palace, more information settled into place in her conscious mind. This would not be easy to explain to Merynbyl. But Rhonwyn had more resources than she'd ever had before in her life.

The trapdoor rumbled upwards, and she climbed the stairs. She chuckled as another of her adversary's memories surfaced: Risick hadn't realised how she'd got into the chamber. He'd assumed she'd found out both the security numbers.

She thought she heard a dull thump in the library as she passed, but no light shone through the door. She carried on down the corridor before being startled by a crash and a loud cry bursting forth from the door behind her.

"Yahhhh!"

She swivelled and instantaneously took in what was happening: Zaryc, a sword in his hand, was belting along the corridor towards her.

With many minds aboard, it took less than the blink of an eye for Rhonwyn to decide on her action. The implant. This was the 'magic' all of Merynbyl had seen. It was how Risick had been impervious. By enhancing mental abilities, it extended the body's capacity. It wasn't magic after all, but technology.

Rhonwyn raised her right arm and backhanded the air in front of her. Zaryc's sword crashed against the wall next to him. She splayed her palm out and up before her and he thudded to a halt several paces away, as if he'd run into a wall. She heard the air leaving his lungs.

"Zaryc, listen to me," she said.

The man continued to struggle, having to regain his breath.

"Zaryc. I'm Rhonwyn again. I'm not Risick. Hear me." She shoved him backwards with the technology, trying to shake him out of his crazed single-mindedness. He immediately started towards her again.

She held him back. The mental extension provided extraordinary strength. If only she could calm Zaryc's mind with it. She stepped back and released Zaryc so abruptly he flopped to the floor.

"I'm not going to kill you!" She bellowed at him.

This, and his impact with the floor, seemed to get through. As he raised his head, Rhonwyn saw confusion swimming in his eyes. She could almost read his thoughts: 'I'm not dead. Why am I not dead?' He'd been utterly desperate.

"Zaryc, please don't try to kill me. Risick's gone. Merynbyl is free." She crouched, maintaining her distance. "I need Kephlen. Would you get him for me, please?" she said.

He gazed at her sidelong as he rose to his feet. But he didn't try to kill her. She rose with him.

"I know my eyes are still wrong, but my voice is my own, isn't it?" she asked him.

His gaze became a squint. He didn't trust her. Of course he didn't.

"Please, bring my friend Kephlen to me. I will collect the people together and let them know. There'll be no more boros mining, no more slavery. Our people can return to their land."

She couldn't stay any longer. She had to convince more than one person at a time or this would take forever. Now knowing she had quick enough reflexes to stop Zaryc if he tried again, Rhonwyn turned away and left him to make his own decision. He didn't follow her.

She went at once to Mistress Berwyn's room. It was in its usual manic state – until the workers realised who'd arrived. The bustle tensed and whoever could retreated as fast as possible. Rhonwyn could smell the fear.

Within an hour, Berwyn had done as Rhonwyn asked: assembled all the leaders of Risick's government. Just like yesterday. And, because of yesterday, they would be nervous indeed. When they were ready, Berwyn herself fetched Rhonwyn. The housekeeper still seemed like she was sleepwalking. Rhonwyn spoke to her as they descended the stairs.

"Is Kymra alright? Is she being taken care of?" She'd been

thinking about her friend, who had mistaken 'atoms' as 'adams'. Sweet, innocent thing.

Berwyn's eyebrows rose. "I wasn't sure what to do after yesterday morning, so I left her in her rooms. She's comfortable, though she's keeping to herself." She paused, her expression troubled. "Very much to herself."

Rhonwyn sighed. "We must take care of her. Send your best healer. And get her parents in, after you explain what he did to her. She'll need them. I assume they still don't know?"

Berwyn shook her head, her face twisted. Rhonwyn swallowed hard. If only she'd been able to prevent this awful thing. Berwyn noticed her emotion, and it seemed to embolden her.

"I will indeed, Rhonwyn. It should never have happened. I'll see to it myself she gets the best of care."

Rhonwyn smiled. "Thank you. I'll come and visit her as soon as I can."

It took hours for Rhonwyn to convince the leaders they were truly free, and to elicit their cooperation. Zaryc and Kephlen were there, too, representing the Resistance. She didn't dare mention the coming hoard of aliens. That would have to wait. She ordered all the boros miners up out of the ground and sent everyone home to digest the news with their families.

Lastly, she informed the inhabitants of the palace of the new developments during the evening meal. The dining hall was abuzz after she'd spoken. Rhonwyn left to give them time and distance to come to terms with this news. She ate in the games room before calling for the magician to be brought to her. Risick hadn't had time to execute him yet. Rhonwyn specifically ordered the guards not to be rough with Talsen. With anyone.

As she waited, she leaned back on the chair, looked up, and laughed. There, caught in the chandelier above, was the missing Gymbal piece. She sat up, still grinning, and fiddled with the Gymbal set, idly placing the pieces on the board.

Rhonwyn, believe it or not, your Gymbal skill will be useful in fighting the invaders.

She almost sank to the floor, her head whirling from the imposition of another consciousness. This was getting worse.

We need to go and we need to go now!

This voice was insistent. Rhonwyn agreed with him, as she struggled to stop herself vomiting. She couldn't take much more of this.

She relaxed on the chair, there in the games room, and closed her eyes, taking deep breaths to overcome the nausea. Each previous host had to submerge itself into her unconscious. One by one they came to her mind, regarded her for a moment, and slipped below the surface, until only one remained.

My friend. My sweet Rhonwyn. Goodbye. You won't stay alone for long. I promise, someone will befriend you and support you as you did me.

"Dyfed." Rhonwyn's voice broke.

Be well and happy, my love.

And he too slipped away into oblivion. All his memories were left, but his precious presence was gone. Rhonwyn sensed it. She was lighter, clearer, but older. And she felt Dyfed's loss all the more.

The door creaked open.

Rhonwyn composed herself, sat up, and faced her visitor.

40

Rhonwyn apprised Talsen of his new situation but suddenly didn't have the energy to explain what had happened to his nephew. Later. She ordered a guard to fetch Berwyn. The woman stood staring at Rhonwyn, jaw slack, until asked what was wrong. It seemed her eyes had returned to their normal colour.

What a relief.

"Please organise a room, and a healer, and make Talsen as comfortable as possible. And find out what happened to his daughter."

"Of course, Your Majesty," Berwyn rattled off, still distracted.

But Rhonwyn was tired and her hackles rose at the title, so laden with memories. She thrust her finger into Berwyn's chest and cried, "Don't you *ever* call me that again!"

Talsen and Berwyn both froze, and the terror Rhonwyn saw smothering Berwyn's face defused her anger in an instant.

"I'm so sorry," she said, reaching out and squeezing Berwyn's shoulder instead. "There must be no more fear in Merynbyl. No more."

A thorny lump rose in Rhonwyn's throat; tears threatened. She turned and fled. The corridors were busy, less than an hour after dinner, and her rapid movement attracted attention. All their staring eyes were too much. She had to get to her room. But as she rushed up to her door, the clock across the hallway – where she'd hidden the key – chimed the hour.

Rhonwyn stopped, glaring at the timepiece, the many tragedies caused by this intruder churning through her mind. *His* time, imposed on *her* people. Life, joy and time stolen from their loved ones. Kymra. Her father. Rhymla – who'd jumped.

That should never have happened.

Dyfed.

The breath in Rhonwyn's chest erupted as a high-pitched sob as she surged towards the clock: an emblem of the time taken from them, the chains thrown about them by Risick's shallow, pointless ambition. She grabbed the top of the clock face and hurled it onto the corridor floor, where its glass front shattered, cogs flying and rolling in every direction.

Abandoning her plan to hide, Rhonwyn stalked further along to the next clock and smashed it too, stamping on the clock casing and kicking the splinters of wood from her path. And then the next. And the next.

She sensed rather than saw the surrounding inhabitants of the palace, frozen like statues, their eyes fixed upon her. But she didn't care. It felt as if her chest would explode. She wanted to erase this Risick-prison they were all in. She had to begin somewhere. There must be something she could do to start the healing. To somehow turn back the time they'd lost. To make it like it had been.

Once she'd destroyed all the clocks on that corridor, she began on the next. Halfway along, someone stepped into her path. She tried to go around them, but hands gripping her shoulders. Rhonwyn looked up.

"That's enough now, dear. You need to stop," Felenya murmured.

Sticky tears puckered Rhonwyn's cheeks as Felenya enfolded her in a tight embrace. She clung to her friend, struggling to breathe through her grief as the singer rocked her from side to side.

"I know. It's alright," Felenya whispered.

Rhonwyn's throat opened just enough to speak.

"He was going to kill you," she wailed.

Felenya shuddered and rubbed Rhonwyn's back.

"He took everyone from me and he nearly took you, too." Rhonwyn's voice broke again. She now knew how clumsy her supposedly 'clandestine activities' had been. With all of Risick's alien technology, she'd been lucky things had turned out as they had – incredibly lucky. No wonder all the Resistance infiltrators had been discovered so quickly; her people were totally naïve compared to the centuries-old Risick.

Rhonwyn buried her face in Felenya's shoulder and whimpered. "Dyfed. I loved Dyfed. And he loved me too. But he's gone." She howled her pain. "I don't want to be alone anymore."

Felenya wrestled Rhonwyn back to arm's length to look at her, an incongruous smile on her tear-stained face. She rubbed Rhonwyn's shoulders once, down and up, wiped her friend's tears away with her thumbs, and took her by the hand.

"Come with me," she replied and led Rhonwyn along the hall, past the staring people. But – Rhonwyn noticed remotely – the looks were not full of fear anymore. They weren't afraid of her. Well, who would be, after that show? She gasped a chuckle at herself. What a performance.

They arrived at Felenya's door and her friend pulled her inside. She had pushed the settee against the side wall and a pillow and blanket lay on it. The last of the sunset was the only lighting.

"Why are you sleeping on the couch, Felenya?" she asked.

Felenya beamed at her, her merry face boldly inappropriate under the circumstances.

"You'll see," she said, and led Rhonwyn into her bedroom, into the dark. She had already drawn the curtains and Rhonwyn slowed so she wouldn't collide with the furniture. But Felenya drew her on, taking her other hand as well and then sitting her down on the edge of the bed. Did she want her to sleep there instead?

"I'll be right back," she said, and stepped into the lounge room.

Rhonwyn sagged with exhaustion and closed her eyes. But they popped open again when a rustling sounded on the bed behind her. She spun towards the sound.

What was that?

Her eyes were adjusting to the dark and she saw the shape of someone already in the bed. But it was only when Felenya returned with a lamp that Rhonwyn could see his face. He was pale, oh so pale. His dark hair was soaked with sweat, the curls clinging to the pillow beneath his head. But his chest rose and fell and, when she reached out for his face, it was warm and she felt his breath on her wrist.

"Dyfed," she breathed. "How?"

"I waited for you," Felenya murmured, "All night I stayed in the sitting room, because you told me that's where he went." She paused. "And then you came out. You dragged his body with you, dropped it at my feet and said, 'Get rid of this.' When you looked at me I saw your eyes and I heard that double voice of his." She sighed, her face slumped with the memory. "And I knew the demon had jumped to you."

Her face lightened. "But he hadn't checked. The demon hadn't checked that he was dead. You remember?" She touched Rhonwyn's shoulder. "You remember my mother was training me to be a healer when I became a singer?"

Rhonwyn nodded and a heavy weight lifted from her heart. "You brought him back?"

Felenya grinned at her. "I've been with him ever since. Just getting him here without being seen took some doing. His fever broke late this afternoon. The poultice worked, thank the heavens. So I only discovered the news when I came down for dinner."

Yes, Felenya did look tired. She'd been up a long time, too.

A groan from the bed gathered their attention. Dyfed gasped

and groaned again and his eyes cracked open.

Rhonwyn leaned over him and wrapped her hand around his cheek. "Hello, Dyfed," she whispered.

He blinked, his eyes taking a while to focus on her face. He frowned. "I'm not dead?" His voice was barely a whisper.

Rhonwyn smiled. "No. And the demon is gone," she added. "He's out of you."

"Ahhh!" he sighed, his mouth curling up at the sides. But his eyes slid closed then and his face relaxed.

"He needs rest," murmured Felenya.

Rhonwyn eased to her feet and followed Felenya out. Once they'd shut the door, she wrapped her arms around her friend. "Thank you. Thank you, Felenya."

Felenya's face shone when she leant back. "I want you to tell me all about it." She released Rhonwyn and made her way to the couch. "But not tonight. I need to sleep."

Dazed, Rhonwyn wandered out to the garden – full of memories – and breathed the free air into her free body on her free world. She climbed up to the high point and lay down. She'd been transformed since she'd last been here. But so much of her was still the same.

The stars were just as beautiful. More so. Her heart warmed at the memory of the meteorite show they'd witnessed two nights ago. What a magnificent display that had been. She'd thought they were angels, but, in fact, it had been Risick's satellite re-entering the atmosphere.

Rhonwyn drew in a long breath and let it out. She needed to say goodbye to one more soul.

"Papa?" she said to the sky. "Thank you for your comfort and your wisdom, all these years since you died. I still miss you, but I'm not alone anymore."

Though she knew it was her own imagination, she heard him again, saw him standing, smiling, cap in hand.

"I'm so proud of you, my brave, brave daughter. Be well and happy, love."

That's what he would have said. He sounded further removed from her this time – so faint. She would never hear his voice again. She wouldn't need to.

Rhonwyn allowed the tears to flow, then wiped them away and returned to Felenya's room. She tip-toed through to the bedroom and curled up next to Dyfed's sleeping form, her head resting on his outstretched arm, her hand on his rising and falling chest.

She would sleep for now. Then she would wake to watch the sunrise with Dyfed. Because that's when the day really began.

THANKS...

For the magnificent cover and interior design:
Tessa Baty – your faith gets us to the final images.

For capturing those incredible images:
Amber-Jayne Bain – my Caravaggio. Wow!
You totally floor me.

For getting flesh, blood and spirit in their rightful
places: Michelle Elvy – you supervise my creation's
growth to maturity.

For making the rubber hit the road:
Christine Borra – plus the giggles, tea and chocolate.

For putting my pieces back together, and all
the ideas: the Zoomers – Iona, Angela, Jane, Denise
and Mary. Brunch soon?

For being my safe haven: Robert – 'I love you'
doesn't seem enough sometimes, but ... *I love you!*

FREE DOWNLOAD

Sign up for Susan's New Releases mailing list and get free short stories. Go here to get started: *www.susanholt.org/free*

IF YOU ENJOYED THIS BOOK ...

Please help me out by leaving an honest review on Amazon or Goodreads.

Thank you so much! We authors are completely reliant on you wonderful readers, so keep enjoying stories and I'll see you in the next book.

Susan Holt is a bubbly and passionate actress and author living in Porirua, New Zealand. After studying linguistics, she followed her dream, moved to Sydney and complete a two year acting course. During that sojourn, she discovered a talent for writing.

Find out more at *www.susanholt.org*